Sanctuary of Evil

Sanctuary of Evil

STEVE BROWN

Chick Springs Publishing
Taylors, SC

First published in the USA in 2003 by
Chick Springs Publishing
PO Box 1130, Taylors, SC 29687
E-mail: ChickSprgs@aol.com
Web site: www.chicksprings.com

Library of Congress Control Number: 2002096626
Library of Congress Data Available

ISBN: 0-9712521-6-5

10   9   8   7   6   5   4   3   2

Author's Note

Acknowledgments

For their assistance in preparing this story, I would like to thank Mark Brown, Sonya Caldwell, Barbara Eberly, Marshall Frank, Missy Johnson, Jackie Kellett, Kate Lehman, Kimberly Medgyesy, Ken McKelvey, Mary Moore, Ann Patterson, Chris Roerden, Ellen Smith, Susan Snowden, Mike Ward, and my favorite Gen-Xer, Stacey. And, of course, Mary Ella.

*To the forensics (CSI) of law enforcement units
in recognition of the dedication, hard work, and
professionalism they bring to each crime scene.*

The world we live in is a much more fragile and resilient place than we have been led to believe.

—Susan Chase

ONE

It appeared that Myrtle Beach PD was looking for someone to talk down a jumper.

"Can you take this one?" asked Dispatch.

"Don't you have someone else?"

"I was told to route everything to you."

"Every dirty little job that comes along," I muttered.

"What was that?" asked the voice over the radio.

"The Host of Kings Hotel, you say?"

"You got it." And the radio in the sedan went silent.

My partner sat in the passenger seat. Daphne Adkins was a bony woman with long arms and legs.

"We're catching a jumper?" she asked.

I said nothing, only wheeled the sedan around and headed in the direction of the Host of Kings.

My partner peered at me through the uneven darkness of the Grand Strand. "Have I done something to tick you off, Susan?"

I smiled at her. "Just your being here ticks me off."

I guess I should introduce myself.

My name is Susan Chase, and these days I'm an agent of SLED, South Carolina's equivalent of the FBI. My family used to fish the Florida Keys, and Daddy pursued that career up the East Coast until reaching the Grand Strand, always one step ahead of the bill collectors. After Mom walked out on us, that left Daddy and me, fussing and fighting until one night, drunk, he fell overboard and drowned.

Being only fifteen, my next stop was a foster home, where

it took me only a few weeks to gauge my chances of becoming the next Cinderella. I hit the streets and lived by my wits, taking a job guarding the beach, and during the off-season, waiting tables. Then some guy asked me to find his kid who'd run away from home. From there I became a private investigator, then an investigator for SLED. Which brings me to the trainee who accompanied me the night I took the call that practically ended my career with SLED.

A crowd had gathered in front of the hotel. Just what a jumper wants. Someone to beg him not to leap to his miserable death. If that's what this guy expected, Dispatch had picked the wrong gal. Climbing out of the sedan, my partner paused to stare at the idiot illuminated at the edge of the roof of the hotel. After all, this is Myrtle Beach, and there's little that isn't highly illuminated once the sun goes down. I shook my head and headed inside, where a uniformed patrolman stopped me.

"Sorry, Miss, but . . . ."

His voice trailed off as he saw the SLED ID on the lanyard around my neck. I pushed my way past him and toward the bank of elevators, where another cop checked my ID before my partner and I were allowed upstairs. Noticing one of the hotel staff near reception, I motioned the guy over as I pulled off my long coat and the business jacket that was part of my navy blue pantsuit.

"Let me have your jacket."

"My jacket?" asked the blond guy, whose name tag said "Eric."

"And give me a woman's name tag and outfit my partner the same way."

Moments later, we took the elevator to where a couple of cops and a firefighter huddled in the stairwell.

"What you doing here, Chase?" Earl Tackett was a stocky guy with a buzz cut and pecs that came from working out. He had twenty years in the military and was working on another twenty with the Myrtle Beach Police Department.

"I'm your negotiator."

"That's bull," said his partner, another well-built guy in

the same blue uniform and equipment belt. "This is more of your grandstanding, Chase."

Tackett reached for his radio. "I'll have to check this out."

"And while you do, hope the guy doesn't go over the edge."

"Hey, we've got someone watching him," said Tackett's partner.

"But is he near enough to prevent the idiot from going over the side?"

"Nobody can get that close."

"That must be why Dispatch called me."

"Listen, you guys," said the firefighter. "They said a negotiator was coming up. If it's Chase, it's Chase. Let's get on with it."

After pocketing my lanyard ID and switching my weapon and extra clip behind my back, I handed off my long coat and suit jacket and shrugged into the hotel's maroon one. I'd already transferred my pad and pen. "I want this door secured and I don't want your people on the roof."

Tackett nodded, then cracked the door and ordered another cop into the stairwell. Daphne and I took the patrolman's place as the door clicked shut behind us.

The roof's blacktop was covered with pebbles, and here and there were huge air conditioners and stubby pipes. It wouldn't normally be all that chilly up here, but a wicked breeze had kicked in from offshore.

"Don't come any closer," said the figure at the edge of the roof.

"I'm with the hotel, not the cops." Lowering my voice, I said to Daphne, "Stay at the door." At this point I was about forty feet away from the guy. "My boss told me to get the info. That's why I'm here." I opened the jacket with both hands as I walked his way. "They sent a girl so you wouldn't be afraid." Now I was about thirty feet away.

The guy was middle-aged, balding, and had a beak for a nose. His face was red from the sun and especially that beak. He wore a pair of plaid shorts and a beach shirt from Ripley's, the aquarium, not the freak show.

"I need to know your room number." Out came my pad and pen from under my jacket.

"Room number? I don't have a room."

I stopped twenty feet away. "Look, fellow, this is not a smart move—to leap to your death from our hotel roof."

"Why not?"

"Our lawyers will have a field day."

"Lawyers? What lawyers?"

"The suits who'll contest any settlement." I turned to Daphne and told her to tell the cops and firemen they could vamoose.

"What was that all about?" asked the guy, stepping away from the edge.

"Mister, you're going to make more profit for this hotel in one minute than it'll make all month."

"How's that?"

"We'll collect on your insurance money."

"But my wife's the beneficiary."

"Sorry, but the hotel has an army of lawyers who will contest the payout."

"But my—my family will need the money."

From next-door someone yelled "jump!" The dummy nodded in agreement. "That's right . . . I have to jump."

"Well, before you do, think about it. If you were staying here, your family might have some wiggle room—a guest wandering about in an area left unsecured, but . . . ." I shrugged. Up and down the Grand Strand green and red lights danced. It was near Christmas and once again I had no one to celebrate with.

"You're trying to trick me. They'd have to pay."

"Mister," I said, stopping less than ten feet away, "the last guy did this, the home office collected a half a million bucks. I hear the guy's kids are working their way through college."

"I—I don't understand. Why are you telling me this?"

"I had to work my way through school. Work and study, work and study, that's all you have time for." I glanced at my trainee who stood at the door to the stairwell. "You're lucky Daphne's not punched in yet. She'd push you over the side to earn another promotion."

The man gaped at the bony woman near the door.

I shivered in the breeze off the ocean. I was missing my

4

long coat. "Look, Mister, can we get on with this?"

"You want me to jump?"

"No, but it's damn chilly up here."

"But if I was a guest . . . ?"

I smiled. "Now you've got it."

"And I can jump anytime, right?"

"Sure," I added, continuing to smile.

"Okay," he said, crossing the pebble-strewn blacktop. "Let's go downstairs."

After he passed me, I said, "Er—mister, it really doesn't work that way."

Before he could respond, an explosion rocked the Grand Strand. Looking toward the center of the Strip, I saw the night light up over the Pavilion and all the rides.

What the jumper did next, I have no clue. After touching my watch to mark the time, I was on the run for the stairwell, opening the door before Daphne could grab the thick metal handle. Pebbles scattered as my shoes scuffed the surface and Daphne stepped back.

Earl Tackett, his partner, and the firefighter made way as I stepped through the door and rushed onto the landing. I took my pen and pad from the hotel's jacket, peeled out of it, and dropped the jacket on the stairs. I snatched my own jacket from the firefighter and pulled out my lanyard ID. Questions along the lines of "what the hell was going on" were shouted as I grabbed my long coat from the fireman and took off down the stairs. Seconds later, both cops and the fireman received their marching orders over their radios.

Below me, the stairwell was empty and I made quick work of the stairs. That is, until we approached the third floor. Here the stairs became crowded as tourists joined us exiting the hotel. "Bomb . . . Kings Highway . . . near Pavilion area," were mentioned.

"What you guys got?" I called back up the stairs as I pushed through the crowd.

"Some kind of explosion . . . ." yelled Earl above the noise of the thudding feet on the stairs.

"Near the Pavilion," shouted the firefighter coming down behind him.

The people on the landing slowed and stared. That made it easier for us to cut ahead and reach the ground floor, where the door was held open as people kept exiting the upper levels. My small group found its way down the hall and entered a lobby rapidly filling with tourists and their kids, some even with luggage. Everyone was headed for the front doors. Some still wore sleeping garb.

How did these people know about the explosion? Then I understood. It would take only one person who'd seen and heard the explosion from their balcony to clear an entire floor.

I forced my way into the revolving glass door behind a father waiting for his family to join him. When the guy stopped, several of us, including Daphne and the firefighter, knocked the guy into the revolving glass, and when the door opened onto the street, the guy went sprawling. Seconds later, his wife and kids reached the wide sidewalk leading to the portico sheltering arriving vehicles. The mom had a babe in arms and another child gripping her robe. When the robe came apart, everyone could see she wore a teddy. The woman snatched the robe closed. Few noticed.

People ran up and down the street, some glancing over their shoulders as if the hotel might collapse at any moment. Farther down Ocean Boulevard the gray cloud continued to hover over the Pavilion. Vehicles honked and tried to move around a patrol car, fire truck, and EMS. Order would have to be restored, but I was heading to the site of the explosion.

Daphne was beside me panting, her lanyard cockeyed around her neck and her coat in her arms. The Host of Kings Hotel jacket probably lay, as mine did, on the steps of the stairwell. From inside the building you could hear a megaphoned voice asking everyone to proceed outside in a calm and deliberate manner.

That was just the problem. After 9/11, nobody wanted to be inside any building where people were hastily decamping, and headlights could be seen in parking garages where vehicles negotiated their way from one level to another, then tried to enter the street. There was a great deal of honking of horns, screaming of parents, wailing of children, and the whine of sirens. Using their whistles, Earl Tackett and his partner were trying to control the traffic. It wasn't working. Even when given notice of an approaching hurricane, it took almost a week to evacuate the residents. Now that the tourists had gone bananas, it might take several days to regain control.

My sedan was blocked, not to mention pointed in the wrong direction. I thrust the keys at Daphne and gripped her hands to focus her attention on me. "Get the car out of here. Leave it at the law enforcement center. Walk in to the scene from there."

"Walk in?"

"No way you'll get a vehicle close."

She glanced at the hotel, where doors adjacent to the rotating one had been wedged back by guests exiting the building. The latecomers were bringing along not only their kids, but also pieces of luggage. Unused reservations be damned. These people were out of here. One of those new Mini Coopers negotiated its way up on the curb and tried to pull a *Bourne Identity*-like move down the sidewalk. The mob stopped the small car cold.

I walked over to where two young women sat on a purple Harley. Dykes on bikes, I would imagine. A muscular brunette with cropped hair revved up her bike and inched down Ocean Boulevard. With tourists crossing a street jammed with all manner of vehicles, the motorbike was no longer king, and it annoyed the brunette no end. Her passenger was a bottle-blonde wearing a string top over a very slight chest. A pair of green short shorts and flip-flops completed the passenger's outfit.

"Going to need your ride," I said, flashing my ID and stepping in front of the Harley.

The purple machine had a long, orange flame painted across the gas tank, but it and most of the engine were hidden by a pair of thick thighs. The driver wore a fringe vest above her jeans, one boot on the front footpeg, the other on the ground to maintain her balance.

"Get out of my way," she ordered, twisting her front wheel at me.

My badge and SLED ID, it would appear, had little effect on her.

"As you like it," I said, stepping to one side.

When the heavy woman twisted the handle to give the engine gas, I reached over and grabbed the brake lever on the handgrip and closed it across her fingers.

She yowled and tried to pull her fingers from under the lever, but my hand remained tight, depressing the brake. There was a yelp of surprise from the bottle-blonde in the sissy seat.

"You bitch," said the driver, referring to me and not her girlfriend, "take your hand—"

Squeezing on the brake again, I shut off her protest. "As you might've noticed, we have what you could call a civic emergency, and you're interfering with the performance of my duty." With my free hand, I pulled back my jacket so the stupid twit could see the Glock on my hip. "You getting off the bike or what?"

She sneered as she did.

"Move to the curb," I ordered.

This, too, she complied with, but her girlfriend remained with the bike. Eyes live with excitement, the bottle-blonde inclined her head in the direction of the gray cloud. "You really going down there?"

I nodded. Not once did my hand come off my Glock. Daphne Adkins gaped, evidently learning something she hadn't been taught in classes at the Criminal Justice Academy.

"Can I tag along?" asked the passenger.

I shrugged as I mounted the bike. I'd need someone to watch the bike once I reached the scene.

"Hey," said driver, stepping toward us, "you can't take my bike *and* my girl."

"Daphne, if this woman tries to interfere, you're to arrest her."

The driver glanced at Daphne, whose hand touched her Glock. Her other hand found the cuffs on the opposite hip.

I straddled the seat, which opened me wide. Harleys are huge monsters, loud suckers, too. Something their owners take great pride in. To the driver, I said, "You can pick up your girlfriend at the site of the explosion."

"If I come down there, I'll get my bike back?"

I glanced at Bottle Blondie with her arms wrapped tightly around my waist. "Yeah, but I can't make any promises about your girlfriend."

Two

There was more stop-and-go as people, cars, or minivans crowded the Boulevard or forced themselves into the flow. Even though I was on a bike, I was stopped by traffic moving away from the explosion and traffic moving in the opposite direction wanting to turn around. I had the bike pointed in the right direction, but I was helpless to go anywhere, as long as I reacted as if I was in a typical urban area.

But I was at the beach.

I nosed the bike against the curb and up on the sidewalk. Pedestrians cursed as I joined them but made way. When I rounded the Host of Kings Hotel, I located the parking area of the beach access, and it goes without saying the area was emptying fast.

"This is just as bad . . . ." The blonde yelped as I goosed the Harley past an SUV and roared toward the thirty-foot wooden walkway leading to the beach. "You're not going to do what I think . . . ."

The remainder was lost in a scream that practically deafened me. I twisted the handle wide open and the bike leaped forward, racing across the narrow walkway. On each side was a railing, but there was plenty of room for the handlebars, though you'd never know it by the way the blonde was screaming and gripping me around the waist. The bike cleared the four or five steps to the beach, went airborne, and thumped into the sand.

The blonde moaned. "Thank God I'm not into men. I don't think I could take another pounding like that."

The front end of the bike almost got away from me, but from my early morning swims in the Intracoastal Waterway, I managed to correct the machine's wobbling nose, bring it around, and point the bike in the direction of the explosion. Ahead of us the beach was clear of tourists; the downside was the tide was in.

"I think I wet my pants," said the woman.

"Nah. The tide's just in."

She giggled nervously. "Thanks. Ever think of making it with a woman?"

"The thought never crossed my mind."

"What a shame," said my passenger, clinging even tighter. "After this, I'm going to want to be with someone."

"You might even be desperate enough to be with a guy."

"I'll never be that desperate." The venom with which she spit this out reminded me of the abusive father in the background of so many screwed-up women. Glancing at the watch vibrating on my wrist, I saw only seven minutes had elapsed since the explosion. Fire engines and squad cars were en route. Their sirens filled the air.

The blonde clung to me, preventing my jacket and coat from flapping in the wind. That was good. A man can pull off his jacket and toss it over his arm without worrying that anything might fall out, but those interior pockets are the hiding places for everything a woman needs but doesn't want anyone to see. Those items remind men that we're women, and that's something a female law enforcement officer doesn't care to advertise, despite the tops you've seen worn by female cops on TV.

Eight minutes after the explosion we were approaching the boardwalk, where a uniformed patrolman on a bike met us coming in the opposite direction. The wind was stiff off the ocean as he and I turned our bikes onto the short street between the Pavilion and The Bowery. We paused at the intersection of Ocean Boulevard, looked both ways, and then dashed past Ripley's Believe It Or Not, the flume ride, and a beachwear shop. At Kings Highway, we stopped our bikes, put down a foot, and gawked at the building across the street.

Sanctuary of Evil

The four-story structure, including the ground-level parking garage, were all in flames. A wrought-iron gate allowing access to the parking garage from the street had been dislodged and blown between two huge potted plants still upright on the sidewalk. So far, the adjoining buildings were untouched by the fire.

Kings Highway had been blocked and patrolmen were on the street directing traffic. Others were stringing crime scene tape to hold back the naturally curious who would wander over from Hotel Row. The crowds weren't there yet, but they would be. This was the Grand Strand and everyone came here for a show.

A ladder truck and two smaller trucks had joined the patrol cars; hoses were being unrolled and firefighters were shouting directions on how best to attack the fire. There was little problem with smoke, since the breeze from the beach immediately blew it inland.

I dismounted the Harley as a helicopter soared in from 501, the main drag into the beach area. When not flying tourists on sightseeing excursions, the colorfully painted Huey was on call for the local television station.

"Stay with the bike," I said to my passenger.

"But I want to go with you."

"You have no ID and I might need your wheels again."

The woman was staring past me. "Look," she said, pointing, "there's a man on the roof."

The helicopter's searchlight was trained on the four-story building. On the roof stood a man waving his hands and shouting to the firefighters below. None of them heard him. The firemen were connecting their hoses to hydrants and the cops were handling traffic. The man on the roof yelled and waved in vain.

"Push the Harley out of the way," I told the blonde. "It's about to get very busy around here."

I walked over to a squad car, removed a bullhorn from its mounting, and adjusted the volume. When I spoke to him, the man on the roof looked down, trying to identify where the voice had come from. Because he wore a business suit, I took a chance that he was carrying a cell phone. I held up my cell and gave him my digits through the bullhorn. The man nodded, backed away from the façade along the front of the roof, and dialed my cell.

"Who is this?" he asked nervously.

"Susan Chase. What are you doing up there?"

"What the hell you think? Trying to get down."

"What's the story on the elevator?"

"The hole extends to the roof and along the elevator."

"Hole?"

"More like a crater in the roof. From the explosion."

"Why didn't you use the fire stairs?"

"The stairs . . ." He coughed. "The stairs are impossible. The garage is in flames."

"Is the rear of the building in flames, too?"

"Yes."

"All four walls are in flames?"

"Yes. Look, do you have someone I can talk to down there. Maybe a guy?"

"What's your name?"

"Glenn Proffitt."

"The owner of the building?"

"Yes, but I had nothing to do with the explosion. You have to believe me."

"I don't remember asking if you blew up your building, Mister Proffitt."

"What are you going to do to get me down?"

"Give me a minute." I crossed the street, passed a cop directing traffic, and stopped where two firefighters were fastening a hose to a fireplug. Tapping one of them on his shoulder, I said, "A moment of your time."

Without looking up, he said, "In a minute, lady. If you haven't noticed, we have a fire across the street."

"And a man on the roof."

The two firefighters straightened up and stared. The man on the roof waved to them. Flames crawled up the sides of the building. There were no apparent windows.

"What the hell's he doing up there?" asked one.

"That's what fire stairs are for," said the other.

"The garage is on fire," I explained.

"The garage?"

They stared at the stucco wall surrounding the street-level parking. Through an opening where the wooden building was offset from the stucco walls, flames slipped through and climbed up the building's sides. The flames were being fed by gusts off the beach, and the first two stories above the parking garage were totally engulfed.

I glanced at my watch. Twelve minutes since the blast. While one of the firemen located his immediate superior, the other ran for a ladder truck. I checked the north and south ends of the building, and then wandered over to a cluster of firefighters.

Under orders from a deputy chief, one of the ladder trucks cranked its engine and began to shift its rear to the front of the building. The driver was assisted by firefighters on the ground who used hand signals to give him directions. The deputy chief spoke into a handheld radio as he walked toward the ladder truck.

"Nothing on the back?"

"No, sir," came the reply.

Generally you can find an unobstructed wall, and up that wall the firefighters would go, if they couldn't bring you down the stairwell. Even if the stairs become compromised, firefighters can usually rope a person down, but in this case, the burning building stood taller than its neighbors, and the wind from the ocean was encouraging the flames to skip the third floor and leap to the wooden façade along the roof.

"Hey, Bob," shouted the deputy chief to the man on the rear of the hook and ladder. "You better get hustling."

Bob nodded and took up a position at the base of the ladder as the turntable mount swung the ladder around. Bob had on an air pack, giving him twenty minutes of air.

As if aware of the threat facing the man on the roof, the deputy chief said, "Zack, take a spare ladder to the adjacent roof. You're the backup if Bob can't bring that guy down. I may have to send you up from there."

Zack and another fireman hustled off to the other ladder truck. Soon Zack and his companion were directing a second truck into position.

Looking behind me, the deputy chief hollered, "How are we coming with that water?"

"In a minute," said a fireman tightening the hose to the fireplug with a huge wrench.

The deputy chief muttered a curse about a drought that had discouraged all training but that taught in the classroom. Something about losing your competitive edge.

Fully extended, the ladder of the first truck was lowered to the building's façade, a rounded false topping painted the same tan color as the building. At the ladder's touch, the façade crumbled to pieces. Down came burning wood, stucco, and not a few bricks. Bob and his companions at the base of the ladder turned their faces away. Some even raised hands in front of the plastic shields protecting their faces.

The phone rang in my hand. It was Proffitt.

"Cracks are everywhere. Any moment I could put my foot through the roof. There's no way they're going to put a ladder on this roof."

I passed this information along to the deputy chief.

"Tell him someone is bringing up a ladder to lay across the roof from the adjacent building."

I passed this along to Proffitt.

Moments later, Zack and his companion were headed up the extended ladder to the roof of the building next door. Each of their free hands gripped an aluminum ladder, one that would be used from one building to the other before flames could climb that side.

Back at the primary truck, Bob had backed his ladder off and had an aluminum ladder brought up. When the aluminum spare was shuttled up the end of the extended ladder, Bob dropped the far end of the aluminum ladder onto the roof. This ladder, too, knocked off more of the roof's edge and created a gap. Down came the aluminum ladder being used for a crosswalk, along with more burning wood and a few bricks.

"Jesus," muttered the deputy chief, "that guy hired the wrong building contractor."

Zack had the same problem reaching the building from the adjacent one. When anything touched the phony walls, the façade crumbled under the weight. They gestured help-lessly from their positions: Bob at the end of his ladder, Zack on the neighboring roof. Glenn Proffitt reported that their efforts had only made more cracks appear in the roof. No way he was approaching the edge. It might give way under-neath him.

"Any way to rope him off?" asked the chief.

That wasn't going to work. Proffitt's building was taller than those beside it. I glanced behind me. A sporting goods shop had had its windows blown out, and in the light from the chopper, a friend of mine was doing a standup for the local TV station. Hmmm. Heather must've commandeered a Harley, too.

As I backed farther into Kings Highway, I could see the flames lick over the edge of the building. For the first time I realized there was an American flag on top of the elevator penthouse, the small structure housing the elevator machinery.

The deputy chief wanted to know if anyone had tried to get inside the parking area under the building. From there they might take the stairs to the roof.

"Too hot," said a female firefighter. She raised the face shield and wiped her forehead. "It's the damnedest thing, chief. When we arrived, flames filled the parking garage."

"Same at the rear," crackled a voice over the radio. "There's a long gate back here and it's open, but there's no way we're going to get inside with the floor in flames."

"Flames inside the garage and climbing all four sides of the building?" asked the deputy chief.

"Got to be arson," I muttered.

The deputy chief glanced at me. Using my cell phone, I was patched though to the command center. The fire department's response time can be incredible out of season. Still, there was chaos in the background.

"Are you watching this on TV?" I asked, after covering my ear to shut out the sounds of the chopper.

"This is already on TV?" asked a nervous voice from the hastily set-up command center.

"That's correct. What's the status of the rescue choppers?"

"One's on its way up from Charleston; another from Shaw

Air Force Base. Twenty or more minutes out."

I looked at the building. Flames now controlled the fourth floor and were reaching for the roof.

"Not enough time." I closed the channel and walked over to Heather's cameraman and tapped him on the shoulder.

"Yeah," he said, without moving the lens glued to his face. The young man had a beard, wore jeans, and a tee shirt with a Rolling Stones bright red tongue.

"What's the phone number of your chopper?"

"Who's asking?"

I walked to where he could see me out of the eye that wasn't glued to the viewfinder.

The camera dipped but righted itself. "Susan, we've got every right to be here."

"Stand still while I take that phone off your belt."

"Hey!" He tried to duck away but had to remain upright to keep his viewfinder on Heather. "You got no right—"

I removed the phone from the pouch, experimented with several different digits, and finally reached the chopper. I could hear the blades in the background as well as over-head.

"Yeah?" asked the pilot.

"Bring the chopper down on the beach. You and I are going to get that guy off the roof."

"Who's this?"

I told him.

"Come on, Susan, there must be a chopper on its way, and much better equipped than mine."

"One from the coast guard, another from the air force, and neither will arrive in time. Now get down here. I'll meet you at the beach."

"Sorry, but I was told to remain on station."

He hung up on me, and just when I considered firing a shot across his bow, Heather stalked over.

"What was that all about?" she demanded. "We're just doing our jobs."

Since her cameraman was filming me, I dialed her station's number and got the producer. Looking into the camera, I said, "This is Susan Chase with the State Law Enforcement

Division. Consider your helicopter impounded. Order the pilot to put down on the beach in front of the Pavilion or I will personally come over to your station and haul your ass off to jail."

I tossed the phone to Heather and headed for the sporting goods shop.

THREE

Heather's cameraman sat on the edge of the open bay, feet on the skid and camera focused on the scene below. Heather stood beside me, her microphone in one hand, the other hand gripping the open door of the chopper. The Coast Guard was seventeen minutes out and the fire had advanced over each side of the roof. Occasionally Proffitt would cough from smoke leaking through the elevator penthouse on top of which the American flag was planted. The fire department was keeping the man soaked, but sooner or later the roof would collapse. A call had gone out for a bag to be inflated for Proffitt to leap onto.

Uh-huh. The guy was supposed to take a flying leap off a building and land on something he couldn't see? I don't think so.

"Mister Proffitt," I shouted over the chopper's engine and the wind passing by the open door, "this is Susan Chase in the helicopter over the Pavilion."

Heather stuck the mike in my face. I'd already taken considerable crap from the command center about involving civilians in our work. Yeah. Like what we were about to do was all in a day's work.

On the roof, Proffitt waved. "Have the helicopter hover low enough so I can grab one of the skids."

"Mister Proffitt, we can't land. We can't even fly over your position."

"Why?"

"Because of the thermal updraft."

"What . . . does that mean?"

"The fire department is going to throw you a vest. When you secure the vest, we'll drop the line to you. It's weighed down, several times more than the vest."

"You're going to pull me off the roof with a cord?"

"Actually a bungee cord."

"I don't know if I can bungee jump off this roof."

"You don't have to. Just hook yourself to one of the vests that's coming your way."

The cameraman focused on the vests as they were thrown on the roof, one thrown by Bob in the flame-retardant suit at the end of his ladder, the other heaved by Zack over the façade from the roof of the adjacent building. We were low enough that we could spot the vests from the light mounted on the chopper. Still, Proffitt remained behind the elevator's penthouse.

"Can you see the vest, Mister Proffitt?"

No answer from the roof.

"Mister Proffitt, look for the strobe lights." I didn't want to tell him the other vest had disappeared into the hole on the other side of the elevator penthouse. Even I could see that gaping hole. The blast had blown a hole straight through from the garage? How was that? "Mister Proffitt?"

"I can't get to it."

The copilot, a teenager whose father was the pilot, tapped me on the shoulder with a pair of binoculars. Everyone was wired into this frequency, even the helicopter's onboard communication system.

I focused the binoculars on the roof. No cracks between Proffitt and the vest. "Twenty feet straight ahead and no-where near the flames."

Proffitt raised his head and shook his head. "No."

"It's just ahead—"

"Dammit! If I go out there, the roof could give way."

A tongue of flame licked over the side of the building, illuminating where the vest lay. Fireman Zack stood on the adjacent roof, hands open wide in a gesture of "what's going on?"

I glanced at the spare vests lying on the long seat mounted at the rear of the chopper. "I don't think I can place a vest any closer than the one the fireman threw."

No reply from the roof.

"Mister Proffitt?"

We hovered and stared at the man huddling behind the small building on the roof.

A girl's voice came on the line. "Daddy, you've got to get into the vest."

Heather and I looked at each other. Who was this?

"Daddy, can you see the vest?" Evidently one of Proffitt's children had been rounded up by the command center.

"Honey, you—you shouldn't have called. It's a bad time."

"Daddy, you have to get into the vest so they can drop you a rope from the helicopter."

No answer. We were definitely losing this guy.

"Oh, hell," muttered Heather from where she stood beside me, "be a man about it."

I looked at her. "What did you say?"

"He's wimping out on us."

"No. What did you say before that?" None of this was going out over the air. Someone in the command center was controlling the feed to the roof.

The cameraman smiled up at us from where he sat with his feet on the skid. "She said 'be a man about it.'"

Heather looked at her cameraman.

I nodded. "That's what I thought you said."

I stumbled to the rear of the chopper and picked up a vest and strapped it on. On the phone the teenage daughter was adamant that her father should cross the roof to the vest. Her father was just as set in his mind that we would have to come up with something safer.

"What are you doing?" asked Heather, sticking the mike in my face when I returned to the open door with two other vests in my hands. The light was trained on me.

I motioned the cameraman to focus on Proffitt; otherwise, those in the command center couldn't see what was going on. He returned his attention to the figure on the roof.

Proffitt came on the line in an attempt to drown out his daughter's pleas. "Listen, people, I'm waiting. Are you going to get me down from here?"

The teenager's voice was replaced by an adult male voice from the command center. The voice instructed Mr. Proffitt to get moving. From the helicopter we could see that all four sides of the building were ablaze and flames were poking their fiery tentacles through the hole this side of the elevator penthouse.

I leaned between the father and son copilots and shouted my idea. The pilot pulled one of his headphones back and looked at me.

"Are you crazy?"

I hooked the bungee cord to my vest. "Maybe so, but you need to keep the command center informed as to what we're doing up here."

The pilot shook his head and replaced the headphone. A moment later, the chopper veered off and rose in the air. His teenage son continued to stare at me as if learning his favorite rock band was not coked out of their minds when they performed.

"Mister Proffitt," I said over my cell, "this is Susan Chase. I have an idea." I had to repeat myself before the command center put me through.

"Where's my daughter?" demanded Proffitt. "Did you cut her off?"

"I think they lost the connection."

"Get her back. This might be the last time I talk to her."

"Do you see the chopper?"

"Yes, but—"

"Keep your eye on it. I'm coming down with a vest."

Heather gripped my shoulder. "Susan, don't do this."

Heather and the pilot weren't the only ones who thought I was nuts. A voice ordered me not to interfere with what the firefighters were doing. It was Theresa Hardy, my boss.

I took my pistol and the clip from my hip and gave them to Heather. Already holding my jacket, she fumbled with this extra equipment and out the door her microphone went. The mike was quickly reeled in as I turned on the strobes strapped to each of the vests. I ignored the whistling air and took a seat beside the cameraman. Double-checking where the bungee cord was secured to one of the skids, I threw the line out. Holding onto the fuselage, I carefully placed my feet on the skid and stood up in the wind.

Making sure my cell phone worked, I got another dose of my boss ordering me not to do this. How did she know what I was up to? The light from the camera was on me, and the wind blew my short, blond hair around and rustled my collar as I stood on the skid. The pilot had stationed his aircraft over Kings Highway. People on the ground looked up. We were getting a pretty good crowd.

"I'll be on this line," I said, motioning to the cell phone I had attached to my ID lanyard.

"Coast Guard fourteen minutes out!" shouted the teenage copilot as if it might prevent me from performing a swan dive from the skid of the chopper.

As the line played out, the fire, the crowd, all those faces rushed up at me. Then the cord grabbed my vest and jerked me to a bouncy halt, just as it had done the time I'd leaped from the Cooper River Bridge. That time I'd been arrested for bungee jumping, and we might have a repeat performance since my boss had been rousted out of bed. Theresa Hardy was known as an early riser.

I settled at the farthermost extension of the flexible cord as the pilot began to make tight circles over Kings Highway. Soon I was swinging about fifty feet over the four lane and suffering the effects of the smoke and heat like any fireman. My eyes ran, my face quickly dried out. It took a couple of swings to get the rhythm, but timing my throw, the third and fourth times I came around, I hurled a vest at the roof.

The first one fell short. The other hit the elevator penthouse, careened off the corner, and slid across the roof to come to rest only inches from the one thrown by fireman Zack. I picked up the phone clipped to my lanyard. It was important that we not lose momentum. Instead, I heard the voice of a well-coached daughter.

"Daddy, you have to get the vest Miss Chase brought down from the helicopter."

Proffitt looked up at me as I passed over the church across the street from him.

"Did you hear me, Daddy? You have to get the vest that

girl brought down to you."

Excellent. The command center was reading my mind.

It was a moment before Proffitt moved, and then he was on the vest in a flash. Returning to the shower of water provided by the firemen, he shouted over his cell, "I've got it! I've got it!"

Someone cut in and spoke to me. "Agent Chase?"

"Who else is on this line?" I asked.

"Just you and me." It was the voice-of-authority from the command center.

"Take me out to sea."

The voice didn't spend time on small talk but issued an order to the pilot, and the helicopter responded by tugging on my vest. We passed about fifty feet over the roller coaster, then The Attic, a local rock 'n' roll joint. Involuntarily, I raised my feet. The smell of saltwater was stronger now.

The voice from the command center said, "Don't forget to leave your vest. The reporter says there are two more in the helicopter to weigh the line down. She'll slide them down the bungee cord. They should stop when they run into your vest. If it's still there."

"It'll be there."

I flipped the phone closed, gripped the bungee cord overhead, and one-handed my way out of the blinking vest as the chopper flew out to sea. This quickly became no fun. My arm began to burn and communicated to my brain that it was time to bail out.

"Susan," said the pilot when I could hold the cell again, "no waves for the last hundred yards and I'm twenty-five feet above sea level."

"Then I'm out of here."

I let go of the cord, dropped like a rock, and just before hitting the water, remembered to take a breath. My feet knifed into the ocean, and when I didn't touch bottom, I relaxed, savoring the coolness of the saltwater. I had the urge to open my eyes and let the water wash away the smoke and dryness. It wasn't so long before my lungs told my aching arms that we needed air and asked if the arms could do something about that.

Breaking the surface, I realized I didn't have a plan to reach shore. I flipped over on my back and waited for whatever was supposed to happen next. Moments later, a jet ski with a wooden platform hanging off the stern took a turn around me. The board was slanted and had rope laced across it. The jet ski came in close, churning the water around me. A pair of arms reached out and grabbed me.

Oh my God, not that arm!

But the hands showed no mercy as they hauled me from the water and laid me across the network of rope. It was then I realized my shoes were missing. Did a girl need a better reason to go shopping? Damn. I was becoming hysterical. Seconds later, the jet ski broke through the waves and skimmed onto the beach.

I was jolted to a stop and my back scraped across the crisscrossed ropes. The two lesbians were there and bent over me. One of them held my long coat. A guy from EMS covered me with a blanket. I felt damp and chilly. The Huey flew overhead, its light searching for something. That something turned out to be me.

"Proffitt?" I asked, sheltering my eyes from the overhead light. Very quickly I lowered the arm that had held my hundred and thirty-odd pounds at the end of the bungee cord. Tears formed in my eyes again.

"The vest caught on the flag pole," explained the bottle-blonde.

"The vest snagged the flag pole, snapping it off at the base," added the brunette. "From what we could see on TV in a minivan, the pole caught in one of the cracks in the roof. Proffitt really went after that rope."

"Yeah," said the blonde, still grinning goofily, "I suppose he was properly motivated."

"By his daughter," I said.

The EMS tech stuck out his hand. "How many fingers, Agent Chase?"

In the overhead light from the chopper, I squinted at his hand. "Three." I swallowed hard, forcing down the bile. Evidently my stomach had just registered what a lunatic thing I had done.

The tech felt my neck.

"Just don't touch my left arm," I said, blinking away tears. "I think it was pulled . . . from its socket."

"You aren't going to believe this," gushed the blonde, "but Proffitt came down with the American flag draped around him. It was on all the stations."

I closed my eyes to shut out the light and hopefully the voices. Not everything worked.

"You're a real hero, Susan."

"Like some kind of superhero."

"Superheroes don't need ibuprofen," I said without opening my eyes. "May I have something for my left shoulder?"

"Stomach okay?" asked the tech.

"Now that I think about it, no."

"Then why don't we try something for motion sickness. You might be going somewhere."

Like I would have the energy to go anywhere. So I lay there as he fed me something for motion sickness and gently washed my eyes with eyewash. In a few minutes, or perhaps it was several days later, I heard a guy say, "They want her at the command center." When he came into my line of sight, I could see he was one of two uniformed patrolmen.

"We'll bring her along," said the EMS tech.

"We're here to make sure you do."

So the three guys transferred me to a stretcher and carried me off the beach. I didn't put up much of a fuss. Next to The Bowery was parked an EMS vehicle. Surrounding it were people. Lots of people. They cheered. My long coat was thrown over my chest by one of the lesbians.

"If you can raise a hand," said the brunette, "you should wave. They're here for you, Susan."

I waved an embarrassed hand, then I was inside the vehicle, the doors slammed, and away we sped. What kind of thanks would fireman Zack get?

The EMS tech said, "The pilot took Proffitt to Myrtle Square . . . to the command center. The doctor ordered him to Grand Strand Regional, but he won't go until he thanks you. That's the reason for the rush."

I wanted to say "what BS." Instead, I shivered.

The tech smiled down at me. "The doctor will give you a sedative if you want it."

I closed my eyes as the truck and its siren screamed down Kings Highway. "And something for my arm."

Moments later, the EMS swung off the road, raced a short distance, made a couple of turns, and came to an abrupt stop. When the doors opened, I saw the parking lot at Myrtle Square lit up like daylight, heard the sound of a helicopter engine winding down, and saw cars with their headlights pointed toward a pair of tents.

I sat up and the tech fastened something around my chest and shoulder to stabilize my arm. He helped me to my feet and down the steps, where the copilot handed me my pistol, clip, and jacket. I didn't know what to do with them. After standing there for a moment, the pilot and his son fitted my jacket over my shoulders and walked me over to another EMS vehicle. As they did, they hooked my Glock and extra clip to my hip. They also disentangled the lanyard and phone from around my neck. The lanyard they stuck in my pocket, the phone was returned to its pouch, and the tech's blanket was rewrapped around me.

The cameraman was filming everything, and Heather was headed for the rear of the other truck. Coming through the flaps of one of the tents was Theresa Hardy, with Mickey De Shields. Mickey, a good-looking black man, had been my partner until Hardy had begun to saddle me with trainees.

In the rear of the other EMS vehicle lay Glenn Proffitt with an IV in his arm. Probably dehydrated. I know the feeling. My mouth felt dry. I brushed back my damp hair and wondered what it did for my appearance. My clothes were plastered to my body but hidden by the blanket. Still, I was barefoot and the asphalt was chilly. I shivered.

Heather shoved the microphone in the man's face. "How do you feel, Mister Proffitt?"

"Relieved."

A grim smile crossed a red face and not one burned by the sun. Up close I could see his thick black hair was turning gray. Well, if tonight didn't do it . . . . Still, someone had pulled a comb through it. Better than I could say for myself. I reached up to touch my hair and remembered my hands were trapped beneath the blanket.

"I wanted to thank you for saving my life, and especially you, Agent Chase, for getting me off the dime."

"Just doing my job." Actually, if someone didn't grab me, I was about to collapse. Now how would that look on TV?

"That's enough," said the doctor from where he sat beside Glenn Proffitt.

We were herded back, the doors shut, and the vehicle was out of there, lights blinking and siren screaming. Someone had to help me stand. I don't know who it was.

"You know, Chase," said the deputy chief, who I'd met at the site of the explosion, "we about had that fire under control when you went Hollywood on us."

Now I knew I was going to throw up.

"Susan?"

It was Harry Poinsett, a senior citizen whose yacht moors next to my boat at Wacca Wache Landing. With my head I motioned him through the police line. Harry hurried over and wrapped an arm around me.

"Rest room," I gasped.

Harry guided me to the porta-pottie where, once I was inside, I promptly threw up.

"Susan," asked Harry from outside, "you okay?"

My face was hot and cold. "Just . . . dandy." I wiped the sweat away, gripped the edges of the toilet, and tried to keep the small room from moving.

"You need a matron in there?"

"I'm . . . fine."

Once I was upright on the edge of the toilet, a damp towel was handed through the door. A dry one followed that. Finally the sweet and sour smell of the porta-pottie was more than I could stand and I had to leave. Not a good decision. Inside one of the tents I leaned against a table while my boss read me the riot act.

I shivered and pulled my blanket tight. There was something I needed to ask . . . . "When did the building collapse?"

My boss frowned, the deputy chief sputtered, and DeShields

found something on the floor absolutely fascinating.

Harry said, "From what we could see from the camera in the helicopter, the roof collapsed only minutes after Mister Proffitt was lifted off."

From behind the light came the voice of the cameraman. "I'll win an award for sure!"

Heather and her companion were asked to leave. Heather protested, saying when she was on a story, she was in all the way, and she had damn well been here from the beginning. So had I, but I was running on empty. Still, Theresa Hardy had chapped me by insinuating that I had acted irresponsibly.

"When did the rescue choppers arrive?"

Harry spoke again. "The Coast Guard arrived a few minutes after the roof collapsed. A couple of minutes later the one from Shaw Air Force Base arrived."

The deputy chief threw up his hands and stalked out of the tent.

"Where's Daphne?" I asked, looking around. Heather and her cameraman were being ushered, under protest, through the flap by a pair of Myrtle Beach cops.

"Good that you're showing some concern for the person you were responsible for," said Theresa Hardy.

I felt a hand against my back. Harry again. My face was cold, but I was sweating.

"Ms. Hardy," he said, "I'd like to take Susan home. She's had enough excitement for one night."

Mickey laughed. "I'd say this was par . . . ."

DeShields' voice trailed off as our boss gave him a withering glare. "Mister Poinsett, I think I should be the one to determine when Susan's shift ends."

"Of course, but while you're making that decision, I'll find a technician who'll see if Susan requires hospitalization."

I did my best to look woozy. It wasn't hard.

"Fine," conceded Hardy, "then Susan goes with you, but make sure she's at the law enforcement center tomorrow morning by eight. People will want answers, and those same people are going to be up all night while Susan's asleep."

I know I should've cracked wise, but it was all I could do to remain on my feet.

"What in the world was that all about?" asked Harry, once we were safely outside the tent.

"When in the company of women . . . ."

Harry gave me a funny look as he opened the door of his Buick. People began to move in our direction. Harry quickly closed the door behind me.

When he was inside and had the engine started, I asked, "How did you get here?" Wacca Wache Landing isn't a short drive away.

"You were on the news."

I didn't understand.

"When you went in the water, I drove up. Lucky for me there's little traffic."

That didn't make sense either, but I was fading fast.

A gawky guy wearing glasses and a bow tie pounded on the glass as we pulled away. I jumped as he shouted through the closed window; then someone fired off a few flashes. I jumped again when my cell phone rang. Fumbling under the blanket, I found the phone. Funny, I didn't think it would've survived my dunking or I might've called ships at sea. Ahead of us, people waved or applauded as the Buick moved out of the parking lot.

"Susan, got a moment?" It was Heather.

"Talk fast. I'm about to fall asleep." I put my head back as Harry passed the civic center, turned right, and headed for the bypass that would take us home to Murrells Inlet.

"You're the reason the chaos on the street ended. Everyone returned to their rooms to watch you on TV."

"I—I don't know what you're talking about."

"You, me, everyone—we were on CNN."

"I don't understand."

"Who's there with you?"

"Harry."

"Give him the phone."

"Harry doesn't like to talk and drive at the same time."

"Then tell him to pull over."

I stuck the phone from under the blanket. "She says to pull over. She needs to talk. To you." After giving the phone to Harry, I leaned against the window and closed my eyes. Seconds later, I was asleep.

Four

With a little help—okay, okay, a great deal of help from Harry Poinsett—the following morning I dragged myself out of bed on the old shrimp boat where I live. Snatching up my gear, along with a Pop-Tart and Pepsi, out the door of *Daddy's Girl* I went. Harry was having none of that and stopped by McDonald's.

Driving in from Murrells Inlet, we heard that only a gas leak could have caused such an explosion. Once the news ended, the DJ speculated that it couldn't have been a gas leak since the explosion had literally gone through the roof and the remainder of the building was still intact. Then he opened the lines to any nut with a conspiracy theory. Probably made it tough for the gas company to get through and squelch the rumor.

I finished my Big Breakfast as we neared where 501 ran into Kings Highway, the main intersection in downtown Myrtle Beach. I can always count on Harry, so in today's perverted world of relationships, a word of explanation is necessary as to why I'm so chummy with a guy old enough to be my grandfather.

When my father died, Harry stepped in and took charge. For that reason I was not displaced at Wacca Wache Landing, a boat dock along the Intracoastal Waterway. Since Harry suffers from an Ivy League education and once worked for the State Department, he has mixed his observations about life along with reading assignments about those who came before me. For example, on D-Day, when the invasion of Normandy took place, the very macho Earnest Hemingway watched from the safety of a ship while his wife, Martha Gellhorn, went ashore disguised as a stretcher bearer.

This is not to take anything away from Hemingway. His stories are highly readable and depressing enough to qualify for any kid's summer reading program. Still, Martha is the one consigned to the dustbin of history, and this is what I mean about Harry Poinsett making sure my schooling was more than *The Education of Henry Adams.*

With traffic slammed in both directions, Harry dropped me off several blocks from the scene of the explosion.

"Don't be late for your eight o'clock meeting, Susan."

"And you get to Atlanta where you can catch your plane." Something else fueling the morning talk shows. Myrtle Beach Airport had been shut down last night.

"I put some Celebrex in your purse," was the last I heard from him as he drove away.

I shrugged my shoulders, loosening up. One of my arms ached when I'd woken up this morning and I'd considered a quick swim in the Waterway to loosen up. Instead, I did some stretches and rolled back the soreness below the pain threshold.

A few minutes later, I flashed my ID and passed under the crime scene tape strung fifty yards away from the destruction. The cops on duty had tired and strained eyes, but their blue uniforms were fresh and only their shoes were covered with ash. Everyone had evidently gone home and cleaned up. Had a decent breakfast, too, if they were lucky. It would be a long day.

A forensic van I thought I recognized was parked in front of the scorched stucco wall, and people in dark windbreakers passed in front of an opening where the iron gate had once protected an entrance to the street-level garage. Dust drifted in the air of an early, hazy December morning; two small fire trucks stood guard, and more uniforms patrolled the area.

Across the four lane, people stared from the sidewalk or the corners of the short street that connected Kings Highway to the Strip, and beyond the Strip, the beach. The sun was burning off the haze, but I could see the ocean was still shadowy dark. The two-block street that began at the Strip and ended at Kings Highway was cluttered with media vans. Dish antennas broadcast images of the destruction and the words of the public information officer to the rest of the world.

I asked a young patrolwoman for permission to enter the scene. In one of her hands she held a clipboard, the bottom of sheets of paper held down by a rubber band. "I don't know, Susan. The lead detective's not here."

"The lead detective's at the chamber of commerce getting his marching orders."

She smiled and checked with the head tech who operated out of this particular forensics van. A couple of minutes later, Jacqueline Marion appeared at the opening at the street-level entrance.

"Another damn investigator?" But her smile betrayed her tone of voice. "Susan's okay," Jacqueline said, raising her voice over the helicopters and generators. "I just have to make sure she keeps her hands in her pockets."

The patrolwoman smiled as she lifted the crime scene tape. I walked past two concrete planters that had stopped Proffitt's iron gate from being blown into the street. The pansies in the oversized planters were covered with ash and the gate had been squarely caught between the two planters and hung there. Mounted on the stucco wall was a card swipe.

While I waited at the entrance, a sudden breeze caused me to jam my hands into the pockets of my long black coat. The coat is water resistant, has a removable insulated interior, and a split tail that flares up when I'm chasing a perp. A high collar makes it almost unnecessary to bother with a scarf.

My friend returned with a yellow hardhat. Jacqueline Marion is a boyish redhead with a sheet of freckles covering her face. Her freckles redden intensely when she's exposed to the sun, even more so when she goes ballistic. Not only did Jacqueline wear a similar head covering, but also protecting her was a dark windbreaker with "Crime Scene" stenciled on the back.

Being careful where I put my feet, I followed her into the

street-level garage. Inside the parking area, she watched with great amusement as I settled the hardhat on my short blond hair. The multidimensional shape of the 'do gives my hair an illusion of movement created by short lengths underneath and on top; longer lengths at the side and the middle give depth to the cut.

Still smiling, Jacqueline asked, "You worry about what that hardhat might do to your hair, but it doesn't bother you to have it blown all to hell?"

I frowned at her reference to last night, finished fitting the hardhat on my head, and followed her over to a monstrous pile of debris.

Rubble had collected in the center, and the two elevators had their metal doors bent inward, one of them collapsing into the car. Techs moved slowly around the scene, snapping shots with their cameras, and a sketch artist stood in a far corner working with his pencil. A Latino muttered "Good luck on this one" and moved on. Luis was a small fellow with a burr cut, almost shaping his head into a square. Instead of still shots, he filmed with a video cam, and I was sure Luis had been outside filming everyone in the crowd. This was so no one could say they hadn't been at the scene if later interrogated.

Around the parking area lay chunks of plastered roof, beams drooping toward the debris-cluttered floor, and scorched and damaged support columns. The outer covering of the columns had been vaporized, revealing their steel and concrete interior. Under the pile of rubble lay the remains of a van or minivan, its scorched and distorted shell covered with grayish-white rubble. Water stood in shallow pools; everything was damp, and with lower-than-normal temperatures, it would remain that way for some time. Atop the rubble, and illuminated by a shaft of dusty sunlight, sat a lone orange plastic chair.

Jacqueline saw me staring at the gaping hole in the garage roof. "Don't worry," she said, "we wouldn't be here if this was as dangerous as hanging from the end of a bungee cord over a thermal updraft."

My head snapped around. "Was it my fault the only

chopper available belonged to the local NBC affiliate?"

"My, my, but we are touchy this morning."

"I didn't mean—"

"I know what you meant, Susan."

Jacqueline and I had met soon after she was hired by the Horry County Police Department, and all the wives knew Jacqueline had joined the force only to sleep with their husbands. She and I formed a small, tightly woven "young girls network" alerting each other to the more sexist cops and those who wanted to play grab-ass.

My attention returned to the rubble in the center of the garage. Maybe the DJ was on to something. This was no gas leak. "What happened?"

"The easiest bomb to make: fertilizer, fuel oil, and a detonator, but I wouldn't trust the instructions you find on the Internet. You might lose more than your fingers."

I shook my head. "Oklahoma City all over again. Any idea what kind of vehicle?"

"My guess is a van. With a hole cut in the top."

"Like a skylight?"

"Larger, and with a thick, metal container under it."

Around us CSI techs continued to photograph in an orderly fashion, and flashes were constantly going off. Twice we had to move or become part of the scene. Small, yellow, triangular markers were placed here and there, marking this and that. There were an awful lot of those little yellow markers.

What she said finally registered with me. "Wait a minute, are you telling me the blast was somehow funneled to the top floor?"

"There appears to have been a metal structure welded around the bomb. It wasn't car molding but metal sheets. Though what we found wasn't flat but peppered from the blast."

I stepped over for a better view of a hole where shattered wood, plaster, and broken wiring hung. The air was thick with the odor of building materials burned and soaked with water. Occasionally, moisture collected at the end of a piece of debris, gained mass, and fell to the rubble. The orange chair remained upright, as if mocking what we didn't know.

"Sweet," I said, looking into the hole. "With the explosion channeled to the roof, Glenn Proffitt's business becomes as much of a target as the investment firm or the abortion clinic below him."

"The doctor's office wasn't OB-GYN?"

"They also perform abortions."

"I thought all those people had gone out of business."

"There's still one in Columbia, one in Charleston, and this one."

Jacqueline looked at the hole with heightened interest. "What better way to disguise an abortion than a trip to Myrtle Beach." She shook her head. "I knew it didn't make any sense—blowing up a business in the middle of the night. It's called the Proffitt Center, you know, Glenn Proffitt, Proffitt Center."

"So I heard." I was trying to make out the vehicle. "What color is that—blue? Light blue?"

"I'd say light blue, but I'd have to run tests—"

"You're not talking to your boss, Jacqueline."

She glanced around to make sure that there was no one within earshot. "Then it was a light blue VW bus. Tough to blow a hole through an engine block, especially when the force of the explosion is straight up. That leaves most of the engine block intact." She motioned me around the rubble. "Come on, Ms. Not-My-Boss, I want to show you what we found after the bomb squad left. It always helps when the sun comes up."

At the rear of the building was a second, grated gate designed to slide back and allow vehicles inside. The force of the blast had pushed the gate outwards, its upper and lower tracks along the stucco wall twisted beyond repair. The guardhouse that had once stood near the rear entrance was, literally, a shadow of its former self. The kiosk had been fried into the rear wall, and all that was left was a shadow burned into the wall. Stucco had cracked and sheets of it had fallen to the floor. Here and there, the grayish color of the concrete underneath had been darkened by the severity of the blast.

Jacqueline led me to the far wall, where we knelt in front of a large sheet of stucco that had been knocked off the interior garage wall. Stuck in the concrete, and under the large sheet of stucco, was a bumper with its ball hitch jammed into the brick.

"Uh-huh," I said, "someone towed a spare to make sure they were as far away as possible."

Jacqueline glanced over her shoulder at the demolished vehicle. "With the intensity of the blast there shouldn't be anything left—"

"But you suspect?"

"Don't quote me," she said, lowering her voice, "but I think when we uncover the vehicle, we'll find more than one sheet of thick metal on the rear floorboard. That, and the metal form, would also direct the blast upwards."

"And something to set it off . . . . Which should be where any leads will be found."

"Yeah. Right, and that's why I work crime scenes and you play Nancy Drew." She stood up and I joined her. "You can run a check on everyone in this state who has access to explosives, but it won't mean this guy didn't serve in one of the Gulf Wars and bring home a hand grenade. Or he's a member of the Guard, an organization that has armaments go missing from time to time, not to mention those gun shows where all kinds of shit is sold. Susan, this guy knew what he was doing, and I don't mean to set off a simple bomb."

"Meaning, because of the time of the night, nobody was supposed to be here."

"Which means it wasn't a terrorist act, but since this is the number one tourist attraction along the Atlantic Coast—"

"Hence, the eight o'clock meeting."

I glanced at my watch—seven fifteen—before walking over to where the long, wrought iron, rear gate was thrust back. The garage opened into a warren of alleys, and the warren was the back door to a good number of small businesses. Here, too, more crime scene tape fluttered in the breeze. Ash shifted along the ground but never got airborne because of the moisture in the air. A metal post allowed access to the garage when no guard was on duty. Now, bent away from the building, the base of the metal post exposed red, white, and blue wiring.

A fat sergeant joined us. At the far end of the alley, his young partner lifted the yellow tape marking the outer ring of the secondary scene. Raising the tape allowed a wrecker to back toward an old brown station wagon parked inside the fifty-yard perimeter.

Beside me, I heard Jacqueline gasp.

"Sergeant," I asked, "isn't it possible the crime scene techs will want to check that vehicle? It is inside the tape."

He glanced at Jacqueline, whose face had become a red sheet, and then he shouted to the patrolman walking beside the wrecker. "Hey, don't you think the techs will want to check that vehicle before it's moved?"

The patrolman appeared puzzled, but finally stopped the wrecker.

"Sorry," said the sergeant to Jacqueline, "sometimes the younger men get a bit overeager."

"Thank you . . . Sergeant," she said, her freckles fading from their bright red.

I was studying the gate that had been thrust into the street. It was a bit longer than most vehicles and tall enough to prevent anyone from climbing over. I noticed that the locking mechanism had been melted away, and below the lock there were grayish spots on the wrought iron. Paint from where the towed-away vehicle had scraped the gate making its getaway?

"Jacqueline, this lock has been tampered with."

"Tampered with?" asked the sergeant. Without thinking, he put out a hand to grasp the gate so he could bend his heavy bulk down and examine the melted lock.

"Don't touch that!" shouted Jacqueline.

The hand was jerked back and the heavy man righted himself and stepped back. "I get it. You'll find this guy's prints somewhere, pull them, and place them here. Well, well," he said, walking away, "looks like you girls are beginning to get on board after all."

Jacqueline let out a snort as the sergeant sauntered off toward the wrecker. When he was abreast of the station wagon he gave it a cursory check, turned back to us, and nodded his approval.

"So," said Jacqueline, watching him go, "to belong to the good ol' boys network, all I have to do is fudge a print here, drop a pistol there."

"What about the gate?" I asked.

"One of the first things discovered by the bomb squad, and a very risky proposition. Not only does melting a lock take time, but a handheld torch emits a bright light, one that someone might've seen."

"Uh-huh. If anyone had been noticed back here, all those TV cameras across the street would be trained somewhere else." I pursed my lips. This close to Christmas much of the Grand Strand was shut down. People would bundle up and walk along the beach, stroll the open shops along the Strip, but to find anyone who'd noticed someone in an alley . . . .

"Where's Proffitt's vehicle?" I asked.

"At his place."

"You're sure of this?"

Jacqueline nodded, which meant she'd gotten the information from someone she trusted inside the department.

I pulled out my phone. "Site cleared for cell phones and radios?"

She nodded again, and I took that to mean that the bomb squad didn't think there were any other explosive devices within the perimeter. I used my speed-dial to call my former SLED partner.

"DeShields," said Mickey on his end.

"Where are you?" I asked.

"Where you're supposed to be—at the law enforcement center," meaning the Myrtle Beach Police Department.

I asked Mickey if he would check the cab companies to see who might've been working the airport last night and dropped off Glenn Proffitt at his business.

"And you can't check this yourself—why?"

"I'm at the scene. If it hasn't been done, you might want to put out a BOLO (Be On The Lookout) for a white American male, age twenty-five to forty-five seen driving a blue VW bus and towing a small car behind it, possibly gray in color, and, later alone in the smaller car, with scratches along one side. Add that he may have been wearing a hood on his jacket like the Unabomber and probably an insulated vest over that."

"That's more than the bomb squad has gone on record saying. You really want to trust your 'scene sense' on this? The Beltway snipers were both black."

"The exception that proves the rule." I glanced out the rear of the garage. "The officers doing the canvass in this neighborhood should ask if anyone saw a bright light. The perp used a torch to cut his way through the gate."

"Susan, the bomb squad has already reported that."

"Mickey, why are you giving me a hard time? You want me to call this in to the desk sergeant?"

"No. I'll run it by Hardy. And I'll have your trainee check the cab companies. But you'd better be right. I don't think you understand how high-profile this whole thing is about to become."

"Sure I do. I'll be lucky to be riding a desk throughout this whole investigation."

I snapped the phone shut and looked around the garage. Under the debris, the floor was scorched black but so were the walls. Glenn Proffitt said he couldn't cross the garage because of the flames. Burning concrete. That had to be a sight.

To Jacqueline, who was signing some paperwork, I said, "Last night the firefighters reported the floor of the garage in flames."

"Gasoline," said Jacqueline without looking up. "We found melted plastic containers everywhere." Returning the clipboard to the tech, she offered more of an explanation. "It's also why the fire went up the sides of the building so quickly and why the firefighters couldn't reach Glenn Proffitt."

"I'm sure someone will be assigned to interview him."

"That would be you." Luis approached us with a cell phone in his hand. A smile crossed her face as Jacqueline asked, "Didn't Proffitt thank you personally before he was taken to the hospital?"

I ignored this remark and headed for a corner.

Luis said, "It's the boss."

Looking up the side of the building from under the

corner, I could see the space separating the garage and the floors overhead. The scorched walls of the building were off-set a good six inches and the wood had been burned away, exposing the moisture-proofing. Reacting to the heat, the material had turned black. At my feet, rubble had collected in a small narrow grate. More grated slots were strategically placed where the wall met the floor, and the floor had a pitch to it.

Jacqueline joined me under a camera mount missing its camera. In all four corners, the small black machines and their cracked lenses either drooped to one side or had vanished. She said, "If Proffitt had used synthetic stucco, it would've had a fire retardant underneath."

"Maybe that's why he didn't."

"I don't follow."

"This could've been his insurance policy."

"I'm sure he has insurance, Susan."

"That's not the kind of insurance I mean."

"Then, if Proffitt got in over his head, this building could go up in flames and he would collect? But wouldn't Proffitt know any explosion after 9/11 would be closely scrutinized?"

"I don't know," I said scanning the pile of rubble in the garage and its blackened walls. "This is way overkill."

"Meaning an amateur got his mixture wrong."

"Or the date of detonation."

"Because Proffitt was in the building."

"That would be the theory." Across the garage, a stairwell door was propped open by a piece of two-by-four. "FBI or firefighters?"

"Firemen and the bomb squad. When the FBI got here, they wanted to go up, but I wouldn't let them. That's what the call was about. My boss says they'll be here by ten-thirty and I'm to give them every consideration."

"I got off on the wrong floor once." I was staring at the busted set of elevator doors. "You have to be buzzed into the investment offices on the first floor, or second floor, if you're counting the parking garage. The office above that, the OB/GYN, had an open area you had to cross to reach the receptionist, and bulletproof glass. Metal doors painted to look like wood and a metal detector built into the door."

Jacqueline said nothing, only stared at me.

I glanced at my watch. "Can we go up?"

Jacqueline was still staring at me.

"Is there a problem?"

"Er—no. Now that it's daylight, but you have to do as I say. That means keeping your hands to yourself."

"Of course."

Jacqueline produced a flashlight from her windbreaker, as I did a penlight from inside my jacket. "Luis, how about coming with us." As we headed for the propped-open fire door, she asked, "Sure you've got the time for this?"

"For a walk-through—sure."

But when we turned up the first body, my tardiness at the eight o'clock meeting became moot, as did the meeting.

Five

On the second floor landing, I joined the others in slipping on a pair of latex gloves. Then we stepped through another propped-open fire door and into a single large room. In the center of the room, light filtered through the hole like a shaft through a rain forest.

Glass was everywhere, and the cubicles everyone complains about working in had been thrown back. Cubicle walls lay against others or leaned against desks like plants flattened by a hard rain. Everything was damp or soaked. The smell of burned or melted material filled our nostrils.

The air was still a bit hazy, but we could see that the elevators and their scarred doors were the only upright structures remaining in the room. In corners were offices with wooden doors, and those doors had been knocked back by the blast or forced open by firemen. Wooden or sheetrock surfaces were dotted with pieces of metal, chips of wood, and the odd fragment of plastic; vents in walls were filled with debris trapped by their filters; and the dual security lights were smashed. On a far wall hung a Christmas wreath locked into a position that defied gravity.

The suspended ceiling had been rocked from its aluminum grids and its opaque glass shattered, melted, or knocked askew. Fractured fluorescent lights hung from their sockets and dripped water. Shattered pieces of the long bulbs had joined chunks of the rectangular insulation on the floor, on desks, or the collapsed cubes. Other than the light through the hole in the ceiling, only our three lights illuminated the gloomy room.

Luis coughed and cleared his throat, Jacqueline's flash discharged and her Nikon clicked, and the carpet squished under our feet. You couldn't help crushing glass or plastic, and the closer you came to the blast area, the more the floor tilted. Office paraphernalia had been blown off a desk and replaced by rubble. The desk teetered precariously near the hole. Burned-out wiring and gutted ductwork hung from the jagged hole as it had in the garage. Water dripped from sprinkler heads and pipes where the system had been severed by the explosion. A melted orange plastic chair—its metal framework twisted—hung in the wiring.

Jacqueline instructed Luis to film all sides of the room, and if he had to, from a distance. Once Luis finished, we skirted the cavity and moved across the room. Wiring snaked across the floor, some of it protected by metal runners, but its machinery had been fried: computers, faxes, even the postage machine. I followed them through a workstation containing a Xerox machine, singed and damp phone books in piles on the floor, and pigeonholes filled with no mail.

I glanced at my watch: 7:35 a.m. "I want a quick look-see in the OB/GYN."

Upstairs, we faced a short hallway, and turning right, we found a nurse's station. Medical files and their plastic slots had been rocked from the wall and scattered across the floor. Cabinets with locked glass doors were busted and gave access to small bottles, which lay on shelves and on a counter below them. Two secretarial chairs sat in the station covered with dust and debris. Christmas and office paraphernalia had been knocked to a vinyl floor, and beyond the nursing station, the linoleum was cracked, the floor littered with melted glass, and the walls nasty enough to embarrass any nurse.

On our right stood a row of examination or procedure rooms. Scratched across the damp and debris-littered linoleum floor were marks where firemen had shoved doors back. At the opposite end of the hall was an opening similar to the nurses' station. More melted glass littered the hall farther down, and the entire wall had been separated from the floor, the sheetrock split. Under us, the floor creaked and a fracture shot down the hall.

"Luis," suggested Jacqueline, "I think we should try the other side."

"Sounds good to me."

We returned to the short hallway and then found another longer hallway filled with storage rooms and doctors' offices. On doors hung decorations or small Christmas wreaths. Jacqueline stuck her head in rooms; Luis filmed and took more photographs. Evidently, you couldn't have too many photos. I followed the others past the fire door on the opposite side of the building and around to the corridor with the fractured linoleum floor.

When Luis headed for the secretarial/waiting room, Jacqueline touched his arm. "Let me go first." She edged past the window with its jagged glass in the lower frame and disappeared inside.

We followed her into a room lit by the same shaft of light through the hole in the ceiling. The bulletproof glass designed to protect the receptionist had been shattered and the waiting room was missing most of its floor. Orange plastic chairs had collected in an orange lump near a hole that distinctly listed downward.

Besides ripping through the reception area, the blast had also demolished the secretarial station and the office of the office manager. In an open area, huge metal cabinets had tumbled over, scattering files across a carpeted floor soaked with water. A plastic Rudolph was melted from his hindquarters back but still had his red nose.

I backed into the hallway, thrust my hands into my coat, and leaned against the wall. Why had someone done this? It just didn't make sense.

I considered lighting up a cigarette, then remembered I'd quit—again—and realized I stood in the "hot zone" where the likelihood of gathering the most evidence existed. A glance at my watch told me I was going to be late for the meeting at the law enforcement center.

I gritted my teeth. Jacqueline and Luis were taking their own sweet time filming and photographing this particular floor, and I had to suppress an urge to ask them to move along. I fingered the penlight in my coat pocket.

"Mind if I check the room across the hall?" I asked.

From the secretarial station came the rapid snap and flash of the Nikon. "I'm not sure about the structural integrity of that hallway, Susan."

"I'm only going in the one across the hall."

"Just be careful. And don't touch anything."

The one across the hall turned out to be a procedure room. The metal operating table had been knocked over and blown into the corner. The surgical arm that fed power from the ceiling hosted a row of electrical cords that had been frayed and melted. Two TV monitors had been blown off their tables, knocked to the floor, and their screens shattered. In the rear of the room a stainless steel sink was littered with debris.

The small room had lost its false ceiling, and pieces of styrofoam and opaque plastic had fallen to the floor along with shards of fluorescent bulbs. One of the pieces of glass reflected something off a metal stool lying on its side. When I put the light on it, the spots disappeared.

Had that been blood?

When I moved the penlight, the dots reappeared across the metal surface. Again they disappeared when I put the tiny beam on the stool. I stepped closer to the overturned table, its wheels locked into place, and one of the stirrups jutting up. The reflection wasn't of blood . . . but a foot with toenails painted bright red!

"In here!"

By the time the others joined me, I was hunched down, staring at the body hidden by the overturned procedure table. At first Jacqueline couldn't see what I was seeing.

"You're putting too much light on it."

"Luis," she said, "turn off the light."

The room went dim. I even turned off my penlight. When Jacqueline moved her light she saw the reflection on the metal stool. She quickly stood up, found the woman with her flashlight, and checked for a pulse. She tried to move the jaw. It didn't move. Luis was told to turn the light back on and to film the far side of the overturned examination table.

"That's why the firemen didn't see her," I said, stooping down in the light from the camera. When I reached for the stool, Jacqueline gripped my arm.

"Careful, Susan, there's nothing you can do for her."

I straightened up, turned off my penlight, and stuffed my hands in my coat pockets. "We're going to have to move her sooner or later."

"But not until we've processed the crime scene," which meant endless measurements, prints, and more photographs. Just thinking about it made me antsy.

"And the coroner has to pronounce."

"Yeah. Right."

Jacqueline reached for a microphone clipped to the collar of her windbreaker and spoke into it. She gave the date, time of day, location, and the names of those present. "What we appear to have is a female body."

"Because of the painted toenails."

Jacqueline snapped off the mike. "Hey, I don't need an attitude."

"I just wish we could move this along."

"I'm sure you do, Susan, but you're stuck with the discovery. If you want to make yourself useful, call this in to homicide."

I didn't get the chance. My phone sounded the theme from *Hawaii 5-0*. I stepped toward the door to take the call. As I did, debris crunched under my feet. "Yes?"

"You're supposed to be at the law enforcement center." It was Mickey DeShields.

"I don't think I'm going to make it."

"You'd damn well better. The FBI is here and someone said the CIA is on the way."

"The CIA?"

"That's right. Now get your butt down here."

"I don't think I can do that, Mickey. I—we found a body."

"Are you serious?"

"As a heart attack."

Jacqueline rolled her eyes. It would be all she could do to keep everyone from clamoring up here and tromping all over the crime scene. And everybody and their sister would have to be notified. Including the CIA.

The CIA. What the hell were they doing here?

"Mickey, I'll get back to you."

"Don't worry 'bout it. I think we'll be coming there."

"They're coming," I said, returning the phone to its pouch on my hip.

"No doubt." She spoke without any trace of humor.

I thought Jacqueline's sympathies were sorely misplaced. I couldn't get the image out of my mind of a hospital gown hiked up to the woman's chest. Where her legs were splayed, the split had been dark and bled. A dry, pink froth covered the woman's face and her eyes were frozen open in that empty stare that always makes me uncomfortable.

"Susan," said Jacqueline, changing the film in her camera, "don't you dare touch anything."

She had caught me scanning the room for something that would ID the dead woman. I returned my hands to my pockets, which was the only way I could be trusted inside a crime scene, especially if I wasn't the primary investigator.

Who *was* the primary on this case? What did it matter? Minutes from now, every member of any law enforcement agency would be crawling all over this place.

I peered around the back of the door. No hook or clothing. But something on the opposite wall. I stepped over, debris crunching under my feet.

"Susan?"

"I'm not touching anything!"

The knob could be a hook, the shadow could be disintegrated clothing, and below that, on a singed counter, a melted brown blob that could be a wallet or billfold.

"I think this is ID."

"Leave it alone."

"But, Jacqueline, her family—"

"Leave it for homicide!"

I closed my eyes, but all I could see was a woman in her late teens or early twenties, no jewelry, and most of her black hair tucked under a surgical cap. Her head was turned to one side; she had a sharp profile, and a set of eyebrows that needed to be plucked. The woman's right arm lay in front of her, the hand cupped, those nails painted the same color as her toes. Pieces of glass, plastic, and sheetrock covered her bare leg, side, and the hospital gown pushed up under her arm. She had no tan, but that wasn't all that unusual this time of year.

"You know," I heard Luis say, "besides the area between the legs, there's no blood."

"Probably the shock of the blast shut down her system." Jacqueline lowered her camera.

"What are you saying?" I asked. "One moment she was alive, the next she was dead?"

"Pretty much so."

How's that? One moment you're here, then the next . . . nothing.

Duh, Susan. That's called sudden death, and the way most people would like to go.

Yeah. In their nineties.

"Okay, Luis, I think we have all we can get until we have the right people up here." Jacqueline fished around in the pocket of her windbreaker and dug out her cell phone. She opened a channel and spoke to homicide.

I was staring again at the overturned table with the stirrup sticking into the air. "Lying on an operating table in the middle of the night . . . there was more going on here than a simple abortion."

"Then where's the doctor?" asked Luis, bringing down his camera from his shoulder.

"That's what I intend to find out." I turned to leave.

"Hey, I haven't cleared that hall for traffic."

But Jacqueline was helpless to stop me. She'd received another call. I stepped into the hallway, and Luis followed me with Jacqueline on her cell.

"Marion here."

I stuck my penlight between my teeth, flattened my body against the wall, and edged across the cracked floor. For my trouble, the floor creaked and the fracture enlarged. Soot drifted from the ceiling to the damp linoleum floor. Very quickly, I shuffled through the door and into the next room.

"Would you repeat that?" came Jacqueline's voice from the hallway.

I shook my head as I came out of the empty room. Luis and his light were filming me from the doorway of the secretarial/reception area. Under my feet, the floor groaned, then splintered, and another ridge in the vinyl erupted. Gaping holes appeared in the hallway between us.

"Don't have anyone go any closer. We'll be right there." Jacqueline closed her phone. "Luis, we're needed elsewhere."

But when Luis returned to the hall, the floor gave way underneath him. Vinyl ripped, plywood splintered, and beams fractured, and there was a thunderous roar as a section of the hallway tumbled into the floor below.

Jacqueline grabbed Luis's arm and they stumbled back as the floor opened up at their feet. Both Luis and Jacqueline sat down hard in the broken glass. Soot floated down from the ceiling, the huge window frame between the hallway and the reception area sagged, and somewhere, off in the distance, I heard the shattering of what had to be the last piece of solid glass left in the Proffitt Center.

Jacqueline got to her feet, shook her pants, and then brushed them off. "Susan, remember that fat sergeant who almost tampered with my crime scene?"

Luis was puzzled, but I nodded.

"He may have found our missing doctor."

Six

Mickey DeShields told me what happened after he got off the phone. Each time he had relayed to my boss what I told him, but one call carried considerably more weight. After the first phone call—the one where I told him to put out a BOLO for a white male, twenty-five to forty-five, blah, blah, blah—Mickey said Theresa Hardy was drinking coffee and eating a donut with the Myrtle Beach chief of police when he brought the information to her.

"Does Chase have any probable cause to back up her assumption?"

"I didn't ask," Mickey said. "I assume she does."

Glancing at the chief of police, Hardy said, "Tell Chase this is no time to be a cowboy and to get down here."

Thankfully, Mickey told me only to make the meeting. My report about the woman's body was the call that got everyone all stirred up. After disconnecting, Mickey realized Hardy was staring at him, and this time she wasn't the only one. Around the long, shiny wood table of the conference room sat the heads of departments: fire, SLED, FBI, ATF, and the local cops. All were staring at him, though Mickey thought he'd lowered his voice to deliver the news.

"Are you serious?" she asked.

"Lieutenant," said Mickey, "you and I need to talk outside."

They did, bringing along the head of the Southern Division of the Federal Bureau of Investigation and the chief of the Myrtle Beach Police. As I saw for myself later, the *feeb* is an average-sized guy with brown hair and brown eyes, fit, though approaching middle age. The chief of police, who I've known for years, is bulky, tanned to the bone, and has a crew cut, probably one of the last in existence. My boss is a heavy woman whose black hair makes her light complexion even paler.

Hardy said, "Tell them what you just told me."

Mickey repeated my story about the woman found on the second floor.

"Details?" asked Jacob Kinlaw, the FBI agent.

Mickey shook his head.

"Did you ask for details?" asked the chief of police.

Gesturing at the conference room, Mickey said, "I didn't think I should. Not in there."

Kinlaw looked at the chief and Hardy. "Well, what are we going to do?"

"I think we should get the particulars from Chase," said the chief.

Kinlaw's eyebrows went up. "Susan Chase? The woman who did the high-wire act over the crime scene last night?"

Hardy and the chief nodded. Evidently, my reputation preceded me.

"You think she's grandstanding again?" asked Kinlaw.

"With Chase you never know," said my boss with a strong lack of support. "She's probably about to go public with the information."

"That would be counterproductive. Is there any way you can stop her?"

Mickey glanced at our boss. "I'm sure it won't take more than a phone call."

"Then for God's sake, call her."

Out came Mickey's phone again, but because of the noise at the crime scene, Mickey couldn't make out what I was saying. It was a moment before he could relay to those outside the conference room that we were clearing the building.

Kinlaw took the cell phone from Mickey. "Clearing the scene? Why is that?"

"We had a . . . situation on the second floor."

"The body—yes. What else?"

"The floor began to give way."

"Is anyone in danger?"

"I think you should ask Jacqueline Marion."

"Who's that?"

"The tech in charge of the crime scene."

"Would you put her on?"

In the parking garage, I thrust the phone at Jacqueline. On this trip out of the building, nobody was taking photographs.

"Yes?" snapped Jacqueline into my phone.

Kinlaw identified himself.

"Agent Kinlaw, I'm trying to clear a potentially dangerous crime scene."

Kinlaw appeared to remember the layout of the Proffitt Center. It had been projected on a screen in the conference room. "Can you take your people out the rear?"

Jacqueline stared through the narrow entrance where her forensics van was parked on Kings Highway, and the reporters waited. When she stopped, we stopped. All except Luis, hustling his camera and gear toward the wrought iron gate blown into the two huge concrete planters on the wide sidewalk.

"Luis, don't go out there."

The Latino stopped and stared at the microphones, heard the shouted questions, and saw the lights of *their* cameras. If the public information officer was around, he was being totally ignored. Jacqueline returned the phone to me, and I was asked by Agent Kinlaw what was going on.

"We stopped."

"Where are you?" asked Kinlaw.

"At the entrance on Kings Highway."

Silence at the other end.

"Now we're turning around and heading for the rear." And that included Luis.

"Hurry, Susan." Jacqueline had taken an angle that would lead her people around the debris.

I followed, only glancing at the dust settling where pieces of the upper floors had fallen into the garage. All of the crime scene equipment had been removed but for the yellow triangular markers on the floor. My phone went dead as Kinlaw disconnected.

At the law enforcement center, Kinlaw returned the cell phone to DeShields. Before they could reenter the conference room, the head of the crime scene technicians appeared outside the door.

"Chief, there's a report coming in about a body found in a dumpster near a pizzeria a little over a block from the primary crime scene."

"Dumped?" asked the city chief.

"I'm not sure. This one was pretty much blown to pieces. Head crushed. Legs missing."

Mickey nodded. "That would be consistent with being on one of the upper floors of the Proffitt Center when the bomb detonated."

"Let's not get ahead of ourselves," said Agent Kinlaw. "Are your people saying they believe this body is related to the explosion?"

"It's not my people," said the head tech. "One of the uniformed patrolmen found the body."

"What's the location?" asked the chief of police.

The head tech told them, explaining where the dumpster would be in reference to the Proffitt Center. "We've had cases like this before. I remember finding a foot, inside a shoe, a quarter-mile from a crime scene. It was after a meth lab blew. "

Kinlaw had a question. "Could this be the doctor?"

"If the doctor was a woman. The preliminary information says it's the body of a woman. Most of her clothing blown off."

Everyone was silent for a moment. The uniformed patrolwoman near the door tried to appear as if she wasn't listening.

"Susan is within walking distance of the second crime scene," volunteered Mickey.

"I'll go with that," said the city chief, nodding. "And she's got a cell with her."

"What about your own homicide people?" asked Kinlaw.

"With the congestion around the crime scene, Chase or the crime scene techs will get there first."

Mickey volunteered his phone and Hardy made the call

and I received *my* marching orders.

"And," said the Myrtle Beach chief, as they returned to the conference room, "I'll have more people assigned to an extensive search of the area. We don't need more body parts showing up over the next few days."

Once they were seated again, Kinlaw worked the conference room by saying, "Agent DeShields, why don't you tell us what you've just learned."

Mickey did, and when he told them about the discovery of the body on the second floor, not to mention the one found in the dumpster, someone from homicide was assigned to investigate both crime scenes.

"That's impossible," said the fire chief as the homicide detective went out the door.

The bomb squad seconded that motion.

But the city chief had more important issues on his mind. "If the building is unstable, we need clearance from the fire department before we proceed."

On the other side of the table, the fire chief opened a line to the command center with a cell phone.

From around the table more than one person asked, "Is everyone safe at the scene?"

The city chief said, "I've been assured that everyone is being removed from the building."

Everyone visibly relaxed.

The fire chief closed the line to the command center at Myrtle Square. "I've got people on the way to check the building." He cleared his throat. "In the chaos of last night, it's possible we might've missed something."

The head of the bomb squad only stared at a piece of paper in front of him.

"Well," said Kinlaw, with a wan smile, "the building was threatening to come down around them."

A patrolman gave me a lift to the law enforcement center, and we sat in his cruiser, staring at the media trucks, reporters, and cameramen.

"Well, Susan, I'm out of here."

Evidently, the patrolman didn't want anything to do with reporters and their antennas aimed at geosynchronous satellites on the horizon broadcasting to the world.

"You don't want to be on TV?" I asked, smiling.

"Not the way they're talking about you." He nosed the sedan away from all those steno pads, cameras, and microphones.

Camera lights were turned on, lighting up an otherwise gloomy day. Since the chamber of commerce is across the street from the law enforcement center, I could only imagine the gauntlet the chamber's director had had to run. I didn't have to imagine long.

"What does it feel like to be a hero, Ms. Chase?"

"How did you feel when you were swinging around on that rope last night?"

"Did you think you were going to die?"

"Did you think Glenn Proffitt was going to die?"

"Have you seen Mr. Proffitt since last night?"

The most inane question of them all came as I made my way across the breezeway. "What's the relationship between you and Glenn Proffitt? We understand he refused medical attention until meeting with you."

"Are you two romantically involved?" was shouted as a uniformed patrolman opened one of the glass doors and allowed me inside.

"Fun, eh?" said the patrolman. "Susan, you'll need your ID to proceed any farther. Things have changed since yesterday."

"So I noticed."

I showed my ID to a young woman at the front desk and she told me everyone was in the conference room. I shrugged out of my long coat, went down the hall, and turned the corner. As I did, I checked my jacket, pants, and blouse. My navy shoes were covered with soot, my pants slightly marred by brushing up against something at the crime scene, and I had a dark smudge over my heart.

I glanced at the locker room where I kept a clean outfit. I didn't have time to change, nor did I want to dampen my white blouse over my undergarments. Not in front of a bunch of men. On the way to the conference room, I went in the bullpen, dropped off my coat, and found my trainee on the phone. Daphne looked up as I approached the desk. The gangly woman checked my attire and frowned.

"Get that taxi report?" I asked.

Daphne fitted the phone between her shoulder and ear as she shuffled paperwork. She found the sheet and handed it to me. As I read the information, she said, "I'm hoping to get off this desk and rejoin you in the field."

"Be careful what you wish for." I returned the sheet. It was part of the official record now.

"Going to the big meeting?" she asked.

"Already late."

"Wish I could join you."

"You think."

Even though the patrolwoman outside the wooden doors of the conference room knew me, I still had to hold up my lanyard ID before I could enter. Even then, she leaned inside as she opened the door and nodded to the Myrtle Beach chief of police.

Legal pads, notebooks, and dayplanners lay on the shiny tabletop. Beside them were donuts and coffee. Behind the officials around the long wooden table was a secondary set of chairs against opposite walls and that is where DeShields sat. Mickey was dressed in all black but for a red tie. Black shades protruded from a jacket pocket. He motioned me to the other side of the table where he'd saved a seat.

Oh, boy.

Everyone looked like they'd been up all night and subjected to too much smoke and media attention. I wondered if I stunk. How could I not?

The fire chief was standing by the projected image of the floor plans of what had once been the Proffitt Center and pointing out that there were no windows on the three floors over the garage, that there were two elevators, two fire doors, and one vehicular exit at street level. The ground floor was for parking and for the flooding from hurricanes that occasionally come ashore.

Sanctuary of Evil

Hurricane Lili had recently done just that. I'd survived; my fiancé had not, and stepping on the deck of *Daddy's Girl* this morning, I'd knocked over a vase of long-stemmed roses. At first I thought my former fiancé had returned from the living dead, and my heart leaped to my throat, but when I bent down and righted the vase, I learned the roses were from Glenn Proffitt. Sorry, I said, tossing the vase and their contents into the Waterway. My heart belongs to another. Someone no longer capable of knowing I exist.

All eyes followed me as I took a seat next to DeShields, and when the chief finished his presentation, I was called on. Brushing back my hair—had I actually come in this room without checking my hair?—I cleared my throat, stood, and related our adventures on the second and third floors. Catching the eye of the fire chief and the bomb squad sitting down the table from me, I explained it had been dumb luck on our part that we had found the dead woman . . . in a dark corner of one of the procedure rooms . . . behind a table . . . and covered by large chunks of debris. I probably went on about this more than was necessary.

"ID?" asked the chief of police.

"Possibly, once they've processed the crime scene."

"What was she doing there?" asked the fire chief.

"From what I saw, it appears she was having an abortion."

Several men sat up. More than one asked, "At that time of night?"

Someone shook his head. "At this time of year?"

I went through the probable cause of death before returning to my seat. I bit my lip. Perhaps the woman had been anesthetized before she'd—

"And the body in the dumpster behind the pizza restaurant?" asked my boss, turning around to face me.

"Oh, yeah." I scanned the table. "Anyone got some extra coffee?" I asked, faking nonchalance.

Everyone looked at everyone else, but it was Mickey who got up and left the room.

When I spoke from my seat, my boss ordered, "Stand up, Chase, to address the group."

I did, describing the second crime scene where the (practically) headless and (definitely) legless woman had been found in a dumpster farther inland, my other stop. "She appears to have been directly over the blast when the bomb detonated. We have no idea if she'd been alerted to the danger and was returning to the procedure room to inform her patient."

I was still having a problem talking to men in the most casual manner about women and what had been done to their bodies, especially when those women had been found in a considerable state of undress. I preferred leaving that to the crime scene techs and their cold, cold hearts.

"Name of the restaurant?" asked the city chief.

I gave them the name, one of gazillions selling pizza along the Grand Strand.

As Mickey returned with my coffee, someone asked, "The restaurant personnel didn't see the woman in the dumpster?"

I smiled at Mickey, sipped my coffee, and said, "The owner of the restaurant told us he could ask his cleanup crew why they hadn't noticed the body, but they were probably in a hurry to return to the bomb site."

"The cleanup crew went to the bomb site?" asked Kinlaw from his end of the table. It was the first time I'd noticed the *feeb.* He wore a dark blue business suit, white shirt, and Ivy League tie. No soot.

"Everyone in the vicinity went to the crime scene, whether they heard the bomb detonate or saw it on TV."

"Why didn't you remain on the scene and continue to search for more bodies?" asked Agent Kinlaw.

"Proffitt said there was no one on his floor or he would've brought them to the roof with him. The owners of the OB/GYN clinic said they didn't know anything about the procedure. An employee was probably performing a late-night abortion."

"And how do you know this?" asked my boss, still canted around. Any moment she'd throw her neck out.

"I contacted the doctors. No one was authorized to be in the clinic last night."

"You contacted *who?*" My boss gripped the table with one

hand, her other on the back of her chair.

"The doctors who own the clinic."

"Chase, the Myrtle Beach chief of police is responsible for assigning who interrogates whom."

"Actually," I said, retaking my seat, "I was more concerned with whether we needed to be searching for that missing doctor who might be out there."

Hardy glared at me, and I realized that she was wearing her one, excellent, Donna Karan power suit, small gold earrings, and a very thin necklace. Black hair still cut as if someone had put a bowl over her head. But it was an outstanding dark blue suit.

A man at the other end of the table got to his feet. The Horry County chief of police was a medium-size fellow with light red hair and a trimmed mustache. He wore a gray uniform and wire-rimmed glasses. Established during the Fifties, the Horry County Police was created when the legislature stripped the sheriff of his power, intent on reducing the Ku Klux Klan's influence in an area beginning to boom with tourism.

The county chief referred to a legal pad. "This operation needs someone to coordinate efforts and I've been asked to assume that responsibility. Still, it'll be the Myrtle Beach chief of police who'll face the media. No one else is to speak to the press, and it has been determined the chief will speak after the news. That's after the evening news, people. We are not going to fuel this fire."

"Has anyone claimed responsibility?" I asked.

"I know you arrived late, Miss Chase, but if you could hold your questions."

I slid back in my chair, taking my coffee with me.

"I don't want to dumb this down," said the county chief, "but since we have so many people in here, I'm going to take it from the top."

Most everyone settled into their chairs.

He continued. "I'll pass along information to those with a need-to-know. In other words, everything goes through me, and when I'm not on duty, Major Fielder." He stepped aside so we could see a balding, middle-aged man sitting behind him. "And I report everything to the chief. He makes the final decision about what goes on the air."

The director of the chamber of commerce cleared his throat. Tanned, and wearing a pinstriped suit, the director had solid shoulders and white hair. Not gray but bleached white by the almost year-round sun of the Grand Strand. His eyes were pale blue. "I'm not comfortable with all these people descending on the Grand Strand."

From behind him, at the other end of the table, the FBI agent said, "We'll use discretion."

The director swung around. "Agent Kinlaw, I appreciate everything the federal government is doing, but I have to remind you that this is going to literally shut us down. I know we need answers and we need them fast and that takes manpower, but this is the Grand Strand and the primary driver of our economy is tourism."

"Mister Director, I think everyone at the table knows that."

The white-headed man gestured at those sitting around the table. "Everyone knows that without the Grand Strand there is no Horry County police, no Myrtle Beach fire department or police department, as we know it. This is not Virginia or Maryland, and the reason for this meeting."

Kinlaw sat there, waiting for more.

There wasn't any, and I wondered how the director could play chicken with this guy. Still, he did, continuing to stare at him.

Finally, Agent Kinlaw nodded. "I understand."

"Thank you." Returning his attention to the Horry County chief of police, the director said, "I apologize for the interruption."

"No reason to apologize," said the county chief after glancing at the FBI agent. "It's something that needed to be said."

"What about overtime?" asked someone.

"Don't worry about it," answered the city chief.

"You're kidding," said another.

The director of the chamber of commerce interrupted again. "If it's a question of money—"

"This came from the governor," said the city chief. "Solve

the case. Catch the bad guy." He looked up and down the table. "That's an order."

After everyone had absorbed this information, the county chief spoke again. "Okay, people, Myrtle Beach is out of school for the holidays. Cots and other provisions will be set up for the visiting media and whoever else needs a place to sleep. The reporters will bunk in at the elementary school, our people will use the middle school, and I don't have to tell you, loose lips do sink ships. For those who want to run their mouths, a tip line is already operational."

"Any leads so far?"

"It's been less than twelve hours, but we have plenty of wild geese for you to chase."

Those at the table groaned. There would be tips from up and down the Grand Strand, and across the country, not to mention the occasional psychic.

"Warrants are being prepared by the solicitor's office for the principals and those subleasing premises in the Proffitt Center. Warrants are also being prepared for Glenn Proffitt's home and his new place of business, along with the homes of the owners of the clinic and the investment house, and that, Miss Chase, was why I wanted you to hold your questions."

I quickly found something on my shoe to brush off and directed my attention there.

"This doesn't mean these warrants will be used, but if someone plays hardball, these warrants can be executed in a moment's notice. Remember, people, this is the Grand Strand, and the quicker we can bring someone in, the better everyone is going to feel," meaning the tourists would once again be returning to Myrtle Beach. "Right now," the county chief added, "the focus of our work is on the clinic."

No one appeared to be surprised, so I had to assume the full extent of operations of the OB/GYN were known to everyone around this table. It also was why my boss had been ticked when I'd called the doctors at home, and I'm sure it didn't go over well with the detectives assigned to the case.

The county chief glanced at his legal pad, then looked at the city chief. "Now we come to who investigates whom. Do you know who you want to perform the initial field investigation with Glenn Proffitt? I understand he's out of the hospital and back at work."

That caused many an eyebrow to go up. In my case, I trembled, remembering last night. My chest seemed to tighten and I had to place my cup of coffee on the floor. Mickey gave me a funny look. I tried to smile.

"Why not Chase?" asked Jacob Kinlaw. "Agent Chase, I understand you received flowers from Glenn Proffitt this morning?"

"What?" I didn't know what to say, but I damned well knew everyone was staring at me. My face flushed and it had nothing to do with my panic attack.

The city chief nodded to the FBI agent. "You're thinking there's already been a relationship established between Chase and Proffitt?"

Kinlaw smiled. "Perhaps one between her and the doctors she's already contacted who own the clinic."

"Chase was out of line there," volunteered my boss.

"Or showing initiative," Mickey DeShields said, speaking up for me.

He was ignored. The fix was in, but I was too pissed to realize that.

"Agent Chase, your boss is right. This is no time for cowboys." Kinlaw inclined his head toward the Myrtle Beach chief of police. "The chief will have to face the media and he doesn't need to be blindsided. As I blindsided you about those roses. Now, why do you think Glenn Proffitt would send you roses?"

I cleared my throat and sat up. "I have no idea. It only said 'thank you' on the card. And his name was signed." I was more interested in how Agent Kinlaw knew about the roses. It had been awfully early when those flowers arrived. And awfully late when I'd gone to bed.

Kinlaw leaned back in his chair and templed his fingers. "It's said that Glenn Proffitt considers himself a ladies' man and surrounds himself with pretty young women."

"I don't see how that has anything to do with anything. Actually, I'd hoped to be partnered with DeShields and work the files of the OB/GYN."

"Susan," said the city chief, "I don't think that's going to work, if I understand what Agent Kinlaw has in mind."

"And what does Agent Kinlaw have in mind?" I asked, turning my glare on the FBI agent.

Kinlaw smiled. "That Glenn Proffitt might mistake you for just another pretty face."

SEVEN

"Agent Chase, can you explain why you want a BOLO put out for a white American male, age twenty-five to forty-five?" Jacob Kinlaw read from a sheet of paper—as our boss glared on.

I stood beside Daphne Akins near the door. The meeting had pretty much broken up and many attendees were heading for more coffee or the rest room. "It's the profile of a typical bomber."

"Yes, but you think this UNSUB drove a light blue VW van and towed a small car behind it, possibly gray in color?"

I stuffed my notebook in one of the inside pockets of my blue jacket and it took me more than one try. "Agent Kinlaw, you have to understand I came late to the crime scene. I was able to see more than those who arrived at first light."

Kinlaw glanced down the table at the few men who remained in their seats. "You don't have to apologize. We're all big boys. Can you confirm the remains of the vehicle in the parking garage as that of a VW bus?"

"The shape of the van is vintage, like hippies used to drive." Oh, hell, now I was sticking it to Jacqueline Marion.

"And the color of the van? How do you know that?" asked Agent Kinlaw.

"Er—that is an educated guess."

"An educated guess?" asked the head tech.

I bit my lip. "The techs on the scene believe the color of the van is light blue."

"I'm not comfortable with guesswork," said the head tech. "I'll have to talk to my people at the scene before something's put out. We don't want another 'white van' controversy."

Oh, man. Jacqueline had said not to quote her on this.

My boss put in her two cents' worth. "Chase, why do you think a small car was towed behind the van? That can't be more than supposition on your part."

"There's a tow bar jammed into the wall of the garage at the crime scene. A sheet of stucco collapsed over it." I tried not to look at those around the table. "It's like finding the body on the second floor. With the right light, you could see it."

Others drifted back into the room to see what they were missing. That went for the patrolwoman guarding the door.

"And the unidentified male with a hood on a sweat jacket and wearing an insulated vest?" asked Kinlaw, reading from my BOLO. "You think he had a hood so he couldn't be identified?"

The chief of police leaned forward. "You believe this man wore an insulated vest because of the cold front that passed through last night?"

I nodded at the chief. "Er—yes, sir, I do."

"What else, Susan?" said the chief. "Spit it out."

"I . . . well, there's the possibility the bomber didn't intend anyone to be injured in the blast."

Several people sat up. "What?" they asked in unison. That was followed by: "What are you talking about? Proffitt was on the roof. You helped bring him down."

I charged ahead, my spavin steed straining forward, my tin lance resting in its stirrup. "That could be the reason why the garage was in flames and Proffitt was trapped on the roof."

"Wait a minute," said my boss, "you can't have it both ways. First you say the perp didn't want anyone injured, but you admit Proffitt almost lost his life in the fire."

I turned to my trainee standing near the door. "Do you have that information from the taxi companies?"

Steve Brown

"And more." Daphne handed me a couple of sheets of paper.

I read from the top one before turning it over to the city chief. "Proffitt arrived fifteen minutes before the blast. He was dropped off by taxi. His car is a red Lexus and still parked at his house. There were no other cars in the street-level garage. Jacqueline Marion said the garage had been filled with gasoline. It's what generated the awesome flames that kept the firemen at bay and forced Proffitt to the roof."

"You think this was supposed to be a crime against property?" asked the city chief, taking the paper from me.

"I believe the perp had no idea anyone was in the building."

"Then how did the women get inside?" asked someone. "You said there were no vehicles under the building."

"What's this all about?" asked several guys as they returned to the room. "I thought the meeting was over."

They were told to sit down and shut up. Or simply to shut up.

The city chief said, "We have people checking cars outside the perimeter. Cars left overnight will have a layer of crud on them. The stuff sticks because of the damp night air off the ocean."

I handed the chief another sheet of paper and had the good sense to let him make the announcement.

Looking up from the paper, he said, "The uniforms have found two cars in the parking garage with crud on them."

"Tell them not to touch those vehicles," said the Horry County chief of police from his end of the table. "We're not making a move without warrants." He turned and spoke to the major sitting behind him. Fielder made a call on his cell phone.

The city chief relayed the same instructions through one of his subordinates to the patrolmen searching the Pavilion parking garage across the street.

"But why didn't one of the women just swipe her damn card and enter from the rear?" asked the representative of the bomb squad. "Why park across the street and pay when you could park for free? There's a keying device at the rear of the Proffitt Center garage."

Agent Kinlaw knew the answer to that. "Because there was always the possibility their vehicle would've been seen. As the unexpected appearance of Glenn Proffitt attests to."

Driving to my interview with Glenn Proffitt, I passed Sam's Corner on Kings Highway. I changed lanes and turned into a narrow parking area that ran parallel to the street. I'd had breakfast, but still felt faint.

I climbed out of the car, stumbled across the parking lot, and onto the sidewalk where I hauled open the heavy glass door. After placing my order, I ran my fingers over a series of formica booths and carefully walked down the long shaft to take a seat at one of the booths. Minutes later, someone placed a chili dog, fries, and beer in front of me.

I blinked as the counterman asked, "Susan, didn't you hear us calling out your order?" Orders at Sam's Corner are to be picked up at the counter.

I apologized, then sat there and stared at the chili dog, fries, and Carolina Blonde, a local brew. I wasn't a bit hungry and wondered what I was doing here. Still, I couldn't move. My hands remained in my lap. They trembled. Was it possible I'd exhausted myself changing into a set of clean clothes? I sat there staring at the customers coming through the front door. Someone spoke to me, but I didn't even turn my head. Maybe I couldn't.

I was still staring at the front door when a slender, brown-haired man appeared in the doorway. My heart rose in my throat, but I swallowed it back down when two other federal agents followed Jacob Kinlaw through the door. Kinlaw left the other agents and walked down the long aisle to where I sat.

"Seems like I'm not the only one who likes chili dogs."

I merely stared at him.

"Agent Chase, are you all right?"

"I'm . . . I'm okay."

"You don't look okay." He glanced at the meal that remained untouched in front of me. "How long have you been sitting here?"

"Not . . . long."

"May I sit down?"

"Okay."

Kinlaw took the seat across from me. He stared at me.

"What?" I tried to raise a hand to brush back my hair and found I couldn't. I cleared my throat. "If you want to order something . . . you have to go to the counter."

"I've eaten here before." He glanced at the food in front of me. "You were able to bring your own food to the table?"

"Agent Kinlaw . . . what do you want?" I glanced at the beer. "Worried that I'm drinking on the job?"

"I think you're in shock and should consider hospitalization."

I straightened up. "What?"

"Susan . . . do you mind if I call you 'Susan?' You may be suffering from post-traumatic stress disorder."

I raised a shaking hand and it was quite an effort. "I'm—I'm okay."

He reached across the table and gripped my hand before I could lower it. "Show me the other one."

I wouldn't. I couldn't.

"Show me," he ordered.

Reluctantly, I revealed the other hand. He took both hands in a pair that were firm and dry. Both of mine were clammy and trembling. He peered at me from across the table. "I take it you usually have more of a tan."

"Maybe it's what I wear. I've changed clothes."

"But you're still wearing the same black coat."

To this I said nothing. Thankfully, I had the long coat on. It was kind of chilly in here.

"Did you eat breakfast this morning?"

"Of course."

"I remember what I ate at your age. What did you have?"

"What is your age?"

"What did you have for breakfast, Agent Chase?"

I told him about the Big Breakfast.

"And how did you sleep last night?"

"No problem," I said, taking my hands away from him and placing them below the table. There they continued to tremble. Why wouldn't this guy go away and leave me alone?

"Take a pull from your beer," he ordered.

"What?"

"I think you need a drink."

"Really, I never thought anyone in law enforcement—"

He reached across the table, picked up the beer, and handed the Blonde to me. "Drink."

I drank. Too much. Tears appeared in my eyes. I coughed and wiped my mouth as the beer threatened to return the way it had gone down. When I rested my hands in my lap, they continued to tremble.

"Drink more."

"But I might not be in any shape to interview—"

"Drink," he ordered.

Once I'd emptied the bottle, he moved it to one side of the table. I could've done that. I think.

"Your boss never should've let you come on duty."

"What about the body I found at the crime scene?"

"The techs would've discovered it."

"And the BOLO put out for the perp?"

"That would've been put out, too, just a bit later."

I relaxed against the firmness of my seat. "So you didn't need me, after all."

"Not if it threatens your health. Unfortunately, there will be plenty of cases in your future."

"I'm okay." Actually, my hands had stopped shaking and I could move my head and look around. People stared at me, and I hoped that was from being on TV last night.

He gestured at the chili dog and fries. "I think you should eat."

No way I was going to eat a chili dog in front of any guy. "You didn't answer my question."

"What question was that?"

"How old are you?"

"Can I say 'thirty-nine?'"

"Would it be the truth?"

"It would've been three weeks ago. And you?"

"Closing in on the big three-oh."

Kinlaw slid from the booth. "I'll just grab a bite." He looked back at the table. "And you should think about eating that chili dog."

"It's cold."

"I'll get you another."

"Could you make it a foot-long? With mustard."

He did, returning with his own foot-long, fries, and a Bud Lite. There was a styrofoam cup of tea for me, and it wasn't the sweet tea Sam's Corner is famous for.

He took a bite of his hot dog. Finished chewing, he asked, "Susan, why did your boss put you on the schedule today? You should be riding a desk."

"I would've been if I hadn't gone by the crime scene."

"Others could've covered for you."

I shook my head. "Nobody covers for me."

"What are you saying, that nobody can do your job?"

"I'm saying I need this job, and being shunted off to interview Glenn Proffitt shows how precarious my position is with SLED."

He stared at me for a moment and then returned to his dog. In a moment, he asked, "You were trained at Quantico?"

"Sex crimes."

"That's not what they call it, nor is it called 'profiling.' It's the 'Behavioral Science Unit.'" After a swallow of beer, he said, "Susan, it's rude to let me eat alone."

I took a tentative bite, then some fries with ketchup, and a drink of tea. The stuff was strong, like someone had filled the cup with iced coffee.

When I was halfway through my dog, Kinlaw asked, "The cardinal rule of the Behavioral Science Unit is?"

"Never think you can 'read' the suspect. Reading a suspect's mind is a fairy tale. Besides, who'd feel comfortable working with such a freak?"

"So there was no reason for you to go by the crime scene this morning."

"Only if I didn't want to be left out."

Kinlaw finished off his hot dog. "I can deal with your competitiveness, but I do want to make sure you have your head screwed on right."

"Ask my shrink."

"I'm familiar with your sessions."

I put down my beer. "If you read my file, then you know I blew away a couple of drug dealers."

"You say that like it wasn't important or the dealers' lives weren't important."

"Take your pick."

"You saved the life of your partner."

"Well," I said, a smile creeping across my lips, "as you pointed out, there was backup outside, so I wasn't necessary on that occasion either."

"Susan, I'm not knocking you, I'm just concerned about your current state of mind."

"What are you doing here anyway, Agent Kinlaw?"

"You can call me 'Jake.'"

"Okay, Jake, what the hell are you doing here?"

"Assessing your current state of mind."

"And how am I doing?"

"You should go home and go to bed, but I don't think anyone would get very far prescribing that type of treatment for someone like you."

"You've got that right." I straightened up in my seat. "I might lose what little hold I have on this job."

"It might interest you to know that no one in that conference room objected to your being there this morning."

"Well, I did find a couple of bodies."

"This was before you found any bodies. Now, based on your experience with the State Law Enforcement Division, which is less than a year, your education—which is merely a GED—and your history of being a cowboy, why do you think anyone would want you in that room?"

"I guess you guys are pretty desperate."

"We are, but it has nothing to do with you." He put the paper plate and napkin aside and rested his hands on the table in front of him. After interlacing his fingers, he said, "Because of what you did last night, it was only natural I checked your file."

"And learned who was sending me roses?"

"Susan, an agent should be open and aboveboard regarding her physical and psychological condition. With the case we have before us, we don't have time for you to be visiting your shrink."

"Then you agree I shouldn't go home and hit the sack."

He smiled.

"You knew about the roses, the ones sent by Proffitt. How's that?"

"Proffitt is a womanizer. It wasn't hard to learn what florist he uses. It was in the dossier put together last night."

Yes. While I was asleep. "You're not trying to make something of the roses, are you?"

"Not at all, but if Proffitt had anything to do with the destruction of his building, he's more likely to reveal it to an attractive woman."

"What bullshit."

That didn't stop him. "You still haven't explained this ability of yours to profile. It's more than I would expect from someone who had spent a few weeks at Quantico."

I put down my styrofoam cup. "I'm an orphan. I pick up things. In a previous life, it was a survival tool."

"And now?"

"I embarrass people."

"As I said earlier, they're all big boys."

"Look, I don't like women being molested and I'm going to step in whenever I see that happen. What do you want me to say?"

"I think you're an asset, but I don't want you running around at loose ends."

I looked past him at the two agents waiting for him at the door. One was examining a tourist display, the other reading a newspaper. "What's really going on here, Agent Kinlaw?"

He glanced over his shoulder. Outside, the narrow parking lot was filling up as lunch customers arrived. As they came through the door, the other two FBI agents made way. "Before I was assigned to this duty I did recruiting."

I blinked. "You're recruiting me for the FBI?"

"With the shakeup at the Bureau after 9/11—"

"That shakeup happened way after 9/11 and the powers-that-be fought it tooth and nail."

"It's not something we in the Bureau are proud of."

"I can imagine. There are terrorists at large. Some with Stinger missiles."

"And we need all the help we can get."

"I don't want to leave the Grand Strand."

His eyebrow arched. "You don't get along with your boss—why's that?"

"I don't consider myself a role model. She does."

"Sorry, but we don't get to pick and choose what people think of us. Have the people from *Oprah* called? The network morning shows or any of the news programs?"

I looked at the tabletop. "I don't know anything about that."

"Then tell me this, Agent Chase, in all honesty, have you intentionally avoided checking your messages this morning?"

It was a moment before I nodded.

He slid from the booth with a quickness that startled me. "I'll be keeping an eye on you." He turned to go, then stopped. "But I do wish you'd consider taking the day off."

"I'm assigned to interview Glenn Proffitt, remember?"

"Perhaps after that."

I smiled up at him. "Based on what you already know about me, you probably understand the odds of my doing something like that."

EIGHT

When I stopped at the sidewalk in the strip mall where Glenn Proffitt had relocated his business, I sat in my sedan and tried to figure out what had happened at Sam's. You'd think a good night's sleep would've been enough. It appears I also needed a beer or two. Perhaps, as Agent Kinlaw said, I was pushing it. Then again, when you come close to death, or hover over a burning building, it tends to alter your perspective. Or numb you into immobility.

Strange how quickly I'd picked up another guardian angel like my former SLED boss, J.D. Warden, and the thought of the job offer irritated me. I didn't want to leave the Grand Strand. I had unfinished business with my former fiancé. Which raised the question: How do you finish business with someone who doesn't remember you?

Glenn Proffitt's condotel operation now occupied a former Ace Hardware, like in mom-and-pop stores before Home Depot and Lowe's came to the beach. A storefront of glass revealed an area where well-dressed women moved with a sense of purpose, workmen were installing telephones, and a receptionist sat in one of those ubiquitous white plastic chairs—the kind found at every Lowe's and Home Depot.

Condotels are condominiums in which you own a week at the beach. If you purchase a week during the prime season, such as summer, or "red," you pay top dollar, but condotels practically give away weeks, called "blue," in January and February. Disney and Marriott have their own variation of time-sharing called vacation clubs. Condotels are governed by a board of directors who assess annual dues and renovation fees, and whose amounts sometimes come as a surprise to their fellow investors. Many condotels have gone to the "vacation club" where "points" or days can be used in the busy seasons or at slack times. Still, you have prepaid for your vacation at the beach and your property will be maintained as well as you insist. Glenn Proffitt makes his money by bidding on the day-to-day maintenance and staffing, but mostly through the reselling of "time-shares."

The receptionist stared at me through the glass wall of the former hardware store. Her mouth moved, but she was speaking to the strawberry blonde standing beside her desk, which was actually a card table. The strawberry blonde struggled into a black pea coat and hurried through the glass door and out to my car. She had freckles across her nose, a Wolff tan, and appeared about my age.

From the other side of the glass, the receptionist continued to watch. She held a cell phone as if every number had been punched except the "send" that would put the call through. I lowered the window as the strawberry blonde bent down to talk to me. Her hands remained in her pockets, and I didn't think they were there to keep warm.

"May I help you?" she asked.

When I reached for my wallet inside my suit jacket, the woman straightened up and her left hand came out of the pea jacket with a .22.

"I'm taking out my ID. That's all."

"Just do it slow."

The moment she looked toward the receptionist, I pulled out my ID and thrust it through the window, jamming the wallet into the woman's abdomen before she could raise her pistol.

"Now imagine if that'd been a gun."

The woman frowned, took the ID, and returned her weapon to her side. "You're Susan Chase?"

Nodding, I raised the window and swung open the car door. Once I was outside, she returned the ID.

"You look a lot taller in person." She fitted the safety on

the small pistol and dropped the weapon in the left-hand pocket of her pea coat.

"I hope you have a license for that."

"Burned in the fire last night, but I've already applied for a new one."

I looked through the glass storefront at the blonde with the cell phone held at the ready. "Time to call off the dogs?"

The strawberry blonde glanced at the woman behind the desk. She pulled her hand out of the pea coat and clasped both hands in front of her. On the other side of the glass, the cell phone came down.

I glanced at the clasped hands. "And the signal to call the cops?"

"Just about anything else."

The woman's hands returned to her coat pockets, and I scrunched down behind my high collar. I felt the coat's tail flap in a sudden breeze.

"I'm Lynda—spelled with a 'Y'—Carlisle. I'm in charge of security. I also oversee repairs during the off-season." The ends of her strawberry blond hair began to flutter in the breeze.

"Okay if we go inside?" I asked.

"Of course."

She stepped up on the sidewalk and I followed her toward the glass doors. "After what we saw on TV last night, we were kind of surprised Glenn would come into work this morning."

"I'm surprised myself. Who set up the new place?"

"Oh, this." She held the door open for me. "I did. It's one of Mister Proffitt's properties."

"Fast work."

"Well," she said with a smile, "I do know who to call to have repairs made on a moment's notice."

The receptionist's eyes were bloodshot, her platinum hair cut in a Cleopatra look, and she sported a chest that strained the buttons of her silk blouse. The smell of paint was in the air, the floors concrete, and from the far end of the longwise room came the sound of a Xerox machine being operated.

The strawberry blonde wandered off, perhaps finding something better to do with her time than harass visiting dignitaries.

"May I help you?" asked the receptionist.

I held my ID over a card table covered with pads, ballpoint pens, and an insulated travel mug advertising one of Proffitt's condotels. She, like the strawberry blonde, visibly brightened after scoping out my ID.

"Oh, Miss Chase, no telling what would've happened if you hadn't gone up there last night. Sometimes Glenn can be such a baby." She glanced at an office behind her with no door. From inside you could hear the lord and master putting things in motion.

"No," shouted Proffitt into a cell phone as he crossed in front of the open door. "I want it done today. Look, I didn't survive that fire last night to put up with this." Proffitt saw me. "I'll get back with you. Or your boss."

The phone snapped shut, and as he strode out of his office, Proffitt dropped the cell into an interior pocket of a blue blazer. His shirt was blue oxford and open at the neck, his pants charcoal gray, and his loafers cordovan.

"Susan, so good to see you again."

He stuck out his hand and I shook it. His face was puffy and his eyes bloodshot. There was a red tinge to his skin, but this I knew to be fire burn, not sunburn.

"Hope you got the roses I sent you."

"A nice gesture, but I was just doing my job."

Proffitt took both of my hands and held me out where all could see. "Everyone, I want you to meet Susan Chase. The woman who saved my life last night."

Several workmen from GTE looked up from where they knelt installing phones. A guy with a tape measure glanced in my direction, and several blondes stuck their heads out of offices also without any doors.

When the blondes started in my direction, Proffitt held them up, too. "No, no, people," he said, still gripping my hands, "don't stop what you're doing. We've got a business to get up and running."

As each woman returned to her card table or office, my

face became as red as Proffitt's. He lowered my hands but didn't let go.

"Can someone scare up some coffee?"

The receptionist scraped her chair across the concrete floor and stood. "I'm not doing anything until the phones are up."

"And then you'll be busy with all the congratulations," he said rather dryly.

"Congratulations?" I asked.

"Yes." Proffitt led me toward his office. "From my creditors."

I couldn't help but chuckle.

"Agent Chase," asked the receptionist, following us into the office to pick up a traveler's mug from Proffitt's desk. "How do you like your coffee?"

"Don't bother. I've had plenty."

"Nonsense," said Proffitt, taking off my coat before I could protest. "Get her a cappuccino."

And that appeared to be that.

The office had no adornments. Sheetrock attached to framing had its basic coat of paint, the floor was concrete bare, and in the middle sat a metal table with a wooden veneer top. There were no phones, but there was writing material and a scarred briefcase with a dented corner.

I mentioned this to Proffitt as I took a seat in one of the ubiquitous white chairs in front of his makeshift desk. "That isn't what I think it is, is it?"

After tossing my coat over the high-backed chair behind his table/desk, Proffitt took a seat beside me. "Forgot all about it until I reached the hospital."

"How did you get it out of the building?"

"Threw it off the roof. One of the policemen brought it by this morning." He smiled. "Now I know why my ex-wife said I should always fill out that tag on the handle."

I nodded. "Before this, you figured only a thief would be interested in your briefcase."

"It's why I never let the thing out of my sight." He glanced at the table with the pens, pencils, and a legal pad. "Now it's all I've got left of my office."

I crossed my legs. I'd taken the time to change into a gray

suit, a black blouse, and boots, all accessorized by fake pearl earrings and matching necklace. "That's not the only surprise this morning."

He smiled. "The doctors thought they were going to keep me for observation, but my girls got me out of there."

When that didn't register, he gestured at the front office. It was then I realized, with the exception of the workmen, there hadn't been any men in the front office.

"Contrary what you might've heard, Susan, businesses don't go broke because of stiff competition and cutthroat practices, but because of a lack of interest. On the part of your employees, suppliers, and your customers."

I gave him a small smile. "But those wouldn't be the ones I'm here to ask about, would they, Mister Proffitt?" I took a narrow pad and pen from my inside jacket pocket.

"Why don't you call me 'Glenn'?"

"If I did, they'd send someone else to question you. Someone who would also call you by your surname."

He returned my smile. Twenty years my senior, this guy had had plenty of time to get his act together. Wrinkles crinkled at the corner of his eyes, there was a touch of gray in his temples, and he needed to lose twenty pounds.

"Susan, would you mind if I asked you a personal question?"

"Depends on the question."

"I wondered, who was this young woman who came flying in to rescue me?"

"Like I said, I was just doing my job." Jacob Kinlaw would be pleased. Glenn Proffitt was blowing off fireman Zack and the vest that had landed as close as the one I'd tossed from the helicopter.

"If that's so, why didn't one of those guys come up there and bring me down?"

"Mister Proffitt, plenty of firefighters risk their lives . . . I'm just the one who got to you first."

"Or I'd be dead."

"I don't know about that . . . ."

The receptionist came through the door with our drinks, and it made me wonder who had made it their priority to have the cappuccino machine up and running.

"Here you are, Agent Chase."

"Thank you."

The receptionist gave her boss his tumbler. "Need anything else?" she asked us.

I shook my head and sipped from the cappuccino. Delicious, and I said so.

"Emily, when will the computers be up?"

"In a few hours. As soon as they connect with the network, they'll feed the records through." On the way out of the room, she stopped to examine the jamb. "The doors are on their way, too."

"Our records are backed up online by a security system," explained Proffitt. "We should be back in business by this afternoon. Tomorrow by the latest."

"Tomorrow is Christmas Eve."

"Thankfully, we had the Christmas party last weekend." He glanced at the open office door. "But everyone knows what has to be done."

I sipped more cappuccino. "Going to mess up more than one person's Christmas."

"And what are your plans for Christmas, Susan?"

In truth, I didn't know. With my fiancé out of the picture and Harry Poinsett winging his way toward St. Louis . . . . Last year had been the first Christmas I'd been part of a family. Now it would be back to square—

"Susan?"

Glenn Proffitt was staring at me. "You left us for a moment."

"Er—right. I don't think many people in law enforcement are going to be off this year."

"I'd hate to think I was the cause."

"That's why I'm here." I took another sip of my cappuccino, set the traveler's mug on the table, and picked up my notebook. Pen poised, I returned to business. "What time did you arrive at your building last night?"

"Back to work?" he said with a smile.

"Just like you."

"Well, to answer your question, just after ten."

"Was anyone with you?"

"No." He suddenly straightened up in his chair, alarmed. "Wait a minute. This wasn't a gas leak like they're saying on the radio?"

"We don't think so."

"A bomb?"

I nodded.

"What kind?"

"It wasn't all that complicated."

"It may not be complicated for you, but break it down. I want to know what they used."

"They?"

"Whoever blew up my building."

"Have any ideas?"

"Who could be mad enough to blow up my building? I'm in the condotel business."

"Like I said, Mister Proffitt, that's why I'm here."

He glanced at my pen and pad. "I don't know who did it and you can put that on the record."

I just sat there.

"Well," he said, shifting around in his chair, "I don't know, and that's a fact. Maybe it's because my building is in the heart of the Grand Strand."

"Why are you located there? It has to be a major hassle during the Season with all those tourists jamming up Kings Highway."

"I got a deal on the property after Hugo came through." When I said nothing, he added, "Everyone is moving to the bypass and beyond. In ten or twenty years, it's going to be a very good investment." He shifted around in his chair. "At least that's my opinion."

I nodded, then said, "Fertilizer, fuel oil, and some method of detonation."

"That's it? Any farmer could've done this?"

"Only if he had a way to detonate the fertilizer and fuel oil."

"So, if this farmer had dynamite to blow stumps out of his fields?"

"Mister Proffitt, if someone had access to dynamite, I doubt they'd be concerned about rounding up a load of fertilizer or fuel oil."

He was silent, but in truth, I was pleased he'd raised the question. Otherwise, I would've wondered why he wasn't curious. Then again, it'd taken him one hell of a long time to get around to the question.

"Mister Proffitt, do you know someone who uses large amounts of fertilizer and fuel oil in their business?"

"Susan, I'm a city boy. All the people I know live along the Grand Strand."

"I thought you owned a farm in the Low Country," meaning below the fall line and not usually associated with the Grand Strand. That information came courtesy of the law enforcement center and one of those cops who had been up last night.

"Oh, that," he said, dismissing his farm with a wave of his hand. "That's for dove hunting."

"But fertilizer and fuel oil are used on the property, aren't they?"

"Er—right."

"I'll need some names of who I should contact there."

"Dave Mendenhall and his wife run the place. Emily can give you the number. Look, Susan, I can tell you Dave didn't do this. He and I go back a ways."

"How's that?" I asked, jotting down the names.

"Dave was my right-hand man, sort of like what Claudia does now, but he got tired of the hassle."

"You hassling him or the work?"

"Both."

"So what's he doing tending your farm?"

"Dave and I hunt together. Dave always said when he retired he was going to have a place like mine. I asked him why he wasn't foreman already. Mrs. Randolph—her husband was the previous foreman and had recently died of a heart attack—wanted to move closer to her children in Ohio."

"Any conflict between you and Mr. Mendenhall?"

"Plenty. Dave had money in the business. He wanted to go slow, but that wasn't my style."

"Where is that money now?"

"Still in the business."

"He couldn't pull it out?"

"Well," said Proffitt with a smile, "not if he wanted to live at Simmerdown."

"Simmerdown?"

"The name of the farm. Simmer down. You know, like to slow down and relax. It's a working farm, but you're away from all this." He gestured at the sparsely furnished office with the missing door.

"How is Mister Mendenhall compensated?"

"I pay him a little more than I did the Randolphs."

"And he's satisfied with that?"

"Well," said Proffitt, smiling, "he does have right of first refusal."

"Do I understand this correctly—upon your death Dave Mendenhall would have a chance to purchase this farm that he loves?"

"Er—yes."

I let that sink in.

"You don't think . . . ?"

"Mister Proffitt, I'm only here to gather information. Let's return to last night. When you arrived at your office, did you see anyone else in the building?"

It was a moment before he said, "No."

"How did you reach your office? Stairs? Elevator?"

He smiled, evidently forgetting any designs his employee might have on his property. "After that flight, it had to be by elevator."

"Rough flight?"

"And long day."

"You were returning from?"

"Cancún. I have a property there."

That also checked with the information that had been given to me before I left the law enforcement center. "Notice anything odd in the parking garage? Cars, any vehicles that shouldn't have been there?"

"There was nothing in the garage when I arrived."

"And you entered the building from where?"

"Kings Highway."

"You have a key to that gate?" The one now hung up between two humongous potted plants.

He nodded. "A card."

"So you . . . ?" I said, making a keep-going motion with the fingers that held my pen.

"Oh," he said, shifting around in his chair. "I left the cab on the street, took my bag and my briefcase upstairs by the elevator. There was no one in the parking garage or on the elevator, and when I reached my office, I turned on the lights and computer and poured something to drink."

"Coffee or something stronger?"

"Actually, scotch on the rocks."

I jotted down his answers as I asked for even more answers. "Your suitcase and briefcase? Where were they?"

"Susan, I didn't blow up my building."

I looked up from my notes. "For the second time, Mister Proffitt, I didn't ask you if you blew up your building." Still, I had to let him run down on this subject before we could proceed.

"The bag and briefcase were carry-ons so they couldn't have held the bomb or they would've set off the detectors at the airport."

I drank from my cappuccino before asking, "Did you share a ride from the airport?"

"No. No."

"Anyone get cozy with you on the plane?"

"Er—no."

"Meet anyone at the airport?"

"No." He shook his head. "Not at all."

"Driver pass you anything in the cab?"

"Of course not."

"Where were you when the bomb went off?"

"In the rest room, thank God. I'd gone to wash my face. I was trying to get some numbers together on an expansion of my operation in Cancún. The drink made me sleepy. That drink just possibly saved my life."

"What did you do? After the bomb went off?"

"For a moment, I just lay there. I guess I was stunned. Then I picked myself up, left the rest room, and found a damn hole in our operations center large enough to drive a truck through." He shook his head. "When I think Emily could've been sitting there . . . ."

"But she wouldn't have been there that late at night."

"Still, the thought crossed my mind."

"You told me on the phone last night that you couldn't go down either stairwell."

"I made it to the garage for all the good it did me. The concrete floor was literally in flames. You couldn't see the elevators from where I stood. So I went up—up to the roof."

I used my pen to point in the direction of his desk. "Take your briefcase along?"

He looked at the floor. "This is stupid, but I went back as soon as I realized I'd left it in my office."

"Went back down from the roof?"

He nodded. "I know I shouldn't have. That hole was very near my office." He shivered. "Think you'll catch the bastards who did this?"

"Where was the cell phone you used to call me?"

"In my jacket pocket on the hook on the back of my office door. The place was a mess, I was coughing, and the dust was slow to settle. There were no flames, but I could see the fire through the hole below me. Papers were everywhere. I was actually on my hands and knees trying to gather up the deal when I realized how stupid . . . ."

A dishwater blonde in her late thirties entered the room through the open door. She had short-cropped hair and wore stonewashed jeans and a white tee. On the front of the tee, it read: "Objects behind this fabric are larger than they appear." The woman wore sandals revealing pink-painted toenails. She was reading from an open manila folder. "Glenn, there are some checks I have a question . . . ." Her voice trailed off as she looked up. She gave me the usual evaluation any competitor gives another, and that was enough to cause me to straighten my spine. "I'm sorry. I didn't know you had anyone with you."

"Susan Chase, this is Maureen Proffitt. My ex-wife."

"His very ex-wife," said the dishwater blonde.

"Maureen used to keep the books. She saw what happened on television and drove in from Hilton Head last night."

"You're the girl on the TV." She slapped the folder shut. "Still robbing the cradle, are you, Glenn? Have you no shame? How old are you, Miss Chase?"

For some reason, I couldn't resist saying, "Not yet thirty." I uncrossed my legs.

"That was my age when Glenn seduced me."

"I seduced you? Seems like it was the other way around."

"Glenn, I was in love with you, but you were in love with yourself."

I cleared my throat. "Do I have to be here for this meeting?"

Both of them looked at me. I tried to start again but the ex-wife cut me off.

"Miss Chase, watch your step around this man. Not only is he still attractive for such an old guy, but he has a silver tongue." She turned to go and thought better of it. "And he collects trophies. His first wife was Miss South Carolina, his second wife does the news in Columbia, and I was the only one who could keep the IRS at bay."

"Maureen, Miss Chase isn't interested in—"

"The more high-profile, the better, and from what I saw on TV last night, you certainly fit the bill." She gestured toward the front of the building. "All blondes out there, if you didn't notice."

I had.

"Maureen, perhaps later—"

"Money missing from your personal account? You want to put off discussing that, Glenn?"

"Is there something I can help you with?" I asked.

"Oh, that's right," said the former wife. "The people on TV said you were with SLED. Why didn't you just land the damn chopper on the roof and lift him off from there?"

"Like I said when you picked me up this morning, Maureen, there was a thermal updraft—"

"Yeah, yeah. I probably missed that when I was throwing some things in a bag. Look, Glenn, we have to talk. I might have to bring in an outside auditor."

"For that you would need a court order . . . . Now if you don't mind, Agent Chase and I have an interview—"

"Have you decided whether to meet with those TV people?"

"As I've told you before, there's no such thing as bad publicity."

"Well, I think it's perfectly tacky." She turned on her heel and left through the doorless doorway.

"Sorry, Susan, but she's upset."

"I would be, too, if money was missing."

"Another cappuccino?" he asked, gesturing at my traveler's mug.

I shook my head and tapped my notepad on my leg, which I'd crossed again.

"I doubt any money's missing. Maureen's been out of the loop for quite a while."

"Anyone not come to work this morning?"

"Just my secretary. I suppose Claudia will be along once she doesn't find me in the hospital."

I glanced at my watch. It replaced the one I'd been given by a special guy to celebrate our first Christmas together. Why had I glanced at my watch? Oh, yeah. "I'd be curious if someone wasn't here this morning. Everyone appears to be pitching in. Even ex-wives."

"Claudia could've stopped by the old location, any number of places. She's probably making sure all the loose ends are tied up."

"That would be Claudia Wasson?" This, too, from the information gathered by the task force last night.

"Yes."

"Does she have access to your checkbook?"

"Of course. I don't have time to write checks."

I just sat there.

"Susan, Claudia has been with me for . . ." He glanced at the open door. "Longer than anyone here."

"Claudia's full name and address?"

"Susan—"

"Mister Proffitt, a bomb destroyed your business and your executive secretary hasn't come to work." Evidently he finally saw the sense in this because he gave me the secretary's full name and address. But being a professional law enforcement officer wasn't all that Agent Kinlaw had in mind, so I asked, "The names, including maiden names, of your former wives and their current addresses?"

"Come on, Susan, you can't really believe they would have anything to do with this."

"Mister Proffitt, the sooner you answer my questions, the quicker I'm out of your hair and you can get your place up and running again."

He gave me the names of the three women. One lived in Myrtle Beach, the others in Columbia and Hilton Head, as the dishwater blonde had mentioned.

"How long were you married to each?"

"Are you sure that's important?"

"Well, Glenn," I said, looking rather coy, "I thought you might make this easy for me. Otherwise, I'll have to go through the public records and that could harm our budding relationship."

Proffitt nodded and answered my question. He also told me there were two children by the first wife. One had been the voice on the phone last night, and that daughter was on her way here by car. There was also a son he didn't have much contact with.

"Someone else driving?" I asked, and this had nothing to do with the job or my budding reputation as a sex object.

"Her mother."

"Good."

"Will there be anything else?"

"Not unless the crime scene techs find another body in your building."

"Another body?" He sat up in his chair.

"Once I have a photograph, I'll drop by and you can ID her. It could be your executive secretary."

NINE

"Someone else was found in the building?"

I nodded.

"Were they on my floor?"

I shook my head.

"Which one?"

"The floor beneath you."

"Good God!" he said, almost coming out of his chair. "They were after the clinic. People told me they performed abortions downstairs."

"You didn't know?"

Proffitt settled back in his chair. "No. They paid their rent on time and paid for a special layout for their floor. All I did was have my general contractor sign off on the project." He gestured at the opening in the wall. "Ask Lynda."

"Lynda?"

"Lynda Carlisle. Security."

The strawberry blonde couldn't tell me any more about the OB/GYN than that she used their gynecological services. She had not heard abortions were performed one floor below her.

"If I'd known, I would have advised Glenn to give them notice."

"Do you have a phone number for Dave Mendenhall?"

The blond and busty receptionist shuffled through a stack of index cards on her makeshift desk. She smiled up at me. "I've been writing down everyone who calls and taking their number. I'm reinventing my Rolodex."

"Dave Mendenhall has already called?"

"Dave was one of the first—on my cell. Someone told him there had been an explosion. He didn't have the details. They don't have TV at Simmerdown. I think it's forbidden." She snapped her fingers. "I need to call Dave. I'm sure he'll be pleased to know Glenn is back in the saddle."

"I'm sure he will be."

I shifted my heavy coat around in my arms to be able to take down Mendenhall's phone number. Emily didn't have an address but a rural route number. She said she could get me directions.

"Should I set up an appointment?" Her hand was poised over a legal pad with "To Do" at the top of the page.

I smiled. "Why don't I just surprise him."

I found Proffitt's ex-wife dusting off a desk she had just finished assembling, a smile of self-satisfaction still on her face. Sheets of cardboard lay in the middle of the floor and a high-backed chair sat behind the desk. In front of the desk sat another pair of the white plastic chairs.

As I entered her office, I threw my coat over one of the chairs. "What's this about missing money?"

A circular carpet covered much of the concrete and would probably remain there once the carpeting was installed. Several mass-produced paintings leaned against the wall, still in their protective wooden corners. A fax machine sat on the floor, as did a portable computer. The credenza was in a crate behind the desk.

"I doubt that would be your business, Miss Chase."

"Agent Chase. Let's call it professional interest."

She took a seat in her chair, leaned back, and studied me. "Aren't you a little young for this?"

I took a seat across from her. "Just tell me about it, Maureen, either here or downtown."

I'll say this for the gal. She was a fast learner. She picked up a folder on the floor and laid it on the desk. Opening it, she turned the folder around where I could see the contents. Inside was a series of faxes from a local bank.

I glanced at the fax machine on the floor. "These are duplicates of your ex-husband's personal bank account, and by the time stamp, they arrived this morning."

"The originals were destroyed in the blast." She gestured at the photostats. "I requested these when the bank opened."

I sat back in my chair. "So it's your nature, first thing after arriving in town, to check your husband's bank records?"

"Only when the originals have been destroyed. Miss—I mean, Agent Chase, I could've gotten a court order, but for some reason, everyone along the Grand Strand is much more cooperative than they've been in the past."

"I'm sure everything will be back to normal by the time the Season arrives."

"And hopefully I'll be back in Hilton Head."

I'd been to Hilton Head, and the only plus I could see was that when the sun went down, the extreme darkness made it easier to accept the fact you might as well turn in for the night. Maybe Hilton Head was for lovers. "Mrs. Proffitt, you seem to think you have interests to protect."

"You're damn right." She glared in the direction of her former husband's office several offices removed. "Glenn has a saying: Ex-wives will get their money when he gets his. He does not make settlements. It would upset the cash flow for his next project, whatever the hell that might be." She gave a careless wave of her hand. "I could go to court and force a lump sum settlement, but that costs money, and when you think about it, it all comes out of the same pot."

"If your ex-husband had died last night, that would've forced a settlement."

She glanced at the desktop. "I might still have feelings for the bastard. That might be the reason I'm here and why I picked him up at the hospital."

"But not good enough reason to be going through his personal bank records."

"You don't see Glenn complaining, do you?"

"Actually, he might have more important things on his mind." I held up my hand before I got more of the same. "I don't care how you learned about the missing money, but this may have a bearing on last night. Tell me what you know."

She nibbled on a lower lip. "When I walked in on you and Glenn"—she had a way of making that sound absolutely nasty—"I wanted to ask Glenn what he was doing writing all these checks to 'Cash.'"

"And that is unusual—how?"

"It means Glenn has been stealing from me and his other two ex-wives." She pointed at the photostats in the open folder on the desk in front of me.

I scooted to the edge of my chair and studied the photostats. In the previous ninety days, two checks had been made out to 'cash,' one for three thousand, another for five, and it appeared Glenn Proffitt had signed both checks because the signature matched that on other canceled checks.

"Glenn doesn't request his checks be returned to him, but I've always believed—"

I held up my hand again. If you don't request your checks, seventy-two hours after being processed, your checks are history. "How long has this been going on?"

She reached behind her chair again and handed me more photostats. "About the same time I had to leave the office."

"Because the divorce was a conflict of interest?"

"Yes, but I wanted out of this circus."

I glanced through the additional photostats she had passed across the desktop. "This is not going to look good to the IRS."

"That is correct, Agent Chase, and audits cost money."

Proffitt smiled grimly from the other side of his table/ desk as we walked into his office. "Now you're going to double-team me?"

"Glenn—"

"Mrs. Proffitt, do you mind?" I asked.

"I just want to know what the hell's going on."

Proffitt looked from one of us to the other.

"Mister Proffitt, do you request the bank return your canceled checks for your personal checking account?"

Her ex-husband opened his mouth, but Maureen said,

"He doesn't want to leave any tracks, but I found them." She smiled and folded her arms across her chest.

"What's going on, Susan?"

"You appear to have a problem with your personal account. There are several checks written for thousands of dollars over the last two years and all made out to 'Cash.'"

He didn't seem to understand.

"You don't remember writing checks for 'Cash' for sums as large as three or five thousand dollars?"

"I would never do such a thing."

"Or," asked Maureen, "are you squirreling away money you don't want anyone to know about?"

He turned on her, the violation of his privacy finally registering. "My personal account? What the hell were you doing in my personal account?"

"Glenn, if you're trying to pull something—"

"People," I tried to say, "this is getting us nowhere."

"He's trying to be a clever son of a bitch."

"And I'd like to know what business it is of yours—"

"Because you're trying to rip me off." She leaned forward, resting her hands on his makeshift desk. "You're not going to get away with this."

I took out my ID and held it between them: Maureen leaning over the desk and Glenn returning the favor by rising from his chair. They both shut up and pulled back.

"Need anything, Glenn?"

The security chief and the receptionist stood at the doorless entry. The natives were becoming restless, and later in the day, résumés would prove once again that you could stuff sheets of paper through a telephone line.

Proffitt waved off both women.

"Are you sure?" asked the strawberry blonde.

"It's nothing."

"Okay."

Once she and Emily moved away from the door, Proffitt said, "I have no idea what you're talking about."

"You son of a bitch, you're trying to pull something."

"Maureen, please—"

She turned to me. "He's trying to hide money."

"And how would I know that?"

She pointed at the folder in my hands. "You've seen the checks. Show him."

"And he'll see what?" I asked. Two could play irrationally as easily as one.

"Checks made out to 'Cash,'" she said.

"What business is that of yours?" asked Proffitt.

"What are you doing with checks made out to 'Cash' and for thousands of dollars?" she asked him.

"You're supposed to know something about accounting. Ask yourself."

"To hide the money from me."

He gestured for the folder. "Susan, may I see for myself?"

I shook my head.

"And why is that?" asked Proffitt, surprised.

"Only once the emotions are stowed away."

"I don't have to take this." Maureen glowered at both of us. "You've seduced her, haven't you, Glenn? I don't know how you did it—"

"Because I was in the hospital?" he asked, leaning back in his chair and smiling.

She looked from him to me and back to her ex-husband. "I'm sick and tired of everyone taking your side. That's why I live at Hilton Head. And I don't want to hear of you buying property down there." She turned and stomped out of the room.

The security guard appeared in the doorway once again. "Sure there's nothing you need?"

"Just a difference of opinion between Maureen and the rest of the world. You've heard it all before."

"Want her escorted off the property?"

"Not unless she leaves her office again."

"Got it."

Once Lynda Carlisle left, Proffitt asked, "What in the devil was Maureen talking about?"

I passed over the folder.

Proffitt opened it, thumbed through several printouts, and looked up. "I never write checks for 'Cash.'"

"Then how did they get written?"

"I have no idea. I'll have Claudia call the bank."

"Claudia's MIA. Besides, your bank will want to know why your signature is on these checks you say you didn't write." I pointed at one of the reproductions. "This is your signature, isn't it?"

He studied the photostat. "It appears to be."

"Maureen got this from the bank this morning. Why would she do that?"

"She thinks she still works here."

"And you act like it. Your ex-wife picks you up at the hospital and the first thing she does is to poke around in your personal financial records—what's up with that?"

"Maureen's always been meddlesome. I'll have the CPA and the bank get together on this."

I let out an exasperated breath. "Glenn, is there any way I can reach you? Maureen said that Claudia Wasson and you are the only ones who have access to your personal checkbook."

"That's correct."

"And she writes your personal checks?"

"Of course."

"Then can we start from there?"

"But I didn't write these and I'm sure when Claudia comes in this will all be straightened out."

"Glenn, focus! If Maureen thinks you're lying, others will think so, too."

"But I'm not lying."

"Good, because you're going to have to explain more than a few checks made out for 'Cash.'"

"What do you mean?"

"The disappearance of your executive secretary—that's going to take priority over a few missing checks."

TEN

I called the chief of police for Horry County. "Has CSI been able to search Proffitt's floor of his building?"

"I understand Jacqueline went in with her boss. They didn't find anything, if you're asking about another body. I think you have a problem with Jacqueline. I heard she was chewed pretty good for giving you access to the crime scene. Susan, if you're going to have a career in law enforcement it might be wise for you to learn to cooperate with other departments."

"Chief, I need a warrant to search the premises of Claudia Wasson." I gave him the address. "How long will it take?"

"What do you have?"

I told him.

"A woman is late for work and you have questions about checks signed by the signatory on the account? It sounds awfully thin."

"Chief, if this was before 9/11, I'd agree, but today it's just another piece of paperwork."

"Susan, is this for real? I don't need you hanging me out to dry like you did Jacqueline."

Gee, but that was hitting below the belt.

"Remember, Susan, everything is being recorded—"

"For quality control purposes—yes, I know."

"What? Oh, I get it. Well, head over to Ms. Wasson's, but wait outside until the warrant arrives."

"Chief, that could take hours."

"Yes, but having a warrant to search someone's home is one of those things that hasn't changed since 9/11."

Claudia Wasson lived in North Myrtle Beach in a twelve-story condo in a gated community. I found the maintenance man in the ground floor parking area and showed him my ID. A Chicano with leathery skin and white hair, he pointed out Wasson's SUV in the parking garage and escorted me upstairs with the haste of someone working in this country without benefit of a green card.

"I'm not with Immigration."

"No comprendo, Señorita."

I said the same thing in Spanish.

"No comprendo, Señorita."

On the twelfth floor, he unlocked the door and left me to my own devices.

"Claudia Wasson," I shouted through the open door, "this is Susan Chase of the State Law Enforcement Division. May I come in?"

No answer.

I tried again, then wandered into the apartment and looked around. I did have probable cause, didn't I? The woman was missing.

Nobody in the bedroom, bath, or kitchen. Or spare bedroom containing a TV in front of a rowing machine.

Nothing. *Nada.*

Wasson's balcony contained several pieces of rattan furniture and the balcony overlooked a beach where senior citizens in brightly colored outfits walked. Through a sliding glass door soiled by the same crud found on the two unidentified cars in the Pavilion parking garage, I saw thick, gray clouds on the horizon, no sun, and a mist not far out to sea. I leaned my head against the glass and sighed. This was Myrtle Beach and the home of Santa in shorts. How could this be happening, and I damn well didn't mean the embezzlement of a few thousand bucks.

I opened the lock by hooking the latch with my pen, pulled back the door the same way, and stepped out on the balcony. Nothing below me but a pool, chairs stacked for the winter, and rectangular pots filled with pansies. I put away my pen, leaned into the railing, and let out a long sigh.

With Chad not remembering me, Harry gone for the holidays, it was probably best I was working.

What a shit I was. Two dead women at the Proffitt Center meant two more families would find little peace this holiday and probably many a holiday to come. I wiped some tears away and returned inside, closing the door behind me.

The bedroom appeared to be furnished by a young girl or the mother of a small child. There were frills and ruffles, especially on the canopy bed. Dolls in a variety of outfits and with an assortment of hairdos lay in upright piles against lacy, pink pillows on a bed that had not been slept in.

Suitcases lined the floor on one side of a walk-in closet filled with dress and casual clothing. Shelves were lined with boxes, under them rows of shoes, and on the back of the door a full-length mirror where I saw a person with yellow hair and dark hollows ringing pale blue eyes. I left the closet quickly. We needed to put out a BOLO for this woman. I made the call.

The county chief fielded this request, too. "Do you have a description of Claudia Wasson?"

"Let me get back with you." I snapped the phone shut and told myself that Glenn Proffitt wasn't the only one who needed to focus.

A cluster of photographs on a pinkish dresser drew my attention. It seemed to me that if a person appeared in more than one of those photographs, that person should be the owner of the condominium and the canopy bed. If so, Claudia Wasson was a dark-eyed, narrow-faced blonde with eyes too close together and who had a tough time smiling. The one time she appeared to have gotten the hang of it was when she stood in the middle of three women, arms around each other's shoulders, all grinning into the camera. If I didn't know better, I would've said one of the brunettes flanking Claudia Wasson was the woman I'd found in the Proffitt Center, right down to the eyebrows that needed to be plucked. Another featured a middle-aged couple; another, a mountain man.

The bathroom held Claudia's toiletries and the kitchen

refrigerator was full of food. I was about to listen to the answering machine on the kitchen counter when I heard someone in the living room.

"Claudia?" called out a guy.

I unsheathed my pistol and tiptoed toward the living room. Glenn Proffitt was sliding back the glass door overlooking the beach. On the balcony, he stopped at the railing and looked down. He shook his head, returned to the living room, and closed the glass door.

Once he entered the bedroom, I holstered my pistol and slipped out of the kitchen, taking up a position near the door as Proffitt searched his secretary's bedroom. I could hear drawers pulled back and their contents studied. The door to the closet was opened, remained that way for a long while, and then closed. When he returned to the living room, I was in the guest bedroom, hiding behind the door.

I heard him come in and open the closet door. He spent little time in the guest room before heading down the hall, but I did hear him pull back the curtain in the half-bath and open the linen closet, both of which were in the hallway. When I heard the answering machine begin to rewind, I returned to the hall.

In message number one, a woman said they should "talk," and the machine indexed the call as being approximately the same time as when I was hanging by a bungee cord over Kings Highway. Surreal to learn how others were going about their lives as you attempted to end yours.

Message number two had come in this morning and was from "Patricia." Patricia was the same voice from the call the previous night. Patricia wasn't worried about Claudia but the whereabouts of someone named Laurie.

"Dammit, Claudia," demanded Proffitt, and startling me on the other side of the wall, "where the hell are you?"

A female voice reminded Claudia the lease was about to expire on her SUV and that she should call "Nina" to roll over the last month into a new lease. A number was left. Message number four was from Emily, the receptionist at the new Proffitt Center; the next from Mrs. Proffitt, asking Claudia to explain discrepancies in her ex-husband's personal checking account.

"Damn it, Maureen," said Proffitt to the machine, "why can't you keep your nose out of my affairs?"

I quickly crossed the living room and knocked on the back of the front door. Proffitt was rewinding the messages, possibly with the intent of erasing one or more. A waste of time since the calls were listed in order. Unless he wanted to erase the last one, the one from his ex-wife.

"Miss Wasson?" I asked from the open door.

Proffitt came to the door and stood in the jamb as if protecting the kitchen from me. "What are you doing here?"

"I might ask you the same question. I thought you had a business to run."

"I need to find Claudia."

"That makes two of us."

Proffitt left the doorway to join me in the living room. He took a quick look around and then sat down on a sofa contrasting with the frilly furniture in the bedroom: dark colors, sharp edges, and a very firm seat.

"I'm beginning to get a little worried myself."

"Her SUV is downstairs," I said, taking a seat in a chair opposite him. It matched the sofa in color, sharp edges, and resistance to your bottom.

"Evidently, her lease is up." He jerked a thumb toward the kitchen. "Message on her machine." He looked around the living room/dining room, then loosened his tie. "I just don't know—"

"Women don't usually disappear off the face of the earth, especially ones as responsible as Claudia Wasson. You're going to have to come up with some kind of explanation. Or suggestion."

"Now why would you think I'd know where she is?"

"Glenn, were you and Claudia Wasson involved?"

"What? Of course not."

I only stared at him.

He got to his feet, and just as quickly, so did I.

"I don't have time for this."

"You had time to come here."

"A waste of time." He headed for the door. "See what you

can do to find her. I've got a business to run."

"There are photographs in the bedroom. I want Claudia properly ID'ed before you leave."

He stopped at the door. "It's the least I can do." He started across the room and stopped again. "But how did you know the photographs were there?"

"Mister Proffitt, just step in the bedroom and point out which one of the women is your secretary. And without touching anything."

Claudia turned out to be the narrow-faced blonde with the dark eyes too close together. The two adults in a single photo were probably her parents, but Proffitt said he'd never met them. Both were deceased, and the only reason he knew this was from the occasional insurance form crossing his desk. He had no idea who the man with huge shoulders, bushy black beard, and red-plaid shirt was.

"Boyfriend?"

"I have no idea. Claudia was a very private person. That's what made her so important to me."

The photograph of the large man gave the impression the photographer had had to work to squeeze him into the frame. He bore no hint of a smile, and that was the only resemblance to Claudia. A shiver ran through me as I stared at the emotionless face. Maybe I should take a sick day.

"Things are not looking good, are they?" asked Proffitt.

"It would help if you were more forthcoming."

"What would you like me to say: That I was having an affair with my secretary? It wouldn't be true, and I don't know where Maureen gets that impression."

"Perhaps because you were sleeping with Maureen when she worked for you."

"That was different."

"How's that?"

"I thought we were in love. Look, Susan, I know the girls in my office are attractive, but they're also smart as a whip. It's taken a long time to assemble this staff and I'm damn proud of them."

"And proud to be seen with them."

Proffitt shook his head. "Claudia was a teetotaler."

"The others were hired to schmooze?"

"Well," he said with a reluctant smile, "you can't always get the complete package."

"You are a dog, aren't you?"

"Oh," he said, feigning innocence, "just because I don't let my wives pick—"

"Ex-wives."

"Ex-wives pick some old hag to handle reception—"

"Along with security, finance, not to mention your personal matters. Maybe if you'd allowed one of your wives to pick your employees, you might still be married to one of those women."

"I really don't know why we're having this conversation."

"For my part, it's business."

"And I need to get back to the office."

I gestured at the photographs. "Then you don't know anyone else?"

Proffitt insisted he didn't recognize the woman who resembled the one I'd found on the second floor of his former headquarters, but he did say the tanned woman in the group shot might be Patricia Owens, a married sister of Claudia's and a forest ranger.

"Where?"

He shrugged. "Who knows? Francis Marion National Forest?"

If you want to know something about a woman, you need to check the bathroom and the bedroom. That's where we gals let our hair down. Don't even mention the kitchen. No amount of takeout or delivery is going to tell you more than little time exists these days to cook. I pulled on a pair of latex gloves and went over both rooms, including the guest bath. Jacqueline would've been proud of me, if it weren't for the serious case of the ass she had.

"Susan," screeched the voice over the cell phone once I had gritted my teeth and accepted the incoming call. "Glenn Proffitt is at the crime scene demanding to see the woman found on the second floor. Now how does some civilian know there's a dead woman on the second floor? The public information officer said there were two bodies found, one inside the building and one outside. I have his statement in my hand."

"I don't think it's likely he'll tell anyone."

"He's telling my boss he'll go to the media across the street if we don't grant him access to the building."

"Show him a picture. All he wants to know—"

"That it's not his secretary. Yes, yes, I know, but that's not why I called. You had no right to release that information."

"I was in a tough spot."

"Yeah. Someone puts pressure on you and you fold."

"Jacqueline, that's not fair."

But she was gone, hanging up on me.

I sat on the edge of the canopy bed, which is not that easy to do with these fluffy, puffed-up sort of beds, and made my own call. This one was to Luis, who'd carried the camera while Jacqueline photographed the crime scene.

"Luis, can you talk?" I had often used Luis as a back door to forensics when Jacqueline would not take my calls.

"I'd better not." His voice sounded cautious, guarded.

"All I want to know is whether Glenn Proffitt can ID the body. This is bigger than any squabble between Jacqueline and me."

"I don't want to get caught in the middle. Jacqueline's freckles are solid red."

"Proffitt thinks it's his secretary. She's missing."

"You never should have told him that we found a body."

"Luis, are you going to call me or do you want me to ask your boss after Proffitt makes the ID."

The Latino sighed. "I'll call, but it's not fair when you get me caught in the middle."

I closed the line to the crime scene and sat there and thought about what a jerk I'd been. My thoughts were interrupted by the front door being unlocked.

I returned to the living room and found two black women in the living room. They carried mops, buckets, and a vacuum cleaner. Both wore matching blue outfits and stared at the latex gloves on my hands. I showed them my ID and identified myself.

"Is there something wrong, Officer?" The skinny one held up a key. "I've got a key and we're to let ourselves in."

"When was the last time you spoke with Ms. Wasson?"

The heavy woman shrugged. The skinny one said, "Don't know. We gets a check in the mail, and I have that key I showed you." She tapped her pocket.

From the inside of my jacket, I took a clipping from this morning's paper. On the front page was a picture of Glenn Proffitt. "Ever see this man here?"

The two women looked at the newspaper clipping. "Ain't that the man on the TV last night?" asked the heavier of the two.

The skinny one was checking me out. "You the woman on the TV, ain't you? You look a lot taller in person."

"This is Glenn Proffitt," I said. "He's the owner of the building that caught fire last night."

"I hear it was a gas leak," said the heavy woman.

"I hear it was a bomb. You know, some of them A-rabs."

"Glenn Proffitt. That's the name on the papers I found last month," said the heavier one.

"What papers?" I asked.

The skinny woman glared at her companion.

"I weren't prying. It was laying out in plain sight."

"What'd it say?"

"I don'ts remember. I jest remember his name was on these sheets of paper I was straightening up." She pointed at a dining room table that would seat at least eight. "It was over there. That's where I saw it."

"Did the paperwork have lines on it? I mean, lots of lines or lines like you would have on school paper?"

"Lots of lines. Lots of numbers, too. They were written in pencil."

"Were the numbers in rows across the page or down the page, you know in a column?"

"They ran up and down the page."

I showed them the photostats from the bank. "Any papers like this you had to straighten up?"

The heavy woman shook her head. The skinny woman lifted her shoulders in a shrug.

I put the photostats away.

"But there was some checks," said the heavy woman.

"Like the ones for cleaning the condo?" I asked.

"They were the same, but not the same."

"Same size, you mean?"

Another nod.

"So they were personal checks with someone's name on them? Did you see the name?"

The heavier woman now looked at the floor.

"Look, Officer," asked the skinny woman, "you want us to clean or you want us to come back later?"

"I want to know the name on the checks. It's very important. In finding Ms. Wasson."

The heavy woman looked up. "The name on the check was Mister Glenn Proffitt. I think he left his checkbook here."

"But neither of you ever saw him?"

"No, ma'am," they said in unison. The heavier one added, "I've been cleaning Miss Wasson's apartment for over four years and I've never seen that—"

My phone sang the tune for *Hawaii Five-Oh*. I held up a hand and took it out. "Yes?"

It was the chief of police of Horry County. I had my warrant. It was on its way over.

"Can we get started cleaning?" asked the skinny maid.

The county chief asked, "Who's that?"

"The maids. I held them up until I got my warrant."

"Just as long as you held them up *outside* the premises, Susan."

"Yes, sir, and thanks again."

Before I got off the phone, he reminded me of the meeting set for less than five hours from now, you know, the one where everyone would play show and tell. At least I had something to tell, if not to show, and I didn't think the guys were going to be all that happy.

"You still want us to clean?" asked the skinny one. "This gonna put us behind if we can't get started."

Remembering what trouble I was already in with the crime scene techs, I said, "I don't think so." Still, I had them double-check the pictures on the dresser.

Both maids identified Claudia Wasson, but they didn't know who the mountain man was any more than Glenn Proffitt had. And they didn't know who the older couple was, or if the two other women in the group shot were sisters or friends. Claudia Wasson had really kept a lid on her private life.

"When should we come back?" asked the skinny one, after we had returned to the door.

"I don't know."

"Is there something wrong with Miss Wasson?"

"I don't know that either."

They looked at each other and then trooped out with their equipment. The door closed behind them.

A half-hour later, I sat in a chaise lounge whose fabric matched the spread for the canopy bed. There was nothing missing from Wasson's bedroom or bath, not even her contacts or medication. A Bible, one that had been a gift from Patricia, was in the nightstand.

There were more medications in the hall closet, many dated, all in orderly rows on the shelf above the extra sheets and towels. On another shelf was a metal file cabinet that could be opened with a bobby pin. Inside were her tax records and other important documents. Wasson was a graduate of Bob Jones University, where she'd majored in business. She was also paid very handsomely for her skills. In the rear of the closet was a locked wall safe. For that, I would need a different type of warrant.

While I sat on the chaise lounge, my phone sounded again.

"Sorry," said Luis from the crime scene, "first time I could call. It's not Claudia Wasson, according to Glenn Proffitt. He looked relieved."

"You showed him a photograph."

"Well, we didn't want the guy puking all over himself. Besides, he's not next-of-kin. Well, here comes Jacqueline. Got to go."

I opened a line to the new Proffitt Center. I'd gotten the number from the receptionist and added it to my speed dial. Also on my speed dial was Chad's number. When was I going to erase it? I couldn't. It would be like erasing him from my life, as his injury had erased me from his.

"Emily, Susan Chase. Has Claudia come in or called?"

"Not yet, Agent Chase. Want me to have her call?"

"You sound as if you're sure she'll be there."

"I don't remember her ever missing a day of work."

"Do you have access to her credit cards? I mean do you have some numbers I could run?"

"I don't know. I don't think people would like that."

"Why don't you and Maureen get any credit information of Claudia's together, and when Glenn returns to the office, ask him if I'll need a warrant for those accounts. If he doesn't return, call his cell phone and get permission."

"We can do that. Maureen can find anything. Even after a building is blown up."

The photographs on the dresser were what held my interest. While on the phone, I had stared at them from across the room. Now I went over and got down on my knees to be at eye level with the surface of the dresser. Six frames on a layer of dust. But the clear spots in the dust didn't always correspond with the photographs. They had not been moved. Some of the photographs had been replaced.

I got to my feet and walked to the bedroom door and stared at the linen closet down the hall. After chewing on my lip, I returned to the chaise lounge, sat down, and flipped open my phone.

"Emily?"

"Agent Chase, what's going on? Maureen went running out of here to pick up Glenn. He said he was too rattled to drive."

"I need to know who's on Claudia's insurance card as the next-of-kin."

There was a sudden intake of air on the other end of the line. "You don't think . . . ."

"Emily, I don't know what to think. Can you help me out?"

"Yes, yes." Paper was shuffled on her end of the phone. "Oh, God, I don't have anything. Everything was destroyed in the fire."

"But you know your insurance carrier, don't you?"

She gave me a name.

After identifying myself to the local agent, I said, "I need a next-of-kin for Claudia Wasson."

"Agent Chase, where can I call to verify that you are who you say you are?"

I gave her the number of the Horry County police chief.

When my cell rang again, I was sitting in the chaise lounge and studying the photostats from Proffitt's bank. Could I make out a difference between a "t" in "thousand" on the check and in Proffitt's name or was I just imagining things? Someone in Jacqueline's department would have to take a look.

"Yes?" I asked, shaking myself out of my stupor. I was running out of gas and it was only early afternoon.

"The next-of-kin for Claudia Wasson is 'Patricia Owens,'" said the insurance agent.

"Just a moment," I said, reaching inside my coat. "Let me get my pad."

"I thought you were in a hurry for this information, Agent Chase."

"Not so much that I'm going to write on a photostat I'm examining."

"Sorry."

I had the pen and pad out. "Shoot."

"Patricia is married to Marty Owens. They live in McClellanville. Patricia works for the national park service. She's a forester. I have a number if you want it."

"Give it to me."

I called Francis Marion National Forest and was put through to Patricia's supervisor. No, I could not speak to Patricia. She had left earlier this morning. Family emergency.

ELEVEN

"Does she have a cell phone?"

"Most foresters don't carry cell phones, Agent Chase. They carry radios. Cell phones don't work all that well in the park." With a small laugh, the woman on the other end of the line explained, "I don't think there's enough business in this part of the state to justify building a tower."

"Have any idea what the emergency was?"

"None at all. Patricia was on duty when she called in. I think she left and went right into Myrtle Beach."

"Her family emergency was in the city of Myrtle Beach, not somewhere else along the Grand Strand?" Much to the chagrin of smaller municipalities, everything along the Grand Strand is simply "Myrtle Beach."

"Yes. Why? Is there a problem?"

"Are there any other siblings, Ms. . . . .?"

"Delores Hamby is my name. Patricia has a sister in Myrtle Beach. I just supposed that was what the family emergency pertained to."

"What is the sister's name?"

"Claudia. 'Wasson' is the family name. Claudia never married. She's one of those liberated types. Oh, Agent Chase, I didn't mean . . . ."

"I know about Claudia, but I thought there might be another sister." I was staring at the woman in the photograph whose body may have been discovered on the second floor of the Proffitt Center. "A younger sibling?"

"Agent Chase, can you tell me what this is all about?"

"I can't go into detail, but I'm standing in Claudia's condo in North Myrtle Beach and looking at photographs on her dresser. I'm just trying to put names to faces. Claudia didn't come in to work this morning."

"Oh, my God! She works in that Proffitt Center. I remember because it has such an odd name."

"So any assistance you can give me would be a help."

"Yes, yes, I understand. Wait a minute. Are you the woman who was on television last night?"

I sighed. "Yes."

"That was quite heroic what you did."

"Actually, it was pretty frightening. Forester Hamby, I need to ask you some questions."

"Oh, yes. I'll be happy to assist you. Will you be coming by the park sometime in the future? I don't want to bother you, but I'm sure my children would love to have your autograph."

"Er—yes, but can you help me with Patricia's siblings?"

"Laura is the youngest and she's an off-and-on student at the tech school in Georgetown."

That would be Horry-Georgetown Technical College. No help there. All schools were on Christmas break. "Her name would also be Wasson?" I asked.

"That is correct. Laura is only nineteen and she's been quite a handful for both older sisters."

"And the parents are deceased?"

"Their mother died of cervical cancer. Their father died at a railroad crossing. This was three years ago." Hamby paused. "There was some suspicion it was a suicide."

Staring at the photograph of the mountain man in the red-plaid shirt, I asked, "What about a brother?"

"You mean John Ross. He used to work for the steel mill in Georgetown, but Claudia was always listed as Patricia's next-of-kin. Agent Chase, if Laurie is with John Ross, you may have a hard time finding her."

"Laurie?"

"Laura is sometimes called Laurie. I guess because she was the youngest. Anyway, when she had a fight with her sisters, she'd go live with John Ross. He has a cabin in the forest. No power, no phone, no nothing. Completely unattached."

I reached for my pad and pen. "Is there someone you know who can give me directions?"

"All you have to do is ask the authorities."

"Wasson has a record?"

"Extensive."

Now I understood why the photographer had found it hard to fit the Wasson brother into the picture on the dresser. The mountain man was larger than life. "So what does John Ross do for walking-around money?"

"Takes tourists into the forest."

"I thought that was his sister's job."

"No, Agent Chase, John Ross takes people into the forest for poaching."

I stood up and walked around, exercising my stiffening shoulder. So what did I have? A missing sister, a possible missing sister, and a brother you could reach only at risk to life and limb. I stopped my pacing, bit on my lip, and stared at the photographs lining the dresser. I called Jacqueline Marion's assistant again.

"Luis, I know the name of the dead woman."

"We do, too. One of the partners came in and ID'd the remains. The doctor didn't know what the nurse was doing here or who the other victim was—the one you found."

"Laura Wasson is the name of the dead woman found in the OB/GYN."

I heard the voice of Jacqueline Marion, who had to be standing nearby. "Who's that?" she asked.

"It's Susan," Luis answered.

"Hang up. If she has anything to say to anyone, she can go through channels."

"Bye, Susan."

"Luis, wait!"

But he was gone.

I sat on the edge of the bed and thought about dead girls, dead relationships, and how I was about to fulfill my prophecy, the one where I'd end up riding a desk.

The phone sang again.

"Chase, here."

Speak of the devil. It was my boss. "You were supposed to interview Glenn Proffitt. If you're through with that assignment, there are plenty of others waiting at the law enforcement center."

"I'm on my way." After closing my phone, I held the instrument at a distance and shot it a bird.

At a pay phone on the street, I made another kind of call. After a few rings, a hoarse voice came over the line, one from my days as a private detective.

The voice coughed. "Why you calling me, Chase? I thought you went legit."

"I need a favor."

"Oh. So nowadays you call them favors."

"They were always favors."

"I don't remember you paying many back."

"Ronnie, I always repay favors, just not in the currency you prefer."

"So what currency you trading in today, pretty girl?"

"You help me, I help you."

"You could really help yourself—"

"Ronnie!"

"Okay, okay." Once again he coughed. "I have a friend in Columbia at the correctional institute."

"What's he in for?"

"Accepting stolen property."

"What's the name?"

He gave it to me.

"I'll see what I can do."

"If you still have a job."

"What's that supposed to mean?"

"I caught your act last night. Stuff like that always chaps the brass, you know, street cops getting face time on TV."

"Ronnie, I need a safe checked."

"Do I get to keep the contents?"

"For once you do."

The gravely voice brightened. "Now that's more like it. Give me the particulars."

"It's in a gated community."

"Good. I like them places where everybody's relaxed and laid back."

I returned to Sam's Corner and had another hot dog. The employees appeared pleased that I was able to move my arms and legs, and only two people asked for my autograph, neither working behind the counter. I took a seat in the rear of that long room and devoured the dog. As I did, Agent Kinlaw appeared in the door, ordered a beer, and joined me.

"Are you psychic?" I asked. "Or do you have a hot dog fetish?"

"Not at all," said the lean man, putting his beer on the table. "I've had a man tailing you since you left Wasson's condominium."

I felt my eyebrows rise. "And why's that?"

He shrugged out of his overcoat and sat down. "The FBI is interested in what you've learned."

"I'll be making my report same as the others tonight." I drank from a Carolina Blonde. It seemed appropriate after visiting the new Proffitt Center.

"After Glenn Proffitt demanded to see the body found at the crime scene I became interested in what you were up to. Susan, you can't go around telling secrets. We might need the leverage."

"Did I, or did I not, get Proffitt moving?"

"You did."

"Next question."

Kinlaw let out his breath. "I can see I'm not going to get very far discussing proper investigative procedures with you. You think Proffitt plays a role in this?"

"As a catalyst."

"I don't follow . . . ."

"Claudia Wasson has cleared out."

"Like in left town?"

"Yes." I chewed and swallowed. "She's been stealing money from Proffitt's personal account for years."

"You know this for a fact?"

I only drank from my beer.

"On what do you base that assumption?"

I put down the remainder of my hot dog, wiped the mustard off my hand, and ticked off my suspicions. "Proffitt says he didn't write the checks, and a secretary you can set your clock by is MIA. Actually, if Claudia Wasson were still in town, I think she would've picked up Proffitt this morning at the hospital and brought him to work. As it was, one of his former wives did."

Kinlaw stopped drinking from his beer. "His ex-wife works in the business?"

I explained that this particular ex-wife received a monthly check and had not gotten a lump-sum settlement.

"So Maureen Proffitt has a monetary interest in her husband's death."

"And Glenn likes the attention." I finished my hot dog. Boy, was I missing a really gooey and greasy chili dog, but you never knew who might show up. This guy was a case in point.

"Where did the ex-Mrs. Proffitt say she was when the explosion happened?"

"Hilton Head."

"Can I have an address?" A vinyl pad and gold pen came out of his inside suit coat pocket.

I opened my own pad and read off the home address of Maureen Proffitt in Hilton Head. Kinlaw would want more so I turned the pad to face him. "Claudia knew the jig was up when the building blew, that there would be all kinds of attention—"

"If not from the IRS, then from the ex-wife. Think she had anything to do with the bombing?"

"I have no idea."

"What did you learn from the search of Claudia Wasson's condo?"

"You'd think the woman was still in town."

"Anything else?"

"I think photographs are missing from the bedroom. The ones on the dresser don't match the spots in dust pattern."

"Wasson thinks we'll believe she died in the blast?"

"Maybe. Do you have someone in the Charleston office available to do field work?"

"Don't worry. We're checking the flights out of this state and Atlanta."

"Wasson's SUV is in her space under the condo so she may have taken a cab. No, what I mean is there's a guy on a farm to the south who needs to be interviewed." I told him about Dave Mendenhall. "I'd like to know where he was last night. He stands to inherit a 'dream come true.'" I told him a bit about the relationship between Mendenhall and Proffitt.

He made a note. "The Charleston office will send someone out. What else?"

"What does her sister know, the forester, Patricia Owens? That's her married name."

"Uh-huh. Well, since a certain someone is loose with their lips, Patricia Owens might know everything about the body found inside the Proffitt Center."

I felt my face heat up.

"Did Claudia Wasson have an answering machine?" he asked.

I drank from my beer to regain my composure. "The sister called. Patricia said they needed to talk. The only problem is I can't locate Patricia."

"What have you tried?"

"First the national forest, then her place in McClellanville, where no one answered, and the hospital, and the morgue." The latter I had worked from my cell phone on the way over and I only hoped I'd remember to pump up its battery. "I think she's on her way to Myrtle."

His eyes narrowed. "Who else did you tell about the dead woman?"

"Look, I didn't tell anyone but Glenn Proffitt."

"Who has a building full of women working—"

"Don't be such a sexist."

"If you'll hear me out."

I finished my hot dog which had turned cold.

"If you had an office full of women and one of them appeared to be missing, they'd be calling anyone they could think of."

I picked up my beer, rolled the bottle in my hands, and stared at it. "Look, the fact a body was found in the OB/GYN was going to get out. You have reporters everywhere, and people who will take money for information. I agree information shouldn't be given out without cause, but I was trying to get Proffitt jump-started. He actually believes Claudia will come in today. I had to shake him up or he was going to stay in that alternate universe."

"You think he's repressing the explosion."

"He's repressing something."

"You actually think Claudia Wasson might've blown up the Proffitt Center to cover up her embezzling?"

"Or she had help. Her brother is one of those back-to-nature types, and there are a lot of people in this part of the state who don't like you *feebs*."

"I'll have the authorities pick up the Wasson brother." Kinlaw shook his head as he wrote. "I hope John Ross is not our man. Eric Rudolph was tough enough to catch."

I put down the beer bottle. "And where the Great Smoky Mountains are tough duty because of terrain, Francis Marion is open to the public. State and county roads cross it, as does the Intracoastal Waterway, and there are plenty of mom-and-pop stores to resupply you."

"I've driven past Francis Marion. It's so thick you could go fifty yards and disappear from sight."

"More like fifty feet. Except there's a possible hole in my theory."

"And that is?"

"It's highly possible the woman's body found in the Proffitt Center is the younger sister, Laura Wasson, sometimes called Laurie."

Kinlaw put down his pen. "You don't kill one sister when you're intent on blowing up the place where your other sister works." He shook his head. "I'm not buying that at all."

"Then you're back to square one, meaning Claudia and her brother had nothing to do with the bombing."

"If that's square one."

"Or," I said.

"Or what? I'm almost afraid to ask."

"I learned that Claudia Wasson attended Bob Jones University. What if Claudia had her brother, after pumping him full of fundamentalist Bible rhetoric, blow the building as a cover-up for her to leave town?"

Kinlaw pursed his lips and tapped his pen against them. He had long fingers, pianist fingers. "So far there's been no message from anyone who can make us believe they had a hand in the bombing."

"How many calls have you received?"

"Not as many as you'd think. After the Beltway Sniper, it's not fashionable to call up law enforcement agencies and claim credit for something you didn't do."

"Were you in Charleston when that guy tried to extort money from the girl's family in Utah?"

"Elizabeth Smart. Yes." Kinlaw sat there in silence as customers filed in the door. "You know, Susan, I'm not all that old, but it doesn't seem as if the world spins on the same axis as it did when I was a child."

"I agree, and I'm much younger."

It was growing dark when we returned to the law enforcement center, and because of the congestion, both Kinlaw and I had to park several blocks away. Which made the media gauntlet you had to run that much longer. The sharks were expecting to be fed and nobody was feeding.

Kinlaw shouldered his way through the crowd and I followed. At the entrance, also fighting to get inside, was a suntanned, solidly built woman in a forester's uniform. She stood near my five-foot-ten, had dark hair, and her eyes were a bit too close together.

"Patricia Owens?" I asked.

"Yes—yes."

"I'm Susan Chase." I showed her my ID. When I did, more flashes went off.

Owens glanced in the direction of the sudden light. "I'm looking for my sister. Can you help me?"

I ushered her inside and into the ladies' room. Once the room was clear and Owens had wiped her wind-burned face with a wet paper towel, she was eager to talk. To a point.

"I need to find my sister."

"Why do you think she's missing?"

Daphne Adkins appeared at the door. "What's going on?" I had called Daphne over my cell. It was easier than fighting through the clogged phone lines or the equally clogged hallways. GTE was everywhere; unless all those people crawling around were the media sneaking a peek. Finally, GTE had to send a supervisor over to check out everyone who claimed to have a work order.

Daphne glanced at Owens as she passed me a photograph. In the photograph, the dead woman's eyes were closed under her bushy eyebrows, her face pale, and her black hair pulled back. I hate these moments.

"Daphne, keep everyone out of here. Mrs. Owens and I need to talk."

"Are you going to fill me in?" asked my trainee.

"Of course."

"Then no one will get in." She stepped outside.

"What is it?" asked Owens, seeing the photograph in my hand.

"We found the body of a young female in the rubble of the Proffitt Center. We need help in identifying her."

Owens gripped the formica counter as if she knew what might come next. Hell, we all know what comes next. Still, I hoped to make it easy on her. "Forester Owens, you aren't the first person to come forward since the explosion and tell us a loved one is missing." Of course, that doesn't mean the person can handle the news.

Owens leaned into the counter for support and bent her head. She breathed so rapidly I thought she might hyperventilate.

"Would you please look at this photograph and tell us if it's anyone you recognize?" I haven't yet learned how to deliver my line properly. I thrust the photograph at her. "Do you know this woman?"

Keeping her hands on the counter, Owens raised her head and gasped. "That's Laurie." Her knuckles grew whiter as she tightened her grip on the edge of the counter. "But—but it looks like she's dead."

"If this is your sister, she is."

"Oh, my God." Between the counter and myself, we caught

her before she hit the floor. Catching her breath, she asked, "What—what happened?"

I told her where the body had been found.

Owens turned away from me, or perhaps she turned away from the photograph. "I told him not to do it."

"Him—who? What?"

"What?" She glanced at me. "Oh, I mean I told her not to do that."

I would not be dissuaded. "What did you tell *him* not to do, Patricia?"

"I—I meant 'her.'"

"Have it your way. What did you warn Laura not to do?"

"Have the abortion."

"You objected to her having an abortion?"

"The whole family did. We weren't raised that way."

"Your parents are deceased. What family are you talking about?"

Owens looked up from the basin. "Me, my sister, that's what I mean."

"Are you sure John Ross wouldn't have objected?"

"No," she said much too quickly.

"How can we contact your brother?"

"I—there is no brother."

"Forester Owens, I can't help you if you aren't truthful."

Both of us glanced at the door as Daphne Adkins raised her voice and turned someone away. What the hell. It wasn't like it was the only rest room in the building. I repeated what I'd said about not being able to help her if she wasn't straight with me. Owens had turned her back to the mirrors and now leaned her bottom against the counter, her hands gripping the counter behind her. Her tan uniform had sweat stains under the arms.

"I . . . I came here to fill out a missing persons report."

"But you knew where your sister was all along."

"That's not true." Glancing at the door, she asked, "I need to know when I can claim the body." A sudden sob escaped from her mouth. Her hands came up to her face, hiding it from me.

There was a knock at the door and a sergeant from the

Myrtle Beach Police Department stuck his head inside. He glanced at Patricia, then said, "I need to talk to you, Susan."

As I joined him in the corridor, Owens followed me out of the rest room.

My boss passed by. "Chase, I've been looking all over for you." Hardy looked at the forester, who now stood between Daphne and me. "Who's this?"

"Sister of the dead woman found in the OB/GYN."

Hardy took the photograph. "Adkins, you come with me. Chase, I may have another assignment so remain in the building." As Hardy took Patricia Owens by the arm, she asked me, "You are fit for duty, aren't you?"

"Of course." In a moment, I wouldn't be. "What is it?" I asked the sergeant, whose kid I'd given swimming lessons to when I'd been a lifeguard.

"Your mother's at the front desk."

I wasn't sure I'd heard him correctly. "Come again?"

"You don't think I couldn't see the resemblance, the hair, the eyes, and the build? It's your mom for sure."

TWELVE

I couldn't forget that face. I saw it each morning before the sleep had been washed from my eyes. The woman was about the same size, had the same yellow hair, and showed an uneasy smile as she stood near the front desk. In the hubbub of people coming and going, no one paid her much attention.

Plain blue dress, no jewelry, and a deep tan. A single beat-up suitcase sat beside her, and I'll give the woman credit, she didn't rush over and throw her arms around me. No. She didn't do that until I tried to shake hands.

"Susan, I'm your mother. Don't I get a hug?"

I hugged her. I think it had something to do with all the people watching, both in the lobby and outside the law enforcement center. Camera lights found us.

The sergeant who had brought me to the lobby said, "Get those reporters away from the door. We can't even conduct our usual business."

"What are you doing here?" I asked.

"I saw you on TV last night." She had my hands in hers and opened me up to see. Her face wrinkled in disappointment. Was there a spot on my blouse? Did I have one of my buttons undone?

"But how did you get here?"

She let go of my hands and both pairs of arms came down. "I took the bus from Miami."

"What can I do for you . . . Mother?" I adjusted the placket of my blouse. No spot there. Or button undone.

"Why, Susan, I'm not the one in need. You are."

"I'm—I'm fine."

She gestured at the interior of the building. "Aren't you going to ask me inside?"

I turned to the desk that stood in a small lobby area. Behind a partition, we could disappear. "May I have a pass for . . . my mother?"

"I don't know . . ." The woman on duty glanced at my lanyard. "Oh, Agent Chase." She extended a hand. "Sarah Ray. I'm on loan from the Florence City Police. Good to meet you." She produced a pass that would clip to the top of a dress and lowered her voice. "I don't know how long they'll allow civilians in here. This place is busting at the seams." She glanced at the suitcase. "From out of town, are you, Mrs. Chase?"

"Miami. My baby was on TV last night. I was so proud." My mother looked me over again. "Funny," she said, "you looked much taller on TV."

I hurried her into the rest room where I had interrogated Patricia Owens. A patrolwoman flushed a toilet, left a stall, and smiled. I nodded, and the woman washed up and checked her hair and lipstick before leaving the room.

"Mother, what are you doing here?"

She was at the mirror, fluffing her curly blond hair. "I should be here. I'm your mother." The purse came off her arm and she set it on the counter between washbasins. Out came a brush.

"But why would you show up now?"

"Because the newspaper people said you were still living on that awful shrimp boat. Don't you think it's time you were married?"

I really didn't want to go there. "How long are you staying, Mother?"

"As long as it takes to get your life in order." She worked the brush through her hair.

"To get my life in order . . . ?"

Daphne Adkins came in. She was obviously put out. "Susan, you said you were going to brief me on what you'd learned outside this fucking zoo."

"Such language," said my mother, tsk-tsking.

"Er—Daphne, this is my mother."

"Nice to meet you, Mrs. Chase." She looked at me. "I'll see you later." And Daphne didn't let the door hit her ass on the way out.

"Mother, you can't just say what's on your mind."

"I can't?" She put away the brush. "Then I wouldn't be your mother, would I?"

"What is this business of getting my life in order? My life is in order."

She took out her lipstick, a color all wrong for her—brown—and touched up her mouth.

"I know about your fiancé."

"My fiancé? What—what are you talking about?"

"It's on TV," she said, running the lipstick around her lips.

"Chad is on the news?" Now it was my turn to grip the counter and hold on.

"They showed the viewing audience where he lives in that rest home, nursing home, whatever."

"Viewing audience?"

She reached over and patted my shoulder. I jerked back and let go of the counter. "This is your hour of need, you're my daughter, and that's why I'm here."

"Mother, I've done quite well without . . . If you're so concerned, where have you been?"

"Susan, I'm willing to put our differences behind us, and make this work."

"What . . . work?"

"Why, our relationship. A mother should be on hand when there are important decisions to be made."

"What decisions?" I asked, trying to regain control of the conversation.

"If you're still living on that old shrimp boat, you could use some help with your finances."

"You're here to help me with my money problems?" That didn't compute for someone who had begged, borrowed, or stolen from me.

"If you gave these nice network people an interview, it

could set me—er—us up for life."

"The network people?"

"Heather told me how uncooperative you've been." Mom picked at something on her plain blue dress. "Of course, I'll need something nicer for the interview." She smiled. "But that's in the works."

"What's in the works? Mother, you're not making sense."

"Heather is very upset with you, Susan."

"There's no way I can talk to Heather."

"You wouldn't want to hurt your friend's feelings, would you?"

"Mother, everyone's been forbidden to speak to the media."

She smiled. "When did rules ever stop my daughter from doing what she wanted? I remember when I tried to ground you . . . well, that's water under the dam."

"Under the bridge."

"Whatever." She looked in the mirror again. "It's all been arranged. Tonight at the Host of Kings Hotel."

I glanced at her suitcase parked under the counter. "You've hardly been here long enough to arrange anything."

"Your friend comped me a suite."

"Mother, don't tell me you asked Heather for a room." And I had to bite my tongue before I almost invited her to stay aboard my "awful shrimp boat."

She took my hand and patted it. "Don't worry, her station is paying everything, and it's a suite. Nothing but the best for my daughter. Think about it: To have the mother of the most famous lifeguard along the Grand Strand staying at the Host of Kings, what could be better publicity for their hotel?"

"I haven't been a lifeguard for years. If you'd been around you'd know . . . ."

Agent Kinlaw tapped on the door and stuck his head inside. I was mortified. This man seeing me with this woman!

He evaluated my mother, who brushed back her hair and raised her meager bustline. "Everything okay?" he asked.

Mother walked over and held out her hand. "I'm Susan's mother, and we're desperately in need of a ride. You look like the kind of man who could help us." After shaking hands,

Mother gently pulled Kinlaw into the rest room. "May I entrust the safety of myself and my daughter to you, Agent . . . ."

"Kinlaw. Jacob Kinlaw. FBI."

An eyebrow was arched. "Are you Jewish, Agent Kinlaw?"

"Haven't had the pleasure."

"Oh, Susan," she said, glancing at me, "grab this one before he gets away. He is *funnnny!*"

I thought I would die!

Mother winked at me. "But make sure he thinks he's doing the picking."

Now I was sure I was going to die. "Mo-ther!"

Still, it wasn't long before we were on our way.

"You know, I have my own car." I sat, slumped in the back seat, arms crossed.

"Your car is a jeep, Susan, and totally unsuitable for arriving at the Host of Kings Hotel."

"No, Mother, I have a car like Agent Kinlaw."

She looked around. "Oh, I'm sure you don't have anything as nice as Jacob's."

They'd been on a first-name basis—at least my mother had—before we'd escaped from the law enforcement center. The local television channel was aiding and abetting our getaway. Fact was, most of the media were busy setting up for the city chief's press conference.

Adding to my funk was the fact that I'd missed the meeting and lost my chance to grill Patricia Owens about the where-abouts of her brother. "My car was nice enough for me to talk down a jumper," I said sourly.

Kinlaw stopped at a light on Kings Highway. "I meant to ask you about that. I didn't see any report filed."

"Now, Susan," said my mother, "you must do your paper-work. How else is our government to keep functioning?"

"Mother, if I'd remained with the jumper at the Host of Kings Hotel, you wouldn't have seen me on TV."

"Nonsense, my dear. I'm quite sure you would've found more trouble to get into."

At the Host of Kings Hotel, Heather and a suite were

waiting. Once Mother freshened up, we were to give an exclusive interview to the local NBC affiliate.

"Well," said Heather, smiling and closing the doors as she backed into the hallway, "I'll let the two of you get reacquainted." And she headed downstairs to inform the management that under no circumstances were they to tell anyone who was up here or on what floor we were staying. That was like telling everyone.

Kinlaw had carried my mother's suitcase into the suite, and surprise, surprise, there was a brand-new outfit waiting for my mom: a tan business suit with matching shoes and accessories. A beautician was on call.

"Mrs. Chase," said Kinlaw, "there's no way Susan can do this interview."

Mother didn't appear to hear him. She held the jacket against her and turned to me. "How does this look?"

"Just fine, Mother." Champagne bottles stood in tall silver bowls on a rolling cart, and soon I was fighting to loosen a cork.

"You didn't even look."

Kinlaw took the bottle. Now I had to look. Whose side was Jacob Kinlaw on anyway?

"At least it'll go with your lipstick," I said.

"Are you sure you want to open this?" asked Kinlaw, holding the champagne. "It's sort of a commitment."

"Hey, Heather knows the rules."

"Yes," he said, returning to the wiring on the cork, "and I wonder where she got the idea you'd play by hers."

"Actually," said my mother, taking a glass from the cart, "Susan's never thought any rules applied to her."

The champagne popped, bubbled over, and Kinlaw hurriedly stuck the mouth of the bottle in one, then a second champagne glass, and finally a third.

He raised his glass. "To the Chase girls."

"Why, Jacob, that is so very gracious of you." Mother downed her glass and asked for more.

Two glasses later—which is not much time when my mother is drinking—dear ol' mom still hadn't been able to change Kinlaw's mind about my speaking to the press.

Mother looked longingly at the tan suit. "I really hate to see this go to waste."

She disappeared into the bedroom, taking along her suitcase and the suit. Kinlaw and I escaped to the balcony, with him bringing along the champagne and a blanket.

"Quite a character," he said, pulling the curtain and sliding the glass door closed behind us.

I plopped into another ubiquitous white chair and propped my feet on the wrought iron railing. Kinlaw wrapped the blanket around my legs and tucked me in. More champagne was poured, and we listened to the ocean wash ashore.

"I thought you were an orphan, Susan."

"Me, too."

"How long since you've seen her?"

"Not long enough." I sat up and brought down my feet. "I'm sorry. I know how that sounds."

"Why is she here?"

"Evidently, to bask in my newfound glory. Soon she'll be working on a book deal."

The FBI agent stretched out one of his long legs, hooked a foot under a small table, and pulled it over to prop his feet on. "She has to accept the fact that you're not going to be interviewed."

I shrugged.

"What will you do?"

"Same as before: deny she's my mother."

"Does that usually work?"

I drank from my glass. "Unfortunately, there are too many children who have decent relationships with their moms and they always encourage me to play nice."

He offered me more champagne. "You sound like a woman who's had one too many sessions with a shrink."

"You don't know the half . . . ." I looked at him as he poured more bubbly. "You know everything about me. I know nothing about you."

"What would you like to know?"

Well, not the question that every gal wants to know.

"Just the facts, sir. Just the facts."

He chuckled. "I was recruited at Duke because I had an ear for languages. I've been with the Bureau sixteen years."

But that has nothing to do with your marital status.

"I had several duty stations. One in Minneapolis."

"Where the woman put together the clues about 9/11?"

He put down the bottle. "Coleen didn't have the complete story. She only had some odds and ends—"

"That she put in a memo and passed along to the higher-ups." I put down my glass between us. "If the people in Washington had their heads out of their asses, 9/11 might never have happened."

"Our generation's Pearl Harbor," he said sadly.

Below us, the waves made less noise than an approaching helicopter with a belly light. So many choppers fly up and down the Grand Strand, I gave it little thought.

"You encouraged Coleen to go public?" I asked.

"On the contrary. I was one of the people who advised her against that trip to Washington. When you look at it through the prism of 9/11, it makes me out to be a pretty bad guy."

"Then you had nothing to do with the memo?"

"A casual conversation at the coffee machine was my contribution, or lack of contribution, to history."

"Telling her not to go public."

"You don't tell Coleen anything. Not even her husband, though he tries to keep her from sticking her foot in her mouth."

"So that's why you've been tagging along."

"Let's just say if I had an agent who did what you did last night, she'd be home today, and if I learned she was working the street, she'd be bundled off to the hospital, after I wrote her up."

"Oh, I don't know. Benign neglect isn't such a bad relationship to have with one's superior."

"I think you're pushing yourself." He glanced over his shoulder at the glass door. "And now this."

I didn't want to talk about *this.* I was watching the chopper working its light along the shoreline. Those on the beach looked up. Some waved. A light breeze played with my hair.

"So how did you end up in Charleston?"

"After Coleen's memo went public, the Bureau came to Minneapolis and moved a few people around."

"They thought you had something to do with the memo?"

"The impression our people in Minneapolis gave was that everyone was four-square behind Coleen."

"You weren't and that earned you a promotion."

"I believe you never go to the Director. Or talk with politicians or their minions."

"Unless it's cleared with your superiors."

Still looking out to sea, he said, "I believe that's a fair assessment of the situation."

"God, but you are a company man."

"I have to be. I have three children and a wife with Lou Gehrig's disease."

I didn't know what to say, but at least I knew his marital status. Still, I didn't understand why he didn't wear a wedding band.

The curtain was pulled back and the glass door slid open. "Oh, good," said my mother. "I thought I might be interrupting something."

"Mother, don't be silly."

Kinlaw pulled his feet off the small table. "I should be going." He leaned over and picked up the glass I had placed beside my chair. I got a whiff of his cologne or aftershave. God, but it'd been a long time since I'd been with a man, or even wanted to. Thankfully, this one was well out of reach.

Mother made way for Kinlaw about the same time the helicopter focused its light on our balcony. When the chopper turned to one side, I saw a man aim his camera in our direction. I scrambled from under the blanket and followed them inside.

Kinlaw made sure the curtain closed behind me. "It's something you're going to have to learn to live with."

"Or not."

"Susan," said my mother, "if you went on record, then they'd leave you alone."

We passed through the living room adjoined by a kitchenette and a nook for dining. I could see another bedroom across from the main room.

"How will you get out of here?" I asked Kinlaw.

He said, "I can brush them off with a 'no comment.' I'm afraid they think you'll say something you'll later regret."

"Susan," said my mother, "you're going to have to speak to the media sooner or later."

"Then I'll take later." Kinlaw didn't want to leave me with this needy woman and an overbearing press. You could hear them rattling around in the hallway. "Would you give me a ride if I meet you downstairs?"

"Are you sure you can get away?" He stood at the door.

If you listened closely, you could hear Heather telling everyone to get lost. Like that was going to happen. "I'll meet you in the garage. Give me fifteen minutes."

He glanced at his watch. "I'll give you twenty and then I'm going to have to get out of here myself. Will they get to you?" he asked, glancing at my mother.

"Don't worry. It's not going to happen."

"Susan . . . ?" pleaded my mother.

Kinlaw's departure stirred up the crowd. As he went out the door, I snatched the electronic keys off the table in the entryway, then stood at the door, listening to see if the reporters followed him to the elevator. It sounded as if they had.

"Mother, come with me," I said, gripping the handle of the door and wrenching it open.

Her face broke out in a big smile. "I appreciate you doing this for me, Susan. We'll have to work out an equitable split of the fee."

"Whatever."

She glanced in a mirror and settled her tan suit on on her frame. She looked rather nice, and the way she'd blotted the brown lipstick, it actually went with the new outfit. As I stepped into the hallway, she said, "Did I tell you I was approached for a book deal?"

Since the reporters figured they had me trapped, they'd gathered around Kinlaw at the elevator, shouting questions.

"She's down here!"

That was my mother, of course, and then she was just another voice hollering for me to wait up. I took off in the opposite direction, opened the door to the roof, and hurried upstairs. It didn't take long before I was, once again, on the pebbled rooftop among air conditioning units and a bunch of stubby pipes. I walked to the edge and looked over the side. The helicopter and I were eye-to-eye, but no one on the chopper seemed to notice—until they were alerted.

Heads jerked up and slowly the nose of the aircraft rose. By the time the light focused on me, I had returned to the rooftop door where reporters were piling out of the stairway. I held the door open and the latecomers forced the herd in the direction of the helicopter's blinding light. When all of them were out of the stairwell, I stepped inside and closed the door. On my way down, I passed my mother and a stray cameraman.

"Susan . . . where are you going?" She was practically out of breath.

"Home," I said, thumping down the stairs.

She leaned over the railing. "But Agent Kinlaw isn't here, my dear. You can talk freely."

The cameraman must've heard the shouts and the pounding because the horde began to scramble down the stairs. I threw back the door to the top floor, hurried down to the elevator, and looked at the floor indicator. One at the garage level, the other at the lobby.

I gritted my teeth and returned to the suite. As I slipped in the door, my mother led the charge of reporters and cameramen to our floor. Unfortunately for them, I had all the keys. Closing the door behind me and falling back against it, I caught my breath and glanced at my watch. Only ten minutes before Agent Kinlaw left me behind. What got me moving was when I heard Heather shout for everyone to back off. She had a key.

I hustled across the living room, went under the curtain, and slid back the glass door. From the balcony, I could see that the helicopter still had its light trained on the roof. I looked at the waves rushing ashore and the people looking up. Children chattered on the adjacent balcony.

I tested the sturdiness of the railing and then pulled off my boots and tucked them upside down in the pockets of my long coat, which I unbuttoned. Using one of the plastic chairs, I grasped the wall between this balcony and the adjoining one, boosted myself up, and fitted my stockinged feet on the railing. The children next door looked up as a dark figure in a flaring coat stepped onto their railing. A woman's voice demanded to know what I was doing, but by then I had leaped to their balcony.

As I leaned against the railing and put on my boots, I heard a child say, "It's Susan Chase."

An open book was stuck in my face by a young boy. "Can I have your autograph?" He was about ten, with a mop of red hair and a pair of pj's under a thermal jacket.

"She was right next door," gasped a little girl.

I took the boy's pen and scribbled my name, wondering why anyone would want it.

The mother snatched the autograph book out of his hands. "You're not asking this woman for anything. She sets a bad example for children."

I eased my way past her as the boy yowled in disappointment.

"No, Gabriel, you're not . . . . Hey! Where do you think you're going?"

Sliding back their glass door, I left the balcony for the bedroom.

"Listen, you . . . ." said the mother.

She followed me through open suitcases, two turned-down queen-size beds, and the sounds of Phish, the rock group both generations can mellow out to without having to send out for grass. In the living room, dad had passed out on the sofa watching a Brenden Fraser marathon. Chips and empty beer cans littered the coffee table.

I cracked the hallway door and peered outside. Straight across from me were the elevators, but both were still on lower floors. Fifteen feet down the hall were the microphones, cameras, and reporters. No sign of my mother. She and Heather were probably trying to figure out how I'd escaped. Poor Mom, she was going to have to return that suit. I closed the door and glanced at my watch. I had eight minutes before Agent Kinlaw left. The children and their mother had caught up with me.

I smiled at the red-headed boy. "Gabriel, how about you stepping across the hall and punching the button for the elevator."

His mother wanted no part of this, but the kid was already gone. I'd given him an open door to slip through.

"Miss Chase, this isn't the sort of example that should be set for children."

What could I say? She was right.

Her son tapped on the door and I let him in.

"I pressed it three times, Susan. I counted."

"Thanks." I peered through the cracked door. The elevators were making their way up and the reporters didn't appear any the wiser.

I stooped down eye-to-eye to the autograph seeker and his sibling. "I really appreciate your help, but what I did was kind of stupid."

The kids stared at me with admiring smiles.

"Nobody in their right mind climbs from one balcony to another in a hotel, or anywhere else."

The children continued to smile. I looked up at the mother, whose mouth was a tight line across her face.

"The elevator?" she demanded, her foot tapping away.

"And never punch all the buttons on an elevator. It might inconvenience other guests."

I still faced adoring smiles. "Well," I said, getting to my feet, "got to go."

I cracked the door again. While I'd been giving my safety lecture, the elevator had reached our floor and was about to close its doors again. I was out the door and across the hall in a jiffy, thrusting my arm between the two rubber bumpers. When the doors bucked back, I slipped inside and punched the button for the garage followed by the "door closed" button. The last I saw, the kids were still smiling at me.

Jacob Kinlaw dropped me off at my car, and I blew a kiss as I got into my sedan. When he disappeared down the street, I drove a couple of blocks, dodged the media, and entered the rear of the law enforcement center.

The city chief passed me in the hall. "Susan, don't you think you should get home? The paperwork will be on your desk in the morning to initial."

"What?" I asked in mock astonishment. "Go home and see myself on TV again? I don't think so."

The chief laughed and slipped out the back door. He thought I was joking.

At Daphne Adkins' workstation, I found a manila envelope with my name on it. Beside the envelope sat a stack of videotapes marked "Myrtle Beach International Surveillance." I unbuttoned my coat and perched on the corner of her desk. Around me patrolmen and plainclothes detectives were answering phones, filling out forms, and placing calls as the wheels of justice, despite the hour, continued to grind. Inside the envelope were photos of everyone who worked for Glenn Proffitt, faxed over by the Department of Motor Vehicles. I shuffled through the collection until I came up with Claudia Wasson.

Sliding off the desk, I turned around to find Jacob Kinlaw behind me. Startled, I stepped back.

"Now what are you up to?" he asked.

I used the folder to gesture at the videotapes. "They were sent over from the airport."

"But couldn't someone else view them? Just tell them what you're looking for." He glanced at his watch. He didn't have to tell me it was past eleven. "You know, I tried very hard not to remind you how late it was."

"And I was thinking we should pop some popcorn and watch a video before turning in."

A skeleton staff was in the conference room and feeling their territorial imperative.

"What you doing here, Chase?" asked Anslow, a Horry County detective who stood at a white board. Uneven lines had been filled in with names, etcetera.

"Yeah," said his partner, "you want to work graveyard, I'll be more than happy to swap."

"I need to check some videos."

Someone with more sense noticed the tapes Agent Kinlaw placed on the conference table. "What you got there?" he asked.

I explained, and most of the guys were happy to take a break. Several restaurants had sent over food for the overnighter, and plenty of gourmet coffee, something almost unheard of in any law enforcement operation. I flipped on the video recorder and sorted through the cartridges until I found the one I was looking for.

Kinlaw was watching the men file out of the conference room. "Does everyone give you a hard time?"

"Only the guys."

He flipped off the lights and took a seat on the other side of the table. I slid a tape into the machine and tossed my coat over the back of a chair.

My cell phone sounded.

I removed it from my belt and that took some doing. For some reason, I was having trouble with my hands. Maybe I was exhausted. Or climbing balcony to balcony was a bit too close to what I'd done the previous night.

"Yes?" I said into the phone.

"What is this? Some kind of joke?"

"Ronnie?"

"No wonder you said I could have the contents. There was nothing inside that damn safe." He severed our connection almost savagely.

As I concentrated on putting away the phone, Kinlaw watched me. He said, "Single girls get all the calls."

"And at all hours of the night."

When I paused the tape, Kinlaw got to his feet and walked to the end of the room. He peered at the black-and-white image of a woman boarding the last flight out of Myrtle Beach. A large screen had been brought in or people would've clunked heads trying to view a screen the size of a TV. The woman held a carry-on but no purse.

"Sure that's her?" he asked.

"It's her." My eyes felt grainy and had begun to burn, but I didn't dare rub them.

Part of the image crossed his body, flashing on his shoulder. "I don't know, Susan. You still haven't explained how she altered the checks."

"Invisible ink." I shut off the machine. "It's available on the web."

He faced me. "Are you serious?"

"When Glenn Proffitt saw those checks, they were waiting for his signature. Everything else is legit, so, when the amount and the payee's name disappeared, Claudia wrote in what she wanted and the word 'Cash.'"

Kinlaw didn't appear convinced.

I glanced at the folder with notes scribbled on it. Daphne Adkins had initialed them and made mention that this information had been included in the official record. "It says here that someone took a cab from Claudia Wasson's condominium right after the explosion. The cab dropped this person—it doesn't give a name or sex—at the airport."

Kinlaw returned to my end of the table. "So you think Claudia Wasson had nothing to do with the explosion?"

"Wasson is an executive secretary, not an explosives expert." I picked up my coat and slipped into it as the tape ejected from the machine. "People like Wasson are creatures of habit. I imagine she was home when the news came on, maybe in bed. It took only a few minutes to call a cab, dress, and open her safe. Then she stuck her passport and a pack of cash in an already packed suitcase and walked away from her former life. She had it planned for months, maybe years." I wrote a message on a sticky note and stuck it to the top of the videotape.

"So Claudia Wasson is where?"

I picked up the folder again. "With the unforeseen death of her sister in the explosion—it says here one of the cars found in the Pavilion parking garage was owned by Laura Wasson—I imagine Claudia will be returning to the States before you can draft the papers to extradite her."

THIRTEEN

M y mother was waiting for me at Wacca Wache Landing where *Daddy's Girl* is moored. With her navy blue cloth coat pulled tight against the night air, and an expression to match, she sat in a golf cart at the end of the pier where I usually take my daily swims.

Just like in the good ol' days.

Water lapped against the hull of my boat and overhead lights illuminated the cove and the boathouse behind it. The parking lot of the Landing held my car and only my car. Harry's Buick was at the airport waiting for his return from St. Louis. Soaring into the night went the remains of a cigarette.

"I thought you had a room at the hotel."

"They threw me out because of you."

"Because of me?" I struggled to connect the dots. "Oh, the interview." I stepped aboard *Daddy's Girl.*

"Everyone was here, but they got fed up and left."

"Here? Who?"

"The reporters—who do you think?"

"Oh."

All I wanted to do was crash. I might not even take off my clothes. I'd almost fallen asleep driving home; the only thing keeping me awake was the recurring ache in my shoulder. I'd probably aggravated it climbing from balcony to balcony.

"All you had to do was give them one lousy interview and I'd be set for life." Mother glanced at the boat as she came aboard, battered suitcase in one hand, purse in the other. "Reminds me of how you used to disappear when there were chores to be done. Now you're stuck with me. I don't have anywhere else to stay."

I glanced at Harry's yacht as I twisted the key in the cabin door. Harry was long gone and I had the key. Maybe I'd be able to clean up any mess good ol' Mom left behind. I don't think so.

I opened the cabin door, flipped on the light, and turned off the whistling alarm. Mother followed me inside and looked around, taking in the essentials: wet bar, battered sofa and coffee table, and rocking chair. A PC sat under the lid of a rolltop desk stuffed with all the paperwork I had in the world, and flanking it were stereo speakers. An expensive print hung over the sofa, but otherwise, well, I'm not really here that much. Or much of a homebody.

"This place hasn't changed," she said, putting down her suitcase.

"I wanted you to feel at home when you returned."

"Susan, if you weren't such a smart aleck you'd have more friends."

"I have plenty of friends."

"Yeah. Drug addicts, cokeheads, and runaways."

I dropped my coat across the end of the sofa. My Glock, extra clip, and cell I placed on the crowded surface of the rolltop. I heard something clatter to the deck as I continued past the bunk beds to the head. Hard to believe a family of five had once lived on this craft, but then again, the sofa opened into a double bed and my siblings and I had been much smaller. For a fleeing moment, I thought I saw a face I recognized in the lower bunk, but Chad wasn't there. It was only me needing a good night's sleep. Or longing to be held.

I went into the head and almost fell asleep before flushing away my sorrows. When I returned to the cabin, my mother had pulled a beer from the small fridge under the bar. The Glock, spare clip, and my cell phone now sat on top of a stack of unpaid bills on the rolltop.

"You need to take better care of your equipment or you're not going to have that job for much longer."

I said nothing, only stood there holding on to the corner of the sofa. It was her party.

She took a seat in the rocking chair given to me by Harry. Considering the two of them never really got along, I wondered if I should tell her. My movements were lethargic, and on my way aft, I'd bumped into the bulkhead and had to steady myself.

Mother looked beyond the battered sofa in the direction of Harry's yacht moored in the adjoining slip. "Lord knows what that man's been teaching you."

"He encourages me to read." I moved some clothing from one end of the sofa and sat down. The end farthest away from my mother.

"He should encourage you to be more appreciative of what your family did for you."

"What?" Had I missed something? Over the past fifteen years.

She swallowed from her beer before going on. "Harry Poinsett always looked down his nose at us. Just because he'd been some kind of diplomat . . . . I was here as long as I could stand it. And I came back for you. More than once. I'll bet you never tell your friends that."

Was it possible this woman could run down? From what I remembered in the past, there wasn't much chance. Mother leaned forward, forearms on her knees, beer bottle held carelessly in her hand. I studied her. From her blouse stuck a pair of bony arms and a pair of broad shoulders I must've inherited, but not the hips. Mom's were much slimmer.

"Susan, we're all the family either of us has."

"Did Grandma pass on?"

"Oh, her. She and I don't see eye to eye. It's like I don't exist."

"I know the feeling" slipped out before I could stop it. Or wanted to.

She sat up. "I'm not going to sit here and listen to your mouth."

"Mother, I've been on my own since I was fifteen. This boat is all I have and I'll be damned if you're going to come aboard and start drawing me up short."

"I didn't travel all this way from Miami to take lip off my daughter."

"Mother, this isn't a conversation I want to have."

"Well, you owe me. I'm your mother."

"Can you be more specific?"

"I gave you life."

"Don't try to hang a guilt trip on me, because the bottom line is, you walked out on this family, or what was left of it, when I was only thirteen."

"You wouldn't leave with me."

"I didn't need a smoke."

She looked around. "Got any cigarettes?"

I sighed. It was impossible to have a conversation with this woman once she began to drink. I got to my feet and dug an opened pack from under a stack of paperwork on the rolltop desk. I lit one, took a drag that perked me up, and reluctantly turned the smoke over to her.

As I returned to my seat, she said, "I think you were nine when you stole your first cigarettes."

"Eleven."

She let out a smoke-filled breath. "That's the way you remember it. You've swallowed what your father said hook, line, and sinker. I didn't disappear after going out for a pack of cigarettes."

"Then why did you leave?"

She glanced away. "I had to."

And whenever she returned home, Mother always waited until my father was away. I would be alone and practically defenseless to her proposals. When it got to be too much, I'd remind her that Daddy loved me more than he loved her. It was about the only piece of self-respect I had left, and I always found a way to throw it in her face.

As an adult I can look back on all that as the pleas of a lonely and disappointed middle-aged woman. Her only son had been killed when a tire broke free at Dayton Speedway and a daughter had died of an overdose in one of the gardens of good and evil in Savannah. That left the youngest, me, as the pawn in my parents' tug of war.

"You could never leave your father any more than I could."

That returned me to the here and now. "You left us!"

"I'm not talking about leaving you, Susan."

"I know you're not talking about me. I've always known I wasn't important to you."

"There goes your mouth again. I was trying to have a civilized conversation. Maybe I should give you a smack across the face like your father did. You always shut up after that."

I'd had enough. "Mother, would you mind if I went to bed?"

She waved the cigarette in my face. "You're not going anywhere, young lady. You and I are going to talk this out."

"Then get on with it." I leaned back in my seat and rubbed my eyes.

"Susan, it's that attitude that makes people—"

I pulled my hands down. "I don't think my attitude has anything to do with what you want to say, right?"

She eyed me as she took another pull from her beer. This was not looking good. She'd probably finished the champagne in the suite before being tossed out.

"You don't have any weakness, do you?" she asked.

"Actually, I'm sleepy and my shoulder aches."

She gestured with the bottle at the ceiling. "I don't have a roof over my head, but that interview, that damn interview could've given me a new start."

"Mother, you aren't going to blow into my life one day and leave the next with a pile of money."

"It wasn't all that much." She took a drag off her smoke. "Not going to be worth much. News is very perishable."

"And who told you that?"

Her shoulders straightened. "Maybe I knew it myself. You've been spending too much time with Harry Poinsett. He's taught you that your family is nothing but a bunch—"

"Harry's never spoken a word against this family."

"I thought I'd never get over the deaths of your sister and your brother, but I did. I went on."

"Mother, I was there when they died, remember?"

"You got that from me. You're a survivor."

Her legs slumped together and the bottle and cigarette rested on her knees as she looked around. Maybe she was searching for a decent memory. Good luck. I'd conducted the same search and always come up empty. Maybe that's why Chad could always fill up this room. I closed my eyes and could see him again.

She was talking.

I jerked awake. "What?"

"I came back several times, but you wouldn't leave. I couldn't stay with your father and you wouldn't leave him."

She was beginning to repeat herself. Or I was losing our train of thought. "If I remember correctly—"

"All you ever remember is what your father told you. It might not be the truth."

"Did you or did you not walk out on this family when I was thirteen?"

"You could've gone with me on any number of occasions, even after your father drowned."

"And where would we have gone?"

"There was my mother's home in Key West."

"Grandma wouldn't have anything to do with us." I glanced at the beer bottle. "Because of the drinking."

"What do you know about my relationship with my mother?" Cigarette ashes tumbled to the floor.

"May I ask you a question, Mother?"

Her reply was a sour look.

"Don't you think it makes sense from my point of view to want stability in my life? Before you walked out—"

"I didn't walk out. You're not going to hang that on me." She took a final drag off the cigarette and dropped the butt to the deck, where she snubbed it out.

I pushed on. "But what I'm trying to say is that I'd already seen my brother and sister die."

"You don't think it upsets a mother to see both of her children die?"

"Both of your children? Don't I count?"

"I didn't mean—"

"I know what you meant. They were always your favorites."

"You were your father's favorite. And you favor him. You're just as hardheaded."

"Like you said: I'm a survivor."

"Susan, I'm not going to let you talk to me like that. When I was your age, I had three children and a husband to take care of."

Oh, not that again! Didn't she understand it wasn't smart to get pregnant by a man who could no longer remember your name? Of course not. My mother was here for the money, and lacking that, she'd settle for beating me up about things I couldn't possibly do anything about. Or the woman I couldn't possibly be.

I could see the next few days very clearly. Listening to her complaints until she finally stole something, pawned it, and left, or I gave her what little money I had and she left, or I left. The cabin door was looking better and better.

I struggled to my feet. "Would you like some coffee?"

She glanced at the empty bottle in her hand. "What are you saying, that I can't control my liquor?"

"I asked if you'd like a cup of coffee."

It was possible that my grandmother was right. Liquor could addle your brain. Grandma said she had the proof. Her husband had died from the sauce, or so she claimed the last time I saw her.

Mother got up and started for the fridge. "I think I'll have another beer."

"Mother, please don't have another drink."

"What are you saying," she asked, turning around at the bar, "that I can't handle my liquor?"

"I just want you to stop drinking . . . so we can have this talk." I gripped a corner of the rolltop desk. Agent Kinlaw was right. I should've spent the day in bed.

But if I'd done that, who would've found the dead woman?

Oh, yeah. Any number of law enforcement officers. They certainly didn't need Susan Chase. Watching my mother pull another beer from the miniature fridge, the thought struck me that it might be ol' Susan Chase who needed law enforcement, not the other way around.

Mother dropped her empty to the deck, and the sound jarred me—right to the heart. A sob rushed up my throat and I lurched over to the cabin door and jerked it open. I stomped out on deck, onto the pier, and hurried past the golf cart to the end of the mooring. What the hell was that cart doing here anyway, and what was stacked in its rear?

"Susan, where are you going?"

Tears formed in my eyes, or was that the Waterway shimmering under the moonlight? The cicadas and a few frogs called to me, as they had many times in the past and in similar situations. A silver flash leaped over the water, hung in the air, and disappeared in the Waterway. Without thinking, I kicked off my shoes, dove into the water, and swam for the far shore. It was only fifty or more feet, but it would put me miles away from my mother.

The water braced me, but I was used to it. I'd swum in the Waterway the day before the bombing of the Proffitt Center. Long, strong strokes pulled me away from my mother's cursing, then her pleading for me to return. Finally, there was only the sound of my body cutting through the chilly water.

My wet clothes proved no burden, just as they hadn't when I'd been younger. I plowed across, leaving everything behind, and then pulled myself out of the water, grabbing roots of trees and hauling myself ashore. It'd been a long time since I'd come over here to think. And have a good cry.

I sat in the bushes and buried my face in the damp crook of my arm. I'd lost Chad and now my mother was reminding me there was no way we could ever reconnect. Life sucked, and I doubted it could get much worse.

I don't know how long I sat there, but when it finally dawned on me that I could stay over here until I froze to death, I got to my feet and picked my way back to the inlet. I was shivering and stepping into the water when the night lit up with flames and the explosion from *Daddy's Girl* pitched me backwards into a tree.

Part Two

Fourteen

Journal Entry One

My name is Susan Chase and for as long as I can remember, which is not very long, I have been a ward of the state of South Carolina. I've heard stories of how crazy people, or in my case, those who have lost their minds, have to eat dog food and live on the street, but that's not how people who have lost their minds are treated in South Carolina. Everything for me is peaches and cream, except I don't remember anything about my past, and I'm becoming rather bored with writing in a journal. And trying to improve my diction.

Journal Entry Nine

The problem with being in an old folks home is that there are very few people to do stuff with. Even my nurse is old. He's an elderly guy with too much time on his hands who comes by and pitches in.

One day we were sitting in the sunroom, where you can see the spring flowers and plants blooming, and I said to him, "Harry, you know a lot of stuff, don't you?"

"Well, my dear, I am considerably older than you."

"And how old am I?"

"I believe they told me you would be thirty next year."

"Oh, yes. My birthday. I remember my birthday."

"Very good. Would you like to tell me your birthday, Susan?"

"I don't think so. I think it's time I have some secrets of my own."

"My dear, everyone here knows your birthday."

I gave him what I thought was a clever smile. "But no one knows if I actually remember the correct date, and that's my secret."

Journal Entry Nineteen

Harry has been very good to me. Every day he works with me on my studies. I seem to pick up stuff very quickly, but I alarm people. They tell me if I continue to scare them, I won't be allowed to leave the property. I tried to leave once and they caught me and brought me back. I wasn't spanked, but I did have to remain in my room. Actually, I think the cute boy in the other wing turned me in. I don't think I like him. But he is very cute.

Journal Entry Twenty-three

For some of my lessons, I have been turned over to Rachel. Rachel is a black woman who cared for me when I was unable to walk.

Rachel had to talk to me because I'd been caught in the bushes with the cute boy and we had our clothes off. I had to promise never to do that again and Rachel had to explain why I bleed every month. Until then, I'd merely been curious. Now I know I can have babies— like the doll I had before I was able to get out of bed. Anyway, I was told if I ever take off my clothes in the bushes, or anywhere else considered a public place, I'll never be able to leave this place. I also had to promise not to see Chad again. That made me very sad. Chad is the only person my age and he has some very nice parents. Well, his mother doesn't like me, but his father is sweet. Bottom line—a phrase I recently learned much to the chagrin of Harry Poinsett—is this: Having all these people bossing me around made me vow that I'll soon leave this place.

Journal Entry Thirty-one

I got out, but they caught me in something called a honky-tonk. Everyone was really upset and I was examined from head to toe by the doctor. He pronounced me healthy, even though I told him about the headache. He said the headache would be gone by morning. Beer really tastes terrible, but it made all the boys happy the more I drank, so I drank more than one bottle. A lot more than one bottle. The people at the home had a meeting about me, and Harry asked if I would like to go home with him for a few days. That sounded neat, and that night I sneaked over to Chad's room and told him about it. Rachel learned I was missing and brought me back to my side. I cried and promised we hadn't had sex, that I only wanted Chad to know why I wouldn't be seeing him again.

Journal Entry Fifty-two

It's been a while since I've written in my journal, and that's because when I left the home, Harry asked what I wanted to do. I told him I wanted to do everything, even if I didn't remember. I really didn't think he'd let me do everything, but damn if he didn't. "Damn" is a word I learned living outside the hospital.

Anyway, the first night I was away from the home, I woke up screaming. It was the same nightmare I'd had before I could get out of bed. There was this loud noise and bright colors. I saw people's faces, especially a blond woman's, and then they were all gone. She was gone.

Harry came running into my room, stubbed his toe, and fell down. I called 911. Everyone thought that was very responsible of me. Harry had a bandage on his head for a week, and I brought him ice packs for a whole day. The following week, Harry turned an old pink jeep over to me and I learned I could drive. I wonder what else I'm going to find out about myself?

FIFTEEN

Harry saw me off in my jeep. "This is going to be a big day for you, Princess."

"*Que sera, sera!*"

Harry gave me a nervous smile as I drove into town.

When I arrived at the law enforcement center, I learned Theresa Hardy was too busy to see me. She remained too busy so Mickey DeShields took me to lunch.

DeShields was a black guy who wore a gray shirt, black tie, tan slacks, and wraparound shades. He watched as I used a white cane, the sort blind people use, to negotiate from my jeep into Sam's Corner. Inside, everyone was overbearingly friendly, but I didn't remember anyone. Some primeval urge caused me to order a chili dog and lemonade. It was delicious. I should trust my instincts more.

"You don't remember me, do you, Susan?"

"Harry Poinsett said I could trust you."

"Then you don't want to see Theresa."

"I don't?" I looked up from where chili ran into my hand. Boy was this stuff good.

"She'll embarrass you back into your place."

I put down the chili dog and wiped my hand. "And that would be?"

Mickey shrugged. "Private-eyeing, I suppose."

"Then I'm out of luck. I don't remember enough about the Grand Strand to make myself useful."

"What did the doctor say?"

"Little by little my memory will return, if I don't press it.

That was the optimistic diagnosis."

"And the other view?"

"You don't want to hear it."

"They say that you were in the same home Chad was in. Any truth to that?"

"His father picked up the co-pay. Anyway, that's what they tell me. They tell me a lot of things these days I don't remember, Mickey."

"How can one of you be worse than the other? It would seem you took the harder lick."

"Chad's was a direct blow to the head. I was flattened by a blast."

"Sounds like doctors splitting hairs, if you ask me."

"Sounded like that to me, too, but the first rule of a hospital is: Never question the word of a specialist. Anyway, with head injuries it's always iffy as to what someone remembers." I looked at him over my next bite of chili dog. "SLED doesn't want me back, do they?"

"When you lost J.D. as your rabbi, you were practically finished."

"J.D." like in J.D. Warden? I'd received flowers from that guy shortly after moving in with Harry. Also from a guy named Jacob Kinlaw, someone else I only knew from his comments in a big thick file I spent most of my time studying.

Mickey was talking. I should be more attentive. It might mean the difference between life or death, like my daily work-outs with that Kung-fu guy who was teaching me some nifty moves with my cane.

". . . tracking down runaways, you located two daughters and one son of SLED employees; one of those parents was a major in Columbia. You were, at one time, very useful to have around, Susan."

I studied him. "You're the one who sent me the file, aren't you?"

"Of course not. That would be against SLED policy."

I felt myself tear up. "Mickey, that file was the only thing that made it possible for me to hang on. Harry thinks it's become my security blanket."

"When I heard you were in a coma, I began making a

copy of everything that crossed my desk." DeShields handed a napkin to me. "Speak of the devil, how is Harry?"

I blotted away my tears. "He says I can't remember my mother, so leave it alone."

"I agree."

I blew my nose, then wiped it. "What am I supposed to do? Swim in the Waterway, work out with that Kung-fu fellow, and wait for my memory to return? I don't have a place to stay or even a job. It goes without saying that most employers don't want to hire a mental case."

"There is a plus side," he said, smiling. "The media moves on. SLED has moved on, too. No way can we justify the manpower that was used to search Francis Marion as we did in January."

"You're waiting for him to trip up, like that guy in the Smokies."

"There are more serious concerns than some guy hiding in Francis Marion National Forest."

"I didn't say there weren't, but I don't have much to do while waiting for my memory to return."

DeShields eyed my white cane. "Hell of a handicap, loss of memory and one bad wheel."

"It might be, Mickey, but I get the impression this is the kind of thing people would expect me to do."

When you're incapacitated, you have plenty of time to learn, and what I learned, if I didn't already know it, was that Francis Marion National Forest is named for the "Swamp Fox" who bedeviled the British during the Revolutionary War. If you've seen the Mel Gibson movie—you also have plenty of time to watch videos when you're laid up—you pretty much have the skinny on Francis Marion. And inside that quarter-million acre forest was hiding one John Ross Wasson, brother of the Wasson girls. Laura had died in the abortion clinic bombing, Patricia worked as a forester in the national forest, and Claudia was in jail for embezzlement. According to a note from Jacob Kinlaw, an FBI agent in Charleston, Glenn Proffitt had cried when Claudia Wasson was sentenced to eight to fifteen years.

The only problem with Francis Marion is that it's an open park, meaning one hell of a lot of people own property there.

Roads crisscross it, and I'm sure that more than one mis-guided person had allowed John Ross Wasson to use their facilities. If just one friend ran a general store, John Ross could sashay in and stock up on whatever he needed. You think Muslim countries should turn over terrorists; then ask yourself why no one ever turned in Eric Rudolph, who finally had to be caught dumpster diving.

According to the file DeShields put together, John Ross had left a long line of busted lips, or women, and busted heads, or men, in his wake. Six-foot-five, almost three hundred pounds, John Ross is the kind of troublemaker you put in the county lockup until he sleeps it off. Or a local judge finally has enough and packs him off to the county farm. His sisters appeared to have a love/hate relationship with their older brother. They never knew if John Ross was going to love them or hit them.

"Sounds bipolar," said Harry as we enjoyed a red sky af-ter the sun had gone down beyond a row of cypress trees you could see from Harry's porch. "Alternating between days of hyperactivity followed by long periods of languidness."

"In English, please. Remember, I was in a coma for over ninety days."

Harry looked over his paper. "That means it's important what day you approach this man. He could be dead drunk or building a rocket to the moon."

"You're kidding, right?"

Harry lowered his newspaper. "Susan, think of how a mania for hideouts fits neatly with long periods of depression and languidity."

I tapped the file. "The report says infrared was used by the army in trying to locate John Ross's hideouts."

"But how would sophisticated instruments assist in locating this man? Something reflecting infrared would be part of his overall plan."

"You're right. It says here that three of his hideouts had material in their roofs used in the space program."

"And how many more places might there be if you were affected with the mania John Ross Wasson displays?"

According to the file, John Ross Wasson had access to fertilizer, and the house he rented in town was heated with fuel oil. He'd been a demolitions expert in the army. But the icing on the cake was that the bastard owned a light-blue VW van, and the van had disappeared off the face of the earth. An old, gray VW bug, with a front hitch, had been found off the road near McClellanville, which is where the initial search had been conducted.

John Ross Wasson was also the perfect candidate for the suspect who'd driven a golf cart onto the pier at Wacca Wache Landing, parked it beside my boat, and killed my mother. It appeared he'd taken it personal when I'd swung over the Proffitt Center, thrown a vest to Glenn Proffitt, and cheated him out of another victim.

Not only had *Daddy's Girl* been destroyed in the attempt to kill me, but so had Harry's yacht. Now we lived at Wacca Wache Plantation. Harry did the cooking, a maid came in once a week, and there was laundry service. John Ross Wasson wasn't the only one living large.

At the Plantation, units went for a quarter of a million dollars and up. The Plantation was "one of the premier golf club communities on the East Coast," or so its sales literature says. Situated upon a historic plantation overlooking the Waccamaw River, beyond its gates was America's favorite golf and beach destination, meaning Myrtle Beach. Inside, residents could enjoy peace and tranquility, along with amenities second to none, including a sheltered garage. Only one shelter per unit though. Even the rich have to rough it.

Because the file DeShields had put together named "Susan Chase" as the target of the second blast, I had to work up the nerve to ask Harry how he was adjusting, since people told me that Harry had spent much of his retirement aboard that yacht.

"My ex-wife would say I've finally grown up."

"You don't miss being on the water?" meaning the cypress and oak trees draped in Spanish moss surrounding Wacca Wache Landing. The marina has full-service docks, wet slips, and dry dock storage.

Harry looked up from his newspaper. Sunlight reflected off the Waterway and the occasional boat sailed by. "It's right there, Princess, and without the dry rot." He returned to his paper. "You and I could go in together on a sloop. You have your insurance money."

"Is this part of my therapy?"

"You've lived on the water all your life. A new boat just might be the ticket."

I glanced at the marina across the road. "Your friends would never vote you back in. You almost blew up the place."

He looked up again and smiled. "With you around, Princess, I'm not worried about being blamed for that particular blast."

"Witnesses say they heard my mother and me fighting the night she died."

"Your mother made the decision to return home and capitalize off your newfound fame."

I slapped the file closed. "And I made the decision to pull Glenn Proffitt off that roof. I must've been a damn fool." I shivered, even though I was wearing a long-sleeved shirt, jeans, and socks with my running shoes.

"And how is Mister Proffitt? I heard they turned his building into an open air park."

My lame leg came off the chair. The doctor said when I was ready to trust my muscles, they'd be there for me, not to rush it. "Harry, I can't just sit here."

"If the authorities are willing to wait for one of his friends to turn him, I say let it go. You must not do anything to jeopardize your career. Look how far you've come."

I hadn't told Harry the bad news about SLED. "You know how many times *Shane* has been on during my convalescence. Finally, even Shane had to call Jack Palance out."

"Ridiculous. This is real life, not some western."

"But I know Francis Marion. I really do. I've been going in there every day since you trusted me with the runabout."

Harry leaned over and tapped the file lying in my lap. "But there's someone who knows Francis Marion much better than you do, my dear, and that's John Ross Wasson."

Sixteen

A few days later, and once I'd built up my nerve, I allowed myself to be thoroughly grounded in the values and beliefs of the church the Wasson family had once attended. After leaving the preacher, I stopped by a liquor store and then drove into Francis Marion National Forest and asked someone where I might find Patricia Owens. The guy wore the tan uniform and Smokey Bear hat of a forester.

He gestured at the pink jeep. "Driving that thing and I'm supposed to believe you work for SLED."

I twirled my cane over my head like the majorette people say I'd never been. "I'm recuperating from the last time John Ross and I met."

"Sorry to hear that, Miss, but that guy's already paid for his crime." Still, he was nice enough to give me directions to her duty station.

Patricia was hosting a plantation that had been deeded over for income tax purposes. Since it was a bit early for tourists and there were no student field trips, I was able to corner her inside the Big House.

Columns marched across the front, and those columns were on a porch several feet off the ground. They tell me that's for when the ocean comes ashore and the river backs up. The interior of the huge building was decorated from antebellum days, the only consideration to modern times being a telephone and a wooden desk. On that desk rested Patricia Owens' forester hat. In the downstairs hallway, a red-velvet rope protected a sofa and cane-bottomed chair. I limped over, unhooked the rope, and sat down. With my good foot, I pulled over the cane-bottomed chair to rest my leg on.

"May I help you?" asked Owens, scrambling to her feet.

I put both hands on my cane and stared at her.

She came from behind the desk. "I remember you. You're that SLED agent I met in Myrtle Beach."

"Actually," I said, glancing at the oil paintings lining the hallway, "I'd prefer to go down in history as the woman who brought your brother to justice."

Owens put her hands on her hips. "Hundreds of people were out there in January and found diddly-squat. What makes you think you can find him?"

"Well, John Ross isn't much for facing people when he pops them. Unless they're women."

"You have no right talking about my brother like that."

"When did you last speak to him, Patricia?"

"I don't have to tell you. I don't have to tell you anything."

"Then what do you want me to tell him when I find him?"

"You won't find him. Now, please move your foot."

I did, and she returned the cane-bottomed chair to where it'd been beside the sofa.

"What happened to your leg?"

"Your brother."

She flushed. "I'm sorry, but you'll have to stand up. Visitors aren't allowed to sit on the furniture."

I stood and leaned on my cane. "Patricia, you and I should be on the same side."

"He's my brother."

"And, from what I've read in police reports, beat you within an inch of your life if you didn't do what he said."

"That's just idle talk," she said too quickly.

"I'm surprised you didn't lose your job that time when he snatched you off the riverbank and dragged you into the park. You weren't heard from for over a week."

"That—that was a family matter."

I pressed on. "When he dropped you off at that general store, you were hospitalized for dehydration, and you didn't even press charges."

"You don't know anything about me or my family."

"He murdered your sister, Patricia."

"She shouldn't have been in that building."

"The preacher took the same tone, and I'll tell you what I told him: I'm bringing John Ross in dead or alive." At least that's the way they put it in the westerns I'd watched while being laid up.

"I knew nothing about the bombing and begged forgiveness."

I only stared at her.

"Look, Agent Chase, I hardly see the man."

"Because Christmas two years ago your brother broke Marty's nose."

"It's not right for you to bring my husband into this. We don't discuss my family."

"Why not? Everyone knows your business. You and Claudia made a better life for yourselves, but Laurie took after John Ross and John Ross took to the woods. Anytime he sucker-punches someone, like he did your husband, he hides in the forest. I'm going to find him and drag him out of there."

"You expect to do what hundreds of others couldn't?"

"I have an advantage." I limped toward the double doors where the morning sunlight streamed through.

"And what would that be?"

I faced her. "Patricia, your brother's slugged any number of women and possibly raped a few, but they won't press charges because John Ross might appear at their door and drag them into the forest. That's my advantage. I want your brother to come looking for me."

When I told Harry that I needed someone close to John Ross who wasn't family, the name Harry came up with was Evelyn Mooney, the owner of a fish camp near the forest. Evidently, Mickey DeShields hadn't been the only one collecting information while Sleeping Beauty slept.

Fish camps aren't what you think, but places where you can eat your fill of seafood, mostly fried. Along the Grand Strand, they're called restaurants so the tourists can comprehend. Evelyn once worked in Murrells Inlet, a place that considers itself the seafood capital of the world. Turned off by the high prices, she'd finally opened her own restaurant.

Evelyn's place had a gravel parking lot ringing a clapboard building and a view of the river. I parked my jeep between a couple of pickups and climbed down. Using my cane, I limped over to the building and knocked on the front door. It was Monday and the restaurant was closed, but Evelyn had agreed I could drop by, as she'd be supervising the serious cleaning that usually happens the first of the week. That cleaning smells of disinfectant and requires heavy-duty brushes and lawn hoses.

The door was opened by a scrawny teenager, naked to the waist, with straggly black hair and a poor attempt at a beard. "Sorry, Miss, but we're not open until four and that's only on Thursdays, Fridays, and Saturdays."

"I'm Susan Chase." The name still sounded odd when it rolled off my tongue. With my cane, I gestured toward the kitchen. "Would you tell Evelyn I'm here?"

He asked me inside and disappeared through a pair of swinging doors in the rear.

The dining area had picnic tables for seating and plywood walls strung with fish netting. There was a counter near the door where you could purchase candy, and across from the counter, gumball machines. On the tables, and the booths lining the walls, sat metal holders of napkins and salt and pepper shakers.

Mooney was removing a pair of heavy-duty rubber gloves as she came out of the kitchen. Hanging from the ceiling ran a toy train on its own track. Before Evelyn reached me, the train passed through an imaginary crossing and tooted its whistle. The dark-haired woman glanced at my cane, tossed the gloves to the boy, and told him to get back to work, that she'd be outside taking a smoke break. The teenager wanted to know when he could have a break. Evelyn said that it'd depend on when he actually got some work done. She said if he didn't work faster, she was going to turn off the train.

"Don't do that, Evelyn," whined the teenager.

"Just put your back into it, Tommy. There's only you and me today, since Lori's had her baby."

She ushered me out the front door and around the side of the building. As she did, she saw the jeep between the two pickups. "I thought you'd graduated to cars." She meant SLED.

"That was when I still had a job."

Evelyn eyed me as I limped across the gravel parking lot to a picnic bench under an oak tree. The wooden table had burn marks along its edges and plenty of names carved into its top. She hoisted herself on the table and planted her feet on the plank seat so she faced the river. On the far side of the water was a solid green wall, and beyond that, Francis Marion National Forest.

"Need a hand?" she asked me.

"Nah," I grunted, "I'm getting better at this."

I fitted my bottom on the seat and used my stronger-than-usual arms to lift me to where I could sit beside her on the tabletop. I lay the cane between us.

Evelyn wore jeans, a white tee shirt, and a pair of black work shoes. She had a moon face and shoulders the envy of any man. Along with those shoulders came very little waist and stocky legs. She shook out a Marlboro from a hard pack.

"Cigarette?" she offered.

"No, thank you."

Matches were slid from the cellophane around the hard pack. After a long drag, she tapped the cane on the table between us. "How you doing?"

"Better than could be expected. Thanks for asking."

"And Chad?"

I looked toward the green wall. On the far side of the river, a great egret fished from an almost submerged branch of a downed tree. "About the same." I was beginning to wonder why so many people asked me about that guy.

"Bummer. I thought he was one of the good guys."

"And Teddy?" I asked, anxiously. It was tough to remember everything I was supposed to remember.

"Absolutely worthless." She elbowed me and flashed a wicked grin. "Everywhere but in bed."

I laughed. This meant nothing to me.

She was silent as we both stared at the green wall. "Ever

since I was a kid, I've loved Brookgreen Gardens. I was looking forward to a wedding there. Must cost a bundle . . . . Sorry, Susan." She glanced over her shoulder at the rear of her restaurant. "Being busy ain't the same as having someone to talk to, and with Lori having had her baby, I'm stuck with Tommy."

I had no idea who Lori was or who was supposed to get married in Brookgreen Gardens.

"You really going to do this thing?" she asked.

I watched the beautiful white egret take wing and disappear behind the green wall. "Yes," I said quietly.

"Well, Tommy's a Wasson, if'n you want to talk to him. Screwed-up family if there ever was one."

I glanced at the restaurant before clearing my throat. "I have the sheriff's report, but I wanted your opinion of John Ross Wasson."

"I guess there aren't many in this county who'd talk to you, and I wouldn't if you hadn't found Lori that time she ran off and drove the whole family nuts." She let out a snort filled with smoke. "The baby of the family gets cut the most slack. I just wish you'd charged us."

I stared at her. "Because we wouldn't be having this conversation?"

"You got that right."

"Evelyn, what you tell me is confidential." Hell, I can't even remember the last conversation we had.

She gestured over her shoulder with her smoke. "And if Tommy tells his people we talked?"

I patted my pocket. "Then we'll have to fix it so he won't."

She glanced at my jeans. "It'll take more money than you've got."

"Come on, Evelyn, John Ross isn't around, isn't about to be, but everyone's still frightened of him?"

"He blew up your boat, didn't he?"

She had a point.

"Let me tell you this, Susan. John Ross is one of the meanest sons of bitches I know. If he wants something, you're better off giving it to him, whether it's your boat, wife . . . or sister. John Ross and I went to school together, and the years he played football we were the most penalized team in the state. If it hadn't been for John Ross, we would've won the state, and if hadn't been for him, we never would've made the playoffs. John Ross would rather fight than talk."

"But you have to agree there's enough evidence to prove he killed his sister when he blew up that OB/GYN."

"Abortion clinic."

I stared at her.

"What??" she asked, letting out a breath full of smoke. "Don't tell me you believe in abortions."

"What I believe has nothing to do with this." Actually, I didn't remember what I believed, but now that you mentioned it—

"He deserves to be brought in for what he did to his sister and that nurse, I'll give you that."

"But the bombing?"

Evelyn stared over the river again. The cigarette burned silently between fingers. Overhead the tree we sat under swayed in the breeze.

"So if someone burned down your business . . .?"

Her head snapped around. "It sure as hell wouldn't be for killing babies."

It startled me, and I watched as Evelyn took another drag off her cigarette and looked over the river again. Everything was greening up, but I felt this growing black spot on my heart. "Evelyn, would you prefer I leave?"

"No. My family owes you."

"Then do you mind telling me if you've ever known John Ross to back down? What I'm asking is whether he's ever failed to get even with someone he thinks wronged him?"

"'Wronged him?' You sure talk funny now that you're with SLED."

I pressed on before I lost my nerve. "Come on, Evelyn, does John Ross let things go or keep a grudge?"

"Are you kidding?"

I looked over the river. "So he'd take offense."

"He sure as hell would."

"Good," I said, setting my jaw, "because I plan on calling him out."

"And what makes you think he'll leave the park?"

"Don't worry. He'll want to settle with me."

She stared at me. "You're nuts."

"The bastard killed the only family I had."

"Come on, Susan, you hadn't seen your mother for years."

I was getting sick and tired of everyone throwing that in my face. "Okay. Then John Ross killed three women and he's going to prison for their deaths."

"Not if Susan Chase gets to him first."

I was taken back. "What do you mean?"

She drew down the last of her cigarette before flipping it toward the water. "I know you."

A shiver of fear rattled me. Was this why Harry and Mickey didn't want me to tackle John Ross? Not only did I not remember Susan Chase, I might not want to. Picking up my cane, I eased off the table.

Before I could reach the gravel parking lot, Evelyn said, "Aw, come on, Susan."

I didn't know whether to return the table or continue to my jeep. You can't run away from yourself. Or, perhaps I could. "Your family doesn't owe me anything, Evelyn. Give my best to Lori and her new baby."

As I shuffled off, Tommy came out the restaurant. "Time for a break?" he hollered across the parking lot.

"Give us a few minutes, Tommy, then Susan might want to talk to you. Come on, Susan. Sit back down and I'll tell you what I know. I'll probably tell you more than you want to know."

But I only stood there, leaning on my cane and staring at her.

She motioned me over. Well, I could at least listen.

After I was seated beside her again, she eyed me over a lit match and a new smoke. "You don't have a chance in hell, you know that, don't you?"

I shivered. Thankfully, Evelyn was too busy blowing out the match to notice.

She said, "You make a big deal of John Ross killing his sister, what makes you think he even knows his sister is dead?"

"After three months. Why wouldn't he?"

She looked at the green wall, then beyond it. "I'm pretty sure John Ross has a radio with him. Hell, he might even have a TV, but the only thing John Ross ever watched was ball games. Didn't care for jukebox music, and whenever I look at any ball game, I don't see much news." Another angry drag off the cigarette, then she said, "You know, people might feed him or shelter him, but who the hell wants to tell John Ross he killed his own sister?"

She might have a point there.

"You think you have a way to lure him out of the park; okay, but think about it. Why wouldn't he think whatever you do is some kind of a con, especially if you try to convince him that he killed Laurie?" Evelyn shook her head. "No, Susan, truth can't pull the bastard out of there or he'd be doing right by my sister."

I gasped. "The baby's father is John Ross?"

"Lori doesn't talk about it, but we're pretty sure." Evelyn took another drag off the new cigarette. "I asked her once if John Ross knew what he'd done, meaning killing his sister by accident. She never answered me."

"What you're saying is I'll have to go in there and pry him out." Was I really up to something like that?

She was still staring at that green wall. "All I wanted to do was tell him about the baby. I never saw him, but I'll bet my bottom dollar he knew I was in there."

I straightened up on the edge of the table. "Then John Ross and I'll just have to compromise."

"Yeah, right, compromise with an animal. You know what animals do when they're finished with their female, their food, whatever? They just lay around."

"And John Ross never backs down."

She looked at me. "I don't know why you're harping on that. You know Marty Owens? He's Patricia's husband. One Christmas, or was it Thanksgiving—John Ross has been in so many scrapes I lose count. Anyway, he broke Marty's nose and Marty took out a restraining order against him."

"And the cops enforce it?"

She smiled. "Well, Marty is the quarterback and

receivers' coach at the high school, and in a football-mad county, any sheriff knows he's not going to be reelected if John Ross kicks *that* coach's butt." More smoke came through her nose. "Marty has what you might call diplomatic immunity."

She appeared to study the river, looking at it almost wistfully. There was a muddy spot where boats moored and people tromped ashore.

I had a sudden flash of inspiration. "Will you tell John Ross I was here?"

Her head snapped around. "Not on your life."

"But I want you to." At least I thought I did.

"Susan, that's just plain nuts. You don't have diplomatic immunity."

"When was the last time he was here?"

She looked away. "Ask me something easier."

"Okay, where would John Ross get the idea he should blow up that clinic?"

"To tell you the truth, I didn't recognize the John Ross I saw on TV. What I think is that John Ross had to be the boss in that family. You know about their parents?"

"Only what was on the report."

"Well, their father was a drunk who found religion, but gave it up after his wife was taken by cancer. After their daddy parked his pickup on that railroad crossing, John Ross, being the oldest, thought he was the patriarch of the family, or some such thing, but he didn't have the head for it. Claudia got a scholarship to that Christian school up in Greenville. Nobody likes that school. They're always picking on it, and that's why the Bob Jones angle was played up. Claudia would go head-to-head with John Ross. Patricia was sneakier, and that's why she and Marty live in the family home and Claudia lived in Myrtle Beach."

"Come on, Evelyn, he didn't want Laurie to have an abortion so he blew up that clinic? Why not blow up the one in Charleston, too?"

"What's to say that place wasn't next on his list?"

I remembered from the file that loads of fertilizer and fuel oil had been found in the garage behind the house John

Ross Wasson had rented in town—enough to make HAZ-MAT nervous, according to their reports. "So John Ross might've had further plans."

"You didn't see my sister getting no abortion, did you? Think about it, all that talk about the sniper in Virginia and it turns out to be a teenager trying to impress the only father figure he ever knew."

Speaking of teenagers, Tommy came out of the back of the restaurant and tossed away a bucket of water.

"Tommy, come over here." In a lower voice, Evelyn said, "Throws papers every morning before he goes to school. Knows where everybody lives in this county."

"Knows those who take the paper, you mean." That just popped out. I have no idea where it came from.

"Hey, everybody's got to read Dear Abby."

Tommy lit up before he reached the table. It was as if he didn't want to chance missing his smoke break if Evelyn could think of something else for him to do. After stuffing his smokes and lighter into his jeans, he ambled over. He wore rubber boots and a baseball cap, no shirt. There was more hair in his beard than on his chest.

"Tommy, this here's Susan Chase. She's looking for your cousin John Ross."

The teenager snorted. "Everybody and their brother."

"Their sister," I corrected him, getting into the swing of things.

The boy didn't understand. I wasn't surprised.

"You have any idea where he is?" asked Evelyn.

"If I did, I'd collect the reward."

"Where would you spend it?" I asked.

"Damn far from here."

"But who's to complain?"

Tommy glanced at Evelyn. "Naw," he said, shaking his head, "there's too many relatives."

"Speaking of that," I said, pulling a sheet of paper from the back pocket of my jeans, "I'll give you ten bucks for every name you can give me that's not on my list," meaning what I'd gleaned from other investigations. I laid the list on the corner of the picnic table.

"Look at the list, Tommy," Evelyn said. "If you can come up with five names, that's fifty bucks."

The teenager smoked his cigarette and checked the list. He glanced at Evelyn again. "And all I've got to do is give you names that ain't on the list?"

"Well, I do need to know where I can find them, and anyone out of state, I wouldn't be interested in."

"I don't think we have kin out of state." He looked at the list again. "There ain't many you've missed."

"Not even five?" Well, well, I impressed myself.

"Yeah, there's five, but I was hoping to make at least a hundred dollars."

SEVENTEEN

Using a map—because I sure as the devil didn't know my way around these parts—I stopped for gas at a general store. It was the same general store where Patricia Owens had been dropped off a week after being snatched and held, supposedly against her will, by her brother in the national forest. Given the number of open roads, I took several wrong turns before noticing the compass mounted on the dashboard.

Duh, Susan, why didn't you speak up before? Maybe she did because I had another flash of inspiration and drove the jeep through a mud puddle. After several runs back and forth, during which someone in an SUV passed and shook his head, I climbed down and made sure my tag was properly plastered. Then I swallowed a half pint of the whiskey I'd bought, and once I'd stopped crying, gagging, and coughing, I wiped the sweat off my face, popped a mint in my mouth, and pulled in for gas.

After pumping from one of two pumps—either high-test or the cheap stuff—I limped into the store using my cane. The building was small, covered with wooden shingles, and had a screened door between the musty interior and a beautiful outdoors. Palmetto trees and loblolly pines swayed in a gentle breeze. It cooled my face considerably.

On my right was a counter with stick candy in jars with large lids, cigarettes locked in a chicken-wire rack, and speaking of the counter, standing behind it was a guy who was a foot taller, twice as broad in the shoulders, and easily double my weight, with a bushy, black beard and blue eyes. He could've been John Ross, and the thought gave me pause.

At the far end of the counter was a mounted and stuffed red wolf, which, if I remembered correctly, was on the endangered species list. At the rear of the building were milk, meat, and beer coolers, and sitting near a cold woodstove were two swamp rats. They wore overalls, muddy work boots, and sat in rockers and smoked corncob pipes.

"Anything else?" asked the mountain man behind the counter once I'd paid for my gas.

"Actually," I said, feeling the liquor, "I've come for John Ross."

"Who?" asked someone behind me.

I faced the men in the rockers, and as I turned, I stepped to one side and gripped my cane. Now the mountain man wasn't directly behind me, unless he moved, and I hoped I'd hear the ground shift when he did.

"John Ross Wasson, the guy who kills women and children."

One of the guys removed a corncob pipe from his mouth. "I didn't know John Ross was in the habit of killing children."

"If you believe what they teach around these parts, he killed a child when he killed his pregnant sister."

The big guy behind the counter said, "I think you'd better leave, young lady."

I glanced at him. "As long as we're in agreement that John Ross doesn't have the nerve to kill anyone face to face."

The wag in the rocker smiled. "I thought John Ross always did his business facing the woman."

His companion's mouth broke into a grin, revealing long rows of yellowed teeth.

"Then John Ross is going to be sorely disappointed, because at his next stop he's going to have to learn to take it in the ass."

"Listen, lady," said the counterman, "you've got your gas, so be moving along."

"What you doing here?" asked the wag from his chair.

"I've come to take John Ross in: dead or alive. Whatever's his pleasure."

"And you would be?"

"Susan Chase."

"I suppose that means something in some parts."

"Only to those who took me seriously."

The wag took a pull off his corncob pipe and began to rock. "Then all I can say is that there must be some very foolish people where you come from, young lady."

"You got relations in these parts?" I asked.

"What's that got to do with anything?" His pipe came out of his mouth and he stopped rocking.

"John Ross made me an orphan when he burned me out. And to let you people know I'm serious, the next smoke you see will be me burning out John Ross."

After a quick lunch, where I again put on my show to the astonishment of the locals, I went looking for the house where Patricia Owens lived. Before I could pull out of the parking lot, a waitress chased me down. She was wiping her hands on her apron when she caught up with me.

"You know where John Ross is?" I asked, feeling the whiskey and leaning out of my jeep and racing my engine.

"I know where he's gonna be, young lady, if you don't watch your tongue." She glanced at the diner. "John Ross is gonna hear how you're talking and come find you."

"Better yet."

Marty Owens was cutting grass when I arrived. He wore jeans over which hung a pot gut. Good thing he also wore a tee shirt. I didn't need to be grossed out this soon after lunch. I turned off my ignition and stayed put until he made a turn around his front yard and stopped at my jeep. The house was red brick with white trim, and its screens and molding all appeared to be in good repair.

I told him who I was.

"Sorry, but I don't want to talk about it."

"I know John Ross is a coward, but I hadn't heard you were one, too, Marty."

Owens glanced up and down the street. A couple of other yards were being cut by women who probably had plans for husbands that didn't include a leisurely ride around their property Saturday morning.

"Miss Chase," said Owens, after killing power to his mower, "I'd be careful what you say about Patricia's brother."

"Why?" I asked, staring at the broken ridge of his nose. "You think John Ross might break my nose?"

His face flushed from something other than the heat. "He sucker-punched me."

"John Ross Owens sucker-punches a lot of people."

"Look, Miss Chase, I don't know what you expect to gain from all this name calling, but John Ross won't hesitate to hit a woman, especially if he's drunk."

"I've never understood why a guy with John Ross's reputation and size has to sucker-punch people. Listen, Coach, I really need your help."

He pursed his lips, then asked, "Okay, Miss Chase, what exactly do you want?"

"Patricia won't help me bring her brother to justice."

"Not many will. They either agree with him or they're too scared to open their mouths."

"Which camp do you occupy?"

"Some of both."

I swung my legs down, planted my feet, and leaned against my jeep. To do this, I had to grip the seat, and it wasn't because I didn't have a good set of wheels. That was the liquor talking. Well, if things went as planned, the liquor would have to do a lot more talking this afternoon.

"Coach Owens—"

"Marty." He wiped his forehead by stretching the arm of his tee shirt. What sleeve there was came away smeared with dirt and moisture. He smiled at me. "I like to be on a first-name basis with those who are about to die."

I returned his smile.

"So, Miss Chase—"

"Susan."

"Okay, Susan, what's the plan?"

"I need John Ross out of that forest."

He shook his head, then realized it was still dripping. He wiped his forehead with the opposite shirtsleeve.

Ugh.

"Sorry, Susan, but he's not coming out."

"What if a girl calls him a coward?"

"Oh, you're figuring on taunting him, then catching him when he comes out? Well, that is a novel approach."

"I don't have to bring him in alive."

"You'd . . . shoot him?"

"Marty, there was damn little left of my boat after that explosion and nothing left of my mother."

"I think I heard something about that." He saw the cane leaning against the seat. "You use that?"

I nodded.

The quarterback and receivers' coach shook his head. "I guess you do need my help. What can I do?"

"Well, Marty, I can't think of anyone better to spread the word that some girl is calling your brother-in-law a coward than someone John Ross can't touch."

"It wasn't my idea to take out the restraining order."

"Patricia's?"

He shook his head, then wiped more sweat away, this time by pulling up the front of his tee and exposing his pot gut. I might not be afraid of this guy's brother-in-law, but this was way too much.

"You know her sister, Claudia, the one caught embezzling? She encouraged me."

"Actually, I'm the one who sicced the FBI on her. It's in the file." Which meant nothing to him. That file, however, had become the center of my universe. "Your brother-in-law likes blitz attacks. Claudia would've been subject to such attacks."

"And knowing that, you still want to do this thing?"

"He killed my mother."

"So it's personal."

"That's what I'm making it. Otherwise, I don't think John Ross will understand."

Good thing Marty gave me the names of two drinking establishments. One of the bars was closed, like in permanently, but at the second one, I polished off the rest of the whiskey before going inside.

Sanctuary of Evil

Driving over, I'd caught sight of a black sports car in my rearview mirror. That car had been there ever since I'd come out of the forest, and that meant I'd be parking my jeep with good visibility all around.

But the Kick Back Bar had only a motorbike and a pickup in the parking lot. The glass front had been painted black, and there was a sign for happy hour that had been up so long, I couldn't make out the hours. Knowing the first shift hadn't turned out and the odds might be in my favor, I sauntered over to the entrance. Well, I sauntered as well as any person on a cane and with a handful of flyers can saunter. Pushing the door out of my way, I stepped inside.

The place was in shadows except for a couple of TVs carrying ESPN. Tables and chairs went all the way back to a wooden wall where cartons of beer were stacked. Coming out of the cooler was a big guy with a case of Budweiser on his shoulder.

"Be right with you."

He hauled the Bud to the bar, let it down with a thump, and looked me over. His brown hair was pulled back into a ponytail and he wore a tee shirt with a monstrous tongue sticking out at me. Where had I seen that red tongue before? I couldn't remember. It advertised something.

"How can I do you, honey?"

The bartender found a dirty cloth under the bar and wiped the counter. Behind him was the cash register, on the wall a calendar that said "Rottweilers Rule," but no mirror or line of liquor bottles. This was a meat and potatoes bar, slimmed down to a bottle of beer and a single bowl of peanuts. A bald biker sat on a stool, an older guy had his head on a table, and in the corner a jukebox played "Sweet Home Alabama."

"I wanted to know if I could put up a flyer."

He looked over my shoulder at the bulletin board near the door. It was filled with posters of tractor pulls, country music concerts, and vehicles for sale, not to mention any number of business cards that always give the appearance of begging.

"If you can find an open space, have at it."

"Don't worry," I said, "I'll make one."

"Here," he said, reaching across the bar, "give me one of those things."

The flyers were printed on pink stationery with a flower border. The one I pinned on the bulletin board, I pinned squarely in the middle.

The bartender looked up. "Are you for real?"

"Sure. Why not?" I returned to the bar and put down the remainder of my flyers.

"I thought you had a bake sale at the church or the school, but this here's a waste of time."

A chain on the biker's belt rattled as he leaned over and read the flyer.

> *Do the right thing.*
> *Turn in John Ross Wasson.*
> *Or you'll lose the reward.*

Theresa Hardy's phone number at the law enforcement center was printed at the bottom.

The biker snorted and looked me over.

Suddenly my mouth was very dry. "Can I have a Blonde?"

"What?"

"It's a beer."

"I don't think we have that brand."

"What about a Coors or a Michelob Lite?"

"What about a Bud?"

"Let's do it," I said, taking a seat a couple of stools away from the biker.

The bartender pulled back the top of a slide-top cooler, scooped a hand in the ice, and pulled out a Bud. He popped the cap on the side of the cooler.

Plopping the bottle on the bar, he said, "Two bucks." Moisture ran onto the hardwood.

I got up from the stool and made a great effort at prying the bills out of a very tight pair of jeans. I almost lost my cane and the biker had to catch it. He grinned as he returned it. That was followed by another evaluation that included not only my jeans but the long-sleeved shirt I wore in the event we had to get down and dirty.

"What's this flyer business?" asked the bartender, taking my money and sliding the bowl of peanuts my way.

"I'm calling John Ross Wasson out. If you want the reward, you'd better get to stepping." I popped a handful of peanuts in my mouth. Some of them made it, others clattered to the bar.

The barkeeper raised his voice, though the biker was only a couple of stools away. "You hear that, Mac? This girl's calling out John Ross."

Mac wore jeans and a black jacket with studs. Hitched to his belt was one of those chains to keep his wallet attached to his britches. On the shoulder facing me was the tattoo of an American eagle with bombs in each claw. Just the guy I was looking for. I think.

The biker took the stool next to me, helped himself to the peanuts, and glanced at the cane. "You use that to get around?"

"Until I go into the swamp after John Ross."

The bartender leaned on the bar so close I could feel his breath. "Unless I remember wrong, there was a bunch of lawmen here the first of the year. They finally decided to call it a day."

"I have more time," I said, "and I'm more dedicated." I was also a little bit drunk.

The bartender glanced at the cane I'd moved to the other side of my stool. "Yeah. Right."

"Hey, I grew up in Francis Marion. My father and I camped on about every rise above water. You don't think I can do this thing?"

"No, ma'am. I have no doubt you're the rooting, tooting lawman who can find and catch John Ross. I just think you're going to have a little trouble on the 'finding' side."

I drank from the Bud. "If he doesn't come peacefully, I'll kill him and float the body out."

They gaped at me.

"Come on, guys, everybody knows John Ross can't kill anyone face to face. I'll have the edge."

"I suppose you will," said the biker as he checked out my chest. Okay, okay, the shirt was a bit tight through there.

The bartender ran the back of his hand up and down my arm. "Haven't you heard, ladies aren't supposed to play rough."

I pulled my arm away. "Hey, look but don't touch."

"Maybe she's one of them gals who likes it rough," suggested the biker.

I made a great show of scratching my chin. "You know, I once killed a woman I wasn't looking in the eye, but she was trying to drown me. A person doesn't have much time to think in those situations."

The bartender straightened again. "Lady, are you for real?"

"Why don't we find out for ourselves?" asked Mac, grinning.

The older guy with his head on the table looked up. "What's with the girl?" he asked.

"She's nuts," said the bartender.

"Nah," said Mac, "she's in heat."

"Got another bowl of peanuts?" I asked.

"Sorry," the bartender said, "you're going to have to share with Mac."

The biker swiveled on his stool, put an elbow on the bar, and smiled at me.

"Actually I wanted a bowl to throw in Mac's face. He's been leering at me and I'm here on business."

"What business?" asked the drunk who had joined us at the bar.

"Your business could get your pretty little ass in trouble," said the biker.

"Thanks for the compliment. I haven't been told I have a small ass in years."

"Kid," said the bartender, "you'd better watch your mouth."

Behind us, more patrons entered the bar. I didn't look. I only had eyes for Mac.

"Come on over here," said the bartender to the new guys. "You've got to meet this girl."

"I've got scrub," said Mac with another leer.

"Yeah, right," I said, looking him in the eye. "You couldn't get to first base without an assist."

The two guys in work clothes ambled over. Without taking my eyes off Mac, I snagged more nuts from the bowl and tossed them at my mouth. Some of them even made it. Out of the corner of my eye, I could see that the newcomers worked for the power company.

"Who's the girl?" ask the larger of the two. His stomach looked like it was about to pop a button.

"I haven't been a girl since puberty." I handed a flyer to each of the new guys, then thrust my chest out, slid my butt back on the stool, and placed both elbows on the bar. You don't need a memory to strike such a pose. It comes standard equipment.

The drunk wanted a flyer, and after I gave him a sheet, he put a hand on the bar, leaned over, and tried to cipher the text. Closer and closer came his head to the bar.

"What's this mean?" asked one of the workmen, looking up after reading the flyer.

"She's calling John Ross out," supplied the bartender.

"Jesus Christ," said the heavy guy. "Give me a beer. I can't wait until hell freezes over."

Beers were passed across the bar. One of the new patrons took the stool behind me and when I turned around to talk to him, Mac the biker began pulling at my bra under the shirt, snapping it.

I swiveled around and faced him, causing him to jerk back. "From the way you're handling the equipment, I figure you haven't taken one of those out for a spin in quite a while."

The bartender chuckled. Once again, Mac leaned close. This guy needed to brush his teeth more often, or drink more beer.

"You know, honey, one day your mouth is going to get you in trouble."

"This very afternoon," said the bartender, "if you don't get your butt out of here."

"Look, guys," I said, picking up my cane, "if you're any-thing like John Ross, all I have to worry about is being sucker-punched."

Dead silence. The jukebox even stopped. Maybe it knew what came next.

"Lady," said Mac, sliding off his stool, "if you don't shut your mouth, I'm going to close it for you, and without any sucker punching to it."

"Hey, take it easy," said the drunk, "she's just a girl."

"No," said Mac, without looking at him, "she's a smart-ass."

Behind me, the workman got off the stool.

"Oh," I said with a smirk, "the guy behind me is going to hold me down so you can pound me."

"Hell, no, lady," said the workman, coming around where I could see him, "we want to watch the show."

The two guys with the power company took the drunk by the arms and steered him over to a chair. I slid off my stool and stood eye-to-chin with Mac. As I did, the hairs on the back of my neck came to attention, a reaction dating back to a time when we were more primitive and wanted to puff up in the face of danger.

"Give her a chance to walk out of here," said the drunk from his chair.

But I didn't want that chance.

When Mac picked up my flyers, I gripped my cane. When he tore them in half, my stick came up between his arms and into his throat.

EIGHTEEN

When the cane came up into Mac's Adam's apple, his head jerked back. That was followed by a gasp and a croak. Then I swung the opposite end of the stick, which was down below his waist, into his crotch. That was enough for this particular biker. He bent over, grasping his crotch with one hand, his throat with the other.

The bartender stared, bug-eyed, but only for a second. He reached under the bar. Unfortunately, that kept him within range of the cane. I snapped my wrist and the cane swung over the bar, braining him.

The blow didn't disable him, but it did sting, and his hands came up empty. By then, I had brought the cane around and swung it level across the top of the bar. The cane slapped him again, this time across the fingers that were checking the damage to his skull. He stumbled back into the cash register and the register rang as the drawer came out, possibly hitting him in the lower back. I don't know. I had turned my attention to the two workmen.

Both came at me, and since I had the cane at bar level, I only had to raise it slightly to slap one of the men across the side of the face. The cane snapped in half and the heavy workman howled. According to the Kung-fu guy, if you want to take the fight out of someone, the element of surprise is good, but what's better is a sudden jolt of pain. The workman reached for his face while his companion was presented with a broken stick that could be jabbed into either eye.

"You want some of this?" I asked, stepping toward him. On my flank, I could see the drunk jabbering into the pay phone.

The second workman backed away.

The biker had recovered to some degree. Still holding his crotch, or perhaps better to protect it, he rushed me with one hand out. I spun around, snatched up a chair with my free hand, and flung it. The chair skidded across the floor, thumping into his legs. The biker's feet were taken out from under him and he landed face-first on the floor.

The momentum of flinging the chair caused me to step toward the bar, where I saw the bartender fumbling under the counter again. Something else from my trainer: Always use the weapon closest at hand. I hooked a foot under the lowest rung of one of the barstools and lifted it with my instep and upraised toes. The stool tried to get away from me, but the adjoining stool kept it moving upwards until I could get a hand on it. As the stool came up, I grabbed a leg between the rungs and swung the stool across the bar, braining the bartender with something a bit more substantial than any cane.

He looked up, a puzzled expression on his face, and then collapsed behind the bar. A baseball bat fell from his hands and clunked to the floor. Out of the corner of my eye, I saw the drunk drop the telephone. Probably called EMS for the wrong person.

As I turned around, I stepped to one side, like I'd been coached: Moving targets are tough targets. Good that I did. The workman I'd hit across the face rushed me a second time. I got a quick glance of blood running down the side of his head as he slammed into the bar. The blow took the breath out of him, and when he stepped back, I stuck a foot behind him. He tripped and landed on his butt. The second workman gaped as I kicked his companion in the face and laid him out across the floor.

I gestured with the stool that was still in my hand. "Sure you don't want some of this?"

"No, no," said the second workman, backing away and his hands coming up. "You stay away from me, lady."

"You'd better get out of here," said the drunk from where he held onto the payphone. "The cops are on the way."

Sanctuary of Evil

Outside the bar, a patrol car from the sheriff's department pulled into the gravel parking lot. Hair in my face, breathing fast—not all of it was an act—I leaned down to its driver.

"There's a terrible fight inside . . . ." It was easier for his partner to step out of the cruiser because I held onto the top of the driver's open door.

"Miss," said the driver, "if you'll let me out."

"Oh, yes," I said, wondering if I could stand without the assistance of the door or my cane, pieces of which I'd left inside the bar.

The two cops hitched up their equipment belts and started for the entrance.

Before I could stagger over to my jeep, the door of the bar flew open and the biker and one of the workmen rushed outside. The guns of the sheriff's deputies were quickly unholstered and trained on them.

"Officer," screamed the workman, "that girl . . . ." His voice trailed off as he realized what he was about to admit.

I climbed into my jeep and reached for my keys. Rising up across the seat, I dug into a pocket and cursed the fact that these jeans weren't relax fit.

"You guys calm down," said one of the deputies.

The drunk stumbled out of the bar and stopped, one hand on the shoulder of the biker, the other pointing at my jeep. "But you're letting her get away."

Faced with two, now three guys who had exited the bar in a hurry, the deputies merely glanced in my direction. Their pistols, however, remained trained on the men at the door.

"Miss?" called one of the deputies.

"Sorry," I said, cranking the engine of my jeep, "but my business is done here."

I headed for Kings Highway, then doubled back and cut through the national forest. It was a few minutes before I realized the black sports car, not a deputy's cruiser, was again on my tail. When I stopped, the black sports car stopped, and I was in no mood to stop long. My body shook and I dripped sweat. I glanced in the mirror, then looked at my trembling hands. I gripped the wheel to stop them from shaking. Not the best time to confront whoever was in the sports car.

Travis Rice was working on the engine of one of his airboats. Airboats are shallow-draft craft driven by airplane propellers and steered by airplane rudders. During the Season, Travis takes tourists through those parts of the forest that allow airboats in Francis Marion. Once again, I was relying on information furnished by Harry Poinsett. Harry wanted me to have a boat with some muscle if I went into the park, and an airboat filled the bill.

Climbing down from my jeep, I limped over to an open-air building with a roof and no walls. Uh-huh. Keep this up and you'll need more than an extra cane. You'll need shoes with steel toes. The open-air shed and a garage were to our left, and that's where I parked my jeep.

I cleared my throat not to startle him. When he looked up, I asked, "How you doing, Travis?"

The airboat was in dry dock, so Travis worked shirtless in a pair of worn shorts and dirty sneakers. He appeared to be in his early thirties and had freckles across his shoulders.

"Susan Chase. Haven't seen you since . . . . I'm sorry, Susan. How you doing?" He shook his head and wiped his hands on a cloth. "That wasn't the right thing to say either, was it?"

"Why not offer me a beer? That always works."

I followed him to his mobile home, where he disappeared inside and left me on a screened-in front porch. A few minutes later, he returned with a couple of beers. He saw me looking through the screen at the far end of the porch and walked over. I accidentally bumped into him when I turned around.

I jumped.

"You okay?" he asked.

"Just a little jumpy."

"Well," he said, handing me a beer, "you didn't sound the same on the phone."

"Travis, I'm not the same."

"No. I don't imagine you are." He took a swig as he watched

the black sports car turn around and head out the dirt road. "They think they can reach the water from here, but this is no boat launch. They oughta pay attention to the 'Keep Out' signs."

"That one didn't have a boat and trailer."

Travis looked again. The black car was gone. "No, it didn't, did it?"

A woman came onto the porch. She was well into her pregnancy. "Susan, good to see you."

I carefully embraced her. What was her name? Jeez, I was going to have to start writing all this down.

The woman patted her abdomen. "This is our third. When are you going to settle down—"

"Vicky, please . . . ." warned her husband from where he'd taken a seat in a large wooden porch chair.

The woman's hand came up. "Oh, I'm sorry, Susan."

"Don't think anything of it . . . Vicky."

She touched her stomach again. "It's my only excuse. I'm due in a few weeks."

"Well, good luck," I said, toasting her after sitting down.

Vicky took a chair between her husband and me. I noticed hers had an especially thick cushion because man, she was huge! Travis and I sipped beer as we sat there looking over a lawn that flowed down to a thirty-foot pier where all sorts of boats were tied up. A flock of redwings lifted off from the green wall across the water from us and disappeared into the darkness of the national forest.

"Travis, I need to use one of your boats. How much for the remainder of the day?"

"For you, nothing."

Harry had told me that Travis and I had dropped out of Socastee High School about the same time. Travis left to support his family; me to run away from an abusive foster home. The football coach wasn't pleased. Travis had had the potential to play college ball.

I dug into my jeans and came out with a hundred dollar bill. I passed it across Vicky to Travis.

"Susan, I don't want your money."

"The money isn't for the boat. It's for your silence."

The boat flew across the black water in shadows from trees draped with Spanish moss and crawling with resurrection fern. In places the moss was almost close enough to reach. For the umpteenth time, I touched my fanny pack where I kept Harry's .45, a vestige of his diplomatic days. The automatic was one of the few items they'd been able to salvage when they'd begun pulling Harry's stuff from the water. I trembled with anger and embarrassment. I'd been in a coma, oblivious to the anguish inflicted on Harry as a result of his mooring next to me.

On my way to my destination, I stopped between two parallel berms of bushes and creepers that would allow some privacy. In the shade of the overgrowth, I pulled on a pair of coveralls. Waterproof boots and a pair of work gloves rounded out my attire, along with elbow and kneepads. I had a shovel and portable welding torch, both purchased at the Super Wal-Mart on the bypass. The coveralls and gloves were from a place where you purchase clothes for working in a garage, the boots from army surplus, and the arm and kneepads from a skateboard shop.

Travis and I'd loaded all this stuff into the boat while his wife made me a couple of sandwiches and packed a cooler. A proper mix of gas and oil filled two five-gallon cans that sat in the bottom of the boat, and Travis flipped me a lighter as I pulled away.

"For luck," he called from his dock.

His wife had looked at him curiously.

Using the map Mickey DeShields had given me, I located the cabin law enforcement personnel had come across in their canvass for John Ross. The building was situated on land rising out of the water, and it sat under three gorgeous oak trees whose leaves and moss made it impossible to see from the air. Trees with distended bottoms and blackened stumps broke the surface, along with a sand ridge that was home to a mass of cabbage palms. The brackish marsh pond was one of those places, where once you're ashore, you could walk fifty feet and disappear from sight. Overhead, a hawk circled, watching my progress.

Sanctuary of Evil

The airboat disturbed a flock of wild turkeys and they scattered as I looped the rise and found the dock marked on a makeshift map. The dock turned out to be nothing more than a set of mobile home steps plunked into the waterline. More cabbage palms leaned over, obscuring any trail.

I circled the island a second time, knowing what I had to do and wondering if I had the nerve to do it. The rise appeared to be about forty feet long and perhaps thirty feet wide. At high tide, which was now, the water lapped into duckweed growing around the circumference. I swallowed down my fear, cut the engine, and let the boat slide across the water. When the airboat thudded to a stop, I looped a line around the blackened pike of a stump and stepped over the side into the water. Crushing spider lilies under my feet, I went ashore. With the engine silenced, the forest was absolutely still but for my squishing feet.

The cabin was constructed of oak logs, notched and fitted together, and had never been painted. The only windows were at each side and the cabin roof needed some new shingles. A cluster of dead leaves had found the lowest point in the pitched roof.

I closed with the building in a hurry, slamming my body against its rear wall. My sore leg did not like the maneuver and let me know about it. Once I caught my breath and wiped the tears away, I announced, "You in the cabin, this is Susan Chase of the State Law Enforcement Division. Throw out your weapons and come out, hands over your head."

No answer from the cabin.

I repeated my warning, adding there were other SLED agents in the vicinity.

Still no answer.

Well, I hadn't expected company.

I crept around the side, shouted my warning again, and waited. Nothing. The door to the cabin was open and yellow crime scene tape blocked the opening.

I wheeled across the front of the structure and raced for the door. Along my way, I tripped and felt a stab of pain in my leg. There was a flash from the doorway, a small explosion, and I continued in the direction I'd fallen.

Steve Brown

I lay in the dirt, smelling the cordite and watching the dust settle. It hadn't been much of an explosion, but it could've peppered me. Pieces of metal rained down on the clearing and holes punched through the tight-leaf clusters of the cabbage palms.

I rolled to my side, mumbled thanks to the elbow and kneepads, and wiped sweat away with the sleeve of my coverall. No way John Ross had known I was coming. Word couldn't have reached him this soon.

I slapped the ground beside me. The bastard!

The late afternoon air was quiet but for the whirl of gnats and a frog that inquired what the hell I thought I was doing. Well, I guess I didn't have to search the cabin but could get right to work.

From the airboat, I took the shovel, the portable torch, some twine, and a couple of pieces of driftwood I'd come across as I'd motored through this heart of darkness. At the front of the cabin, I thrust a shovel into the sand and began turning it over. When I finished the plot measured six feet by two feet and no more than six inches deep. Minutes later, I'd burned John Ross's name into one of the two pieces of driftwood with the welding torch. From my pocket I took some twine, knelt down, and formed a cross. Finished, I used the back of the shovel and pounded the cross into the soft ground. Next came the extra cooler I'd brought along.

I flipped back the styrofoam lid and took out an almost-full wine bottle with a rag instead of a cork stuffed into the mouth. I shook the bottle, making sure the detergent had mixed properly with the gasoline, then faced the cabin door still reeking of cordite and dust. The crime scene tape dangled from both sides of the door, cut in two by the mini explosion. I fished Travis's lighter from my jeans and lit the cloth hanging from the mouth of the wine bottle.

"This is for you, Mom, wherever you are."

The flame caught and I threw the bottle through the open door where it smashed against the rear wall and burst into flames. When the flames showed themselves through the matching windows on each side of the structure, I limped back to my boat. Plodding into the water, I lifted my line from around the blackened stump and heaved myself into the airboat. Seconds later, I was anxiously negotiating my way among the bald cypresses as the sun began to go down.

On my return trip, I steered the boat between the same set of overgrown berms. This became a bit dicey because I was pretty much pumped up and almost rammed ashore. Pines and their tangles hid me as I stripped off the gloves, coveralls, arm and kneepads, and weighed them down with the portable welding torch and shovel. I sunk the cooler by smashing a hole in the bottom and giving the styrofoam some weight. I threw everything into the deepest part of the river.

Travis was watching the smoke rising above the tree line deep inside the national forest as I cut the engine and glided toward his dock. I waved at Vicky, who stood at the screened door. She turned away, disappearing into the doublewide. Once I was clear of the boat, Travis winched it ashore to sit beside the one he was working on. Finished, he wiped his brow and stared at a helicopter hovering near the column of smoke.

"Well, now it begins," he said.

The following morning, Harry and I were drinking coffee and sitting on his porch when the phone rang. It was my former boss and she was ready to talk.

"It'll save DeShields having to come down to Georgetown County and pick you up."

"Thanks for your interest in my affairs, Theresa."

"Chase, just report to the front desk before eleven a.m. or I'll put out a warrant for your arrest."

I wore a blue business suit, white blouse, and flats. Not only did I look professional, said Harry, but it was the uniform of choice by SLED females. The outfit had no noticeable effect on Mickey DeShields. He had a concerned look on his face when Theresa Hardy led me away.

"Follow me," she said.

Men and women eyed me as I trailed Hardy out of an open area where desks and chairs were pushed together. I limped down the hall with my new cane and entered a room with a large mirror on the wall. Hardy gestured for me to take a seat in the straight-backed chair facing the mirror. On the other side of the table were two more chairs.

She read me my rights. "Do you understand?"

"I've heard them enough on TV."

She asked me to sign a form I hadn't noticed on the table. It was my rights in writing.

"You can consider your job in jeopardy."

"That job belonged to Susan Chase, not me."

"Chase, I don't have time for games."

"Or Susan Chase, it would appear."

"Do you deny you threatened Patricia Owens at her place of work yesterday?"

Looking into the mirror, I said, "I did no such thing."

Harry was right. I did look better in this getup, but I was going to have to do something about my hair. While recuperating, I'd forgotten to have it cut. Or was this the way I knew Chad would remember me from our stay in the nursing home? Where was that guy anyway?

"Are you saying you didn't threaten Patricia Owens?"

"I threatened to bring her brother to justice."

"You have no official standing to do such a thing."

"Then you'll need to do something about the reward, because, as a private citizen, I plan on bringing the bastard in."

"As a member of a law enforcement agency, you aren't eligible for rewards."

"Which way you want it, Theresa?" I asked, leaning forward. "Either way, you're going to have a lawsuit on your hands."

"You'd sue for what?"

"Either my job or the reward."

"You're just trying to make trouble."

"I'm trying to make a life for Susan Chase."

"I think you're going to have to explain yourself."

Again I spoke to the two-way mirror. "Let me make this perfectly clear. I don't remember who I am, and I don't give a damn if you believe me or not, but I have plenty of people trying to help me remember. Now, if that many people believe in Susan Chase, then I have an obligation to her."

"You're not going to get away with this, Chase."

"Don't call me that name," I said, pushing back my chair. "I'm sick and tired of being called by her name."

She smiled as she took a seat. "Oh, you're good, but I think I'll stick to what you've done in the last forty-eight hours. You're sure to remember that." Her pad came out and she placed it on the table. "I want you to think before you answer: Who set fire to John Ross Wasson's cabin in Francis Marion National Forest?"

"How would I know that?"

"You were seen in the vicinity."

"What time was that?"

She gave me a time.

"I think I was at Drunken Jack's. You can ask Harry Poinsett."

She referred to her notes. "You didn't get there until seven-eighteen."

I shrugged. "I don't have a job. The hours run together."

There was a tap on the window behind her.

Hardy picked up her pad, got to her feet, and headed for the door. "Remain here."

Like, where was I going?

She returned with a guy from the forest service. A silver-haired, stocky man, he took a seat across from me. On the table between us, he placed a manila folder and his Smokey Bear hat. His name tag said "Gibson."

"Agent Chase," he said, nodding in my direction.

"She's suspended," snapped Hardy, taking the other chair. "There's no reason to honor her with such a title."

"What do you have?" I asked the forester.

"Miss Chase, I can put you at Travis Rice's. From Rice's, you took one of his airboats into the park."

"A cabin you knew the location of," interrupted my boss, or former boss, whichever way she was having it, "because you gleaned that information from our files."

"I think everyone knows where that cabin is."

"Susan, you can play this cute, but you're looking at a

prison sentence, so I'd watch what you say."

"You have witnesses that place me in the park?"

"Of course or—"

"Do you mind if I question the forester, Theresa?"

Hardy sat back in her chair and shook her head. "A perfectly good career—"

"When it suits SLED for me to have one." I directed my question to Gibson. "Do you have witnesses that place me in the park at the time of the fire?"

They did not, but an airboat had been seen, and I had questioned Patricia Owens.

"And what did I question Owens about?" I asked.

"She said you threatened her."

"Her or her brother?"

Gibson referred to his notes. "Her . . . brother."

"Thank you. Now, is she the only witness who corroborates I was in the park?"

"There was the forester who gave you directions."

"Susan," asked Theresa Hardy, "what about that airboat coming from the direction of the fire? You're going to tell us there was more than one airboat in the park."

"The airboat was seen coming from the fire?" I asked Gibson. "Is that something you can corroborate?"

"In all fairness, Miss Chase, there are too many directions you could have come from."

"Boaters saw you," inserted Hardy. "We have a positive ID."

"What was I wearing?" I asked her.

"Jeans and a long-sleeved shirt."

Gibson glanced at the folder again. "Travis Rice says you were at his place yesterday, renting an airboat. His wife confirms this. You paid one hundred dollars. Cash."

"What was I wearing?"

"Jeans and a long-sleeved shirt. Sunglasses."

"Go on."

"Susan," asked Hardy, "why are you playing this game? You borrowed an airboat, went into the park, and burned down that cabin." She shook her head wearily. "And dug that phony grave."

"Pardon me?" I leaned on the table once again.

"Miss Chase," said the forester, "there was a mock grave site near the cabin with John Ross Wasson's name burned into a crude cross."

I leaned back in my chair. "Interesting." I smiled at the mirror behind them. "No. Make that 'colorful.'"

"Then you admit to being on the airboat?" asked Hardy.

"Yes, but I don't admit to torching Wasson's cabin."

"Then what were you doing in the park?"

"Putting out flyers."

"Miss Chase," said the forester, "it's against federal regulations to post signs in the park."

"I'm an agent of the State Law Enforcement Division. That gives me some leeway."

"Come on, Susan, you didn't post flyers anywhere near where you set the fire," said Hardy.

"Pardon me, but are you trying to make my case?"

Hardy ground her teeth.

"Are you saying you didn't go near the cabin, Miss Chase?" asked Gibson.

"That would be the last place Wasson would be. Why would I go there?"

"Would you allow a matron to examine you?" asked my former boss.

"For what?"

"Cuts and bruises." She looked at me closely. "Burns from where you fired Wasson's cabin."

I pushed back my chair so quickly that they jumped. I got to my feet, rolled up my sleeves and showed them there were no cuts or bruises. I turned my palms out, then in the other directions. I did the same with my pants so they could see as high as my knees. I pulled my blouse out and held up the front.

Hardy blushed. Gibson looked away.

I turned my back to them and pulled my blouse almost over my shoulders. "Had enough or want me to moon those in the observation room?"

"Sit down," ordered Hardy. "I noticed you're sunburned."

"Yes, I am, Theresa. Most people who live along the Grand

Strand are. We have to make the tourists envious."

They leaned back in their chairs and stared at me.

"Susan, I want your ID, Glock, and badge."

"What an idiot," I muttered, glancing at the floor.

"What did you say?" demanded Hardy. She gripped the edge of the table, aghast.

"You're totally insensitive to your subordinates. You need to be written up, and when I leave, I just might do that."

Again the tapping on the glass behind her.

Hardy got up again and left the room.

"Agent Chase," asked the forester, lowering his voice after the door had closed, "what's going on?"

"Right now, my boss is being told I can't give up my weapon, ID, or badge. They were all destroyed in the explosion that killed my mother."

Mickey DeShields was waiting for me in the parking lot behind the law enforcement center. He leaned against my jeep, meaning the seat, as it was the only place he could touch without getting dirty from all the mud from Francis Marion. I needed to get that jeep washed or hope my memory would return so I could remember the most elementary precautions, my dear Watson.

DeShields watched me limp over with my new cane.

I said, "You tracked my whereabouts yesterday."

"That doesn't mean the report is complete. There are guys at a bar who deny you were there when a woman matching your description and your jeep were seen in the vicinity."

"What'd you expect? They got their asses kicked."

He glanced at the law enforcement center. "I expect you to be careful. What you're doing is not safe." He rolled off the seat. "Follow me. I have something for you."

This chat didn't appear to call for chili dogs and lemonade at Sam's. Instead, Mickey's car stopped behind an abandoned motel over a mile from the law enforcement center and several blocks off the beach. I pulled in behind his sedan. By the time I limped over, he had his trunk open and tossed me a paper bag from Bi-Lo at the Beach.

I fielded the sack and glanced inside. A bulletproof vest was wrapped around several other items. I unwrapped the vest. Previously, I'd seen these only on TV, but I'd recognize them anywhere.

"Who was on the other side of the glass while I was being interrogated?" I asked, sorting through the stuff in the bag.

"Just about anyone who could talk his way into the observation room." He looked at me closely. "You sure you don't remember anything?"

There was a pistol and an extra clip wrapped inside the vest. "What's this?" I asked, pointing at the hammer.

"Well, you fake it as well as anyone."

I looked up from the bag. "From what people say, I get the impression I was a con artist in an earlier life."

"You wouldn't be far wrong. To answer your question, that's called a hammer shroud. Do you remember where you used to get those quick-draw fanny packs?"

"No."

"Well, that's your gun of choice."

I turned the weapon over in my hands, then shrugged. "What good will it do me? I must be way out of practice. I only took Harry's pistol—"

"You're a snap shooter. Just point and shoot."

"Really? Sounds neat."

"'Neat?' You have been spending too much time with Harry Poinsett."

The other items were a SLED ID and badge and paperwork in the form of a series of small cards. "Where'd all this come from? This is official-looking stuff."

"The packet was sent to my home instead of the office, which means you have a friend in Columbia. There's also a copy of your gun permit, driver's license, and credit cards."

"Harry helped me get my driver's license, and I've reapplied for my credit cards."

"Then you'll have an extra set." He glanced down the alley that hid us from the street. "Don't let anyone see them, do you understand?"

"Yes." I dropped them back into the paper sack.

"Susan, how long is this going to last?"

"Pardon me?"

"How long before you're going to be you again?"

"I wish the hell I knew."

"But isn't this charade getting a little old?"

I fitted my rear on the back bumper of his sedan and let out a long sigh. "You're not the only one who thinks I'm faking it. The doctor says to stop worrying and just let it happen, but I'm tired of being an outcast."

"People still care about you." He gestured at the bag.

"And it's suffocating me."

"So if I took you for another chili dog . . . ."

"I'd sit there wondering if I was making a fool of myself."

He nodded. "You need a vacation. From us."

Tears appeared in my eyes. I placed my cane against my hip and wiped them away. "I sure as hell do."

He eyed my cane but said nothing.

"Don't worry, Mickey, I'll make sure the leg is better before I leave, but where I'm going I won't need my memory."

NINETEEN

It was exactly one week from the date that I'd informed everyone with the surname of "Wasson" that it would be best if John Ross turned himself in before I went into the national forest and dragged his ass out of there.

I ate a very good breakfast, cleaned up Harry's kitchen, and left a note. Harry had decided to make himself scarce by staying over at his new girlfriend's. It appeared Harry's stock had risen by moving out of a marina and into a set of overpriced condominiums.

After locking up, I hoisted my pack on my shoulder and walked to Kings Highway. Since most of the people at the Plantation were either retired or got into work later than six a.m., no one asked me if I needed a ride. And I didn't leave through the gate but went over the back wall. If anyone saw me in the dawn fog, they didn't raise an alarm, and if they had, the alarm would've been raised for a redhead in a red tube top and a pair of white short shorts tight enough to give you a wedgie. At Kings Highway, a trucker stopped and I hauled myself aboard.

"Where you headed, little lady?"

"Below Georgetown."

He shifted the mechanical monster into gear. "On my way."

He wanted to ask questions—you know, the usual stuff about my availability—but I encouraged him to talk about trucking. Truckers are suckers for that.

Soon we reached Mount Pleasant, where I climbed down and waved good-bye. Once he was out of sight, I crossed the four lane and hitched a ride with a traveling salesman going in the opposite direction. The salesman wanted to stop for breakfast. I agreed to stop in Georgetown, and it wasn't long before he was telling me how his wife didn't understand him and how he'd known when he picked me up that the two of us were going to get along just fine.

When he put his hand on my thigh, I told him I wanted out of there. Totally apologetic that I had misunderstood his intentions, he tried to reassure me that there was nothing to be concerned about. Actually, the frantic looking about I was doing was me searching for my turnoff. Soon my backpack and I were on the side of the road and the salesman's tires were squealing away.

The next car that stopped was told "no thanks," and I didn't even have my thumb out. Hey, what an outfit. It could create rides out of nowhere, if you didn't mind the insects that came along with the magic.

When the traffic slowed to a trickle, I crossed Kings Highway and discovered a black sports car waiting for me. An electric window was lowered and I found myself staring at the face of Chad Rivers. Strands of brown hair fell across his forehead.

"So you're the guy who's been stalking me."

"But I stopped. I was afraid I'd frighten you."

"You did." I hoisted my pack on my back and crossed in front of the Corvette.

"Susan, don't go," he said, climbing out of the car. "I was sent to give you a ride."

I threw a finger in his direction. "Stay right where you are! In the car."

He sat back down and closed the door.

I came over to the passenger side. No way was I going to stand on the side of the highway and become roadkill. When the window was lowered on my side, I asked, "What do you mean: you were sent to give me a ride?"

"Harry called and said you'd need a ride to Francis Marion. I'm sorry I wasn't there in time. I didn't mean to invade your space. I just wanted to see you again, and Harry said this was the best way."

Lowering my pack to the ground, I bent down to the

window. "But why didn't you just drop by? It would've been much easier than getting up this early."

"I get up early every day and drive around. Nobody's there to ask you the same questions over and over again." Chad glanced at the floorboard. "The time I came to see you, the guards were joking about the crazy girl I wanted to see. I didn't think it was a good time."

"So you stalked me to see if I was nuts?"

He nodded. "Pretty much so."

"Chad, would Susan Chase have known your car?"

"I suppose. Wait a minute, I thought you were Susan Chase."

"I'm have a hard time referring to me as her." Or was that her as me?

"Join the crowd. All these people saying I'm 'Chad Rivers' and explaining our relationship. I finally asked my dad to put me back in the hospital. They pretty much leave you alone in there."

"Except in therapy."

He smiled. This guy had the cutest smile. "When my folks wouldn't send me back, I ran away. I know it sounds stupid since I'm in my thirties, but I ran away from home."

Gee, Chad, that's what people say I'm doing.

"In Charleston I ran into some of my relatives. I didn't know I had relatives in Charleston. They called the cops and I was picked up. I finally went to work at the family boatyard, but everyone was so nice it about drove me nuts. Nowadays, I spend most of my time driving around and waiting for my memory to return." He patted the dashboard. "Burn a tankful of gas everyday."

"Chad, what do you remember? About me? About Susan?"

"I get a flash from time to time." He smiled. "And you have your clothes on."

I flushed and looked at the ground.

"Sorry. My bad. I don't know if you're interested, but Harry and my father want us to get together."

I looked up. "They think we'll remember each other?"

"They think we're a breath of fresh air to each other. So,

when you get back from wherever you're going . . ." He tried to look beyond me, but there was nothing but the darkness and silence of the pine forest. "Would you mind if I called you?"

"Only if you promise to forget you ever saw me out here."

"Forget?" he said with a laugh. "Hell, I'm the world champion in that department."

A piece of orange duct tape wrapped around a pine tree marked a spot a little over three hundred yards down the road. From there, I found my way through the bushes, scrub pines, and spring flowers to the cove where Travis Rice was pretending to fish. It was a narrow stretch of water that widened as it approached the river. Palmetto trees shadowed Travis's boat as well as a skiff that was moored in lily pads near shore. Dawn fog still hung over the cove.

I swung the pack off my shoulder and stepped from the riverbank into the aluminum runabout. With one hand on his fishing rod, Travis helped me aboard. Just at that moment, his line tightened.

"Hold on! I've got something here."

I laughed. Travis wasn't pretending.

He glanced at me as he worked the line. "You sure you remember how to live in the wild? They have alligators and black bears out there." He was trying to check out my outfit and beach the fish at the same time.

"No problem," I said. "I even brought along my *Girl Scout Handbook.*"

Two days earlier, Harry had opened the door to get the morning paper and found a pack containing everything the intrepid explorer needed. Inside the pack was a copy of the *Girl Scout Handbook.* I lugged the pack inside the condo while Harry examined the card.

"Who's it from?"

"Jacqueline Marion."

"Wait, wait," I said, thumping the pack on the end of the dinner table, "don't tell me. Another friend of Susan Chase." I opened the pack and saw the goodies inside, most of which

I had no clue how to use.

Harry handed me the card. He had tears in his eyes.

"Jesus, Harry, please don't cry."

He wiped his eyes. "Didn't mean to, but now I know for sure you're going to do this damn fool thing."

I put an arm around him, took the card, and read it. The card wished me luck, and jotted under the inscription was a note from Jacqueline reminding me to watch my back.

"You ask me to sneak out," Travis said, reeling in whatever he'd caught, "and you're parading around like a streetwalker?" He was referring to my red tube top and white short shorts. Perhaps even my wig.

I held my arms open and caused the boat to wiggle. "I'm hiding in plain sight. I saw it in a movie on TV."

In contrast to my tube top and shorts, Travis wore jeans, baseball cap, and flannel shirt. He watched as I removed the red wig, then returned to landing his fish. "For a moment I didn't think you were as serious as when you slipped me that note."

"Did Vicky buy the idea I'd only stopped by to apologize for the cops bugging you?"

"Not until you didn't show again."

"Well, I had to give John Ross the opportunity to get the word."

"Yeah. Right."

The line snapped, the rod kicked into the air, and the fish was off. My intrepid fisherman cursed, then apologized for his language and offered me some coffee. There was a spare mug and thermos. I leaned forward, took it, and thanked him.

"You know, Susan, I get the idea you've been planning this a long time."

"But I don't want you or Vicky linked to me."

"Don't worry," he said, refilling his mug. "It doesn't take much imagination to see your pregnant wife being dragged off in handcuffs and questioned in some dark room until she's about to bust a pipe. That'd sure put an end to making babies." He gazed into the fog separating us from the main

Steve Brown

body of water. "I'm sorry we had to tell the cops about your first visit."

"No problem. Another good reason for me to wait a week before doing this thing."

I looked at the wooden skiff tied at the stern of the runabout. It was about ten feet long and came to a point. On the rear, and to one side, was mounted a thin trolling motor. There were no oarlocks, but lying on the bottom of the wooden boat was a pole for pushing the boat through the shallows. The draft would be about six to eight inches with me standing in the boat, and those times I'd raise the trolling motor out of the water. I should be able to go about anywhere and be heard by damn few.

Travis took a final sip of his mug, reached over the side of the boat, and washed it out. "You brought Carey home and that's all that matters to me. More?" He gestured with the thermos.

I shook my head. Harry had reminded me who "Carey" was, in case the subject should come up.

Travis recapped the thermos. "Just how many runaways have you found, Susan?"

I sipped from my mug and dodged the question. "Carey was smart enough to try it only once."

He put down the thermos, picked up his fishing rod, and began to reel in his broken line. "But what do you say that makes them stay home? That was over five years ago, but the look on Carey's face whenever the subject comes up—"

"I took her by the county morgue." Harry had told me that was a trick of Susan's, too.

"Jiminy. Well, I guess that would do it."

After changing clothes, I lay in the bottom of the runabout while Travis ferried the skiff and me into the forest. A half-hour later he throttled back on the engine.

"Why do you believe this is the place?" Travis raised his voice over the sound of the idling engine. "I'd be in the deepest part of the forest."

"It *is* the deepest part of the forest, if you factor in a road system and a general store."

"You know, Susan, John Ross might be long gone by now."

I looked up from the bottom of the runabout. "I don't think so. These days there are too many people who scrutinize strangers. Ready for me to sit up?"

"Give me a minute."

Bushes became thicker and scraped the sides of the aluminum boat. Palmetto fronds and dwarf palmettos caused Travis to twist the tiller handle one way, then the other, as large green leaves reached over the sides. He had to wrench his shirt out of the clutches of a swamp rose. It showered me with petals.

"I heard planes with infrared are mandated to fly over this area and report the findings to those on the ground."

"And that's why the system doesn't work. The locals are informed of the flyover."

The boat stopped, jamming into pickerelweed, their purple spikes rising higher than the sides of the boat.

"You really think people around here would protect that lousy bastard?"

I didn't have to answer his question because he said, "We're here."

I sat up. The runabout was engulfed in duckweed, spider lilies, and cardinal spears. A cottonmouth slid off a log and under a lily pad.

"When do you want me to come back?" asked Travis.

"Four days from today."

I gave him a copy of my map and pointed at what appeared to be nothing more than one big green space. A two-lane county road cut through the space and the general store was marked on the map, but the store was several miles away.

"Harry and I think I should be able to loop through here in those three days. The fourth is my cushion."

Travis studied the map bathed in a portion of sunlight compared to the desolateness across the water. We were between two worlds: the green and vivid colors of the sandbar contrasting sharply with the stagnant, black waters dotted with the occasional pike-like stump.

"Does this thing you're doing bother Harry as much as it

bothers Vicky and me?"

"More."

"Do you have a weapon?"

I nodded.

"Well, I don't know what I'll be driving. It could be the runabout or the airboat or maybe the launch, but I'll pull you and the skiff wherever you want to go."

I touched the map several miles from our current location. "Here. If this place doesn't work out."

He took the map, folded it, and stuck it in his jeans. "I'll arrive after the tourists call it a day. I think it's best we run at dusk and you don't get out of the boat or even show yourself. I think it should appear I've found a boat and I'm towing it in as salvage."

"If you're coming at dusk, then I'll meet you in three days. I appreciate everything you're doing for me, Travis."

"Well, don't you get yourself killed. Harry would never forgive me."

I waited a few minutes before poling in the opposite direction. It was about eight a.m. and the dawn fog had disappeared, the sun had broken through, but this part of the park was quiet. The pole moved me across great stretches of open water, except the occasional spot that turned out to be too deep. In those areas, I didn't have to use the motor but allowed the momentum of the boat to move me along. A compass was strapped to my arm, my ears and eyes strained for any sight or sound, and I trolled a line in the water seeking out the first fish to bite. Harry had taken me fishing last week and taught me how to fillet.

Finally a bass hit and I reeled it in. That afternoon, after checking one dead-end creek after another, not to mention paths that terminated in piles of trash, I tied up. Digging a small pit, I started a charcoal fire and wrapped the fish in aluminum foil and laid it over the coals. I'd brought along some corn that I cooked in its husks and a bottle of cherries for dessert. Water came from a large, plastic bottle and I was careful to take only a few sips. While the fish cooked, I surveyed the area with binoculars and found a stork in a bald cypress tree framed by a rising moon. He appeared to be about as lonely as me.

After my meal, which happily tasted like what Harry had prepared over the grill on his porch, I allowed myself two cherries, drank from the heavy water bottle, and repacked the skiff. Harry said it'd be smart if I arrived after dark wherever I stopped. That way, there would be no fires and, hopefully, I'd learn to live without lights.

A woman was talking.

"What?" I asked, sitting up.

The woman was leaning over me. "This is not a good idea, Susan."

"What?"

"You shouldn't be out here."

I'm sure we were somewhere, but I had no idea where. I had eyes only for this woman. She was young, beautiful, and blond. Around her the air glowed.

"A young lady doesn't go into a swamp alone."

I found myself saying, "I can't be the woman you want me to be, Mother."

This was my mother? The woman's face was tanned, her blond hair short, and her blue eyes demanding.

She shook her head sadly. "You're too much like your father. Too much the tomboy."

I woke up screaming.

I shivered and pulled the poncho liner tight around me. The air mattress squished under me, so much so that I put out a hand to steady myself. Fireflies fluttered, mosquitoes were kept at bay by a greasy balm, and some animal hung from a branch. Gold-green eyes staring at this fool having a nightmare. It was several minutes before I could go back to sleep.

The first passersby were practically on top of me before I saw them. They were in a slow-moving launch with a very quiet motor. Rods and reels stuck from the stern and lines trailed in the water behind the boat. When I finally heard them, I poled behind a tree.

The fishermen came through, drinking beer and looking as if they were not the least bit concerned with my where-abouts. A forester passed by later in the day. He stopped to examine the remains of a wooden boat left to rot on a peat bar. I recognized him as Gibson, the guy who'd been in the interrogation room with Theresa Hardy. Maybe he was looking for poachers. Yeah. Right.

The camouflage poncho liner blended into the background of the forest. That clever item had come from my former boss, J.D. Warden, who now lived in Montana. And each morning I cut and mounted new bushes fore and aft to break up the lines of the skiff. I also used the paint Travis left behind to disguise the boat in gray, black, brown, and dark green. You can learn many a helpful hint watching the History Channel.

Once, when I was poling toward sunlight and the open water beyond, a boat stalled out and floated my way. There was nothing I could do but lie low. I did, and soon I could hear the fisherman cursing that he'd not taken the time to top off his spare tank. He threw out an anchor and waited for someone to pass by. That meant almost an hour with me lying on the bottom of the boat and the horseflies trying to stick their snouts under the poncho liner. Finally the sound of another boat.

To make sure he wasn't missed, the fisherman fired off a shot. The other boat cut its engine, and there began a shouting match between the two about how close the first fisherman had come to his rescuer with that pistol shot. The rescuer threatened to leave the stranded man in the park. That wasn't going to happen. The adrift fisherman had a pistol.

The rescuer quickly siphoned fuel into the primary tank and was soon out of there. It was several minutes before the fisherman could bulb-pump enough fuel into his engine; then he was gone, spraying the air with more curses. By then it was nightfall and I'd missed my chance to catch and fry something to eat. That night, I had to settle for a power bar.

Travis was just where he said he'd be three days later. While his runabout idled, he scanned the water behind him. "I'm not saying the foresters don't know what's going on— they stopped me and asked if I'd seen you—but we've got to watch it."

"What'd you tell them?"

He looked down where I lay across the bottom of the wooden skiff. I'd arrived at the sand bar several hours earlier. It was good to be in the sun again.

"Don't talk, Susan."

I shut my mouth.

"One of the foresters said if I saw you, that I should tell you to turn yourself in. He also marked a couple of areas on a map he thinks you should check out." Travis peered at me as he tied off the skiff. "This was an older guy by the name of Gibson, but it could be a trick. You'll have to make that decision. I'm only in charge of transportation."

A pack was thrown in the bow along with a sack of ice. The rope tightened and the skiff trailed along bringing me with it.

"Vicky sends her best, some canned goods, more beer and ice, and word that we'll probably be at the hospital three days from now."

Two fishermen came roaring through. The next minute their boat sputtered and went dead. They drifted by as I ducked under the poncho liner and cursed. No wonder foresters are kept busy with people who run out of gas. And why don't we hear more about them? Why would the dopes want to talk about it?

I'd finally had enough. How was this slinking around going to work anyway? I stood up and threw off the poncho liner. Since I was less than thirty feet away, it startled the stranded fishermen.

"Enough already!"

Both fishermen wanted to know if I was intent on giving them a heart attack; then they asked, as I poled away, what I was going to do for them.

"Nothing!"

Steve Brown

They must've mentioned the incident to the forest service because the following day that area of the park was swarming with launches. I could faintly hear their engines as I was, at the time, miles away.

My arms ached, my shirt became pasted to my back, and once again, I had no time to cook. Dinner was another power bar and a hearty drink of water. Come the morning, a gray rain soaked everything and lowered the temperature. I fitted my head through the poncho and poled on, making several stops to bail out the accumulating water. The following day, I came across the girl.

She was a brunette of about twenty and sitting on a rise in the middle of a swamp pond. Her long stringy hair hung in her face and she squealed as I poled over. Her dirty face was gaunt, her jeans and white blouse streaked with mud. Bare feet.

"Calm down," I said. "Who are you?"

She scrambled forward on a spit of sand, then splashed into the water. "Are you the girl?"

I didn't understand what she meant.

"Are you the girl come for John Ross?"

"Er—yes." I really should get my pistol. Holding onto the pole, I started moving toward the bow. "Do you know where John Ross is?"

"Did you bring candy?" she asked, gripping my boat and peering inside. "John Ross said you'd have candy."

"I can take you away from here. We can head for the highway."

My arm was pointing in the direction of the highway and my other hand holding the pole—when something hammered me in the back. The blow knocked me over the side and into the water. I never heard the shot.

TWENTY

The pool of water I fell into was dark, brackish, and gave a delicious sense of relief. Unfortunately, swamp water is not very deep and I had to decide whether to "lie low" or return to reality. The reality I returned to was almost more than I could bear.

Both of my hands were gripped and I was dragged onto the spit of sand extending into the water. Initially the breath had been knocked out of me, but I had had the good sense, probably from living around water so long, to take a breath before going under. My head was twisted to one side, providing me with more air as I was dragged ashore.

Who was pulling me ashore? The girl?

If so, she'd gone after my boat, after dropping me unceremoniously in the sand. My back ached, and I lay sprawled on my side. Thank God for the bulletproof vest. From where I lay, blackened stumps protruded from the water, rays of light broke through the shadows, and there was the sound of an approaching engine. I was soaking wet.

The girl squealed at what she found, and the boat came ashore. Heavy feet hit the sand near my head. I closed my eyes and drew up into the fetal position, hands at my feet.

"What's this?" asked a male voice. "No blood?"

"Where's the candy?" asked the girl from farther away.

I was rolled over on my back, and a bearded face leaned down for a closer look. Blue eyes, black hair, and sunburned face. Out of the corner of my eye, I could see the bow of his boat, and, in his hand, a high-powered rifle.

My hand came out of my boot, and I brought up a knife

and stuck it under his chin. "John Ross Wasson, I presume."

His head rose very slowly as I sat up. His eyes became very hard.

"Put down that rifle, and if you make any sudden moves, I'll gut you like the fish I ate last night."

The blue eyes continued to focus on me as he placed the rifle in the sand. A .306 with a scope.

"Easy does it." My voice was hoarse, my back ached, but my knife remained at his throat—until something hit me on the side of the head and everything went very dark.

I woke up with the worst headache and backache. I was strapped to the base of a tree with my hands tied behind me. I was wearing some kind of vest and it was soaked with water, as were my clothes. Across from me was a young brunette. She sat on her haunches, rifle across her knees. Behind her was a camouflage tent; to the left, a cooler; to the right, a Hibachi grill. Sticking out of the tent was an air mattress.

I moved my head and it throbbed with pain. Tears came to my eyes. "What . . . happened?"

"I'm sorry I had to hit you."

"Why . . . ?"

"You were going to kill John Ross."

Someone moaned and it wasn't me.

Despite the pain and tears, I turned my head and looked at the man sitting next to me. I was tied to a thin pine and so was he, both of us in a u-shaped stand of bamboo and the ground made of sand. Blood ran down the side of Wasson's face and onto his camouflage tee shirt. His pants were made of the same material. Like me, he was wet and wore waterproof boots.

"What's going on?" I asked.

The brunette was a stocky girl and much younger than me. She looked sad. "I don't know what to do."

"If you have any sense, you'll turn me loose. I work for SLED."

Her head canted to one side, her eyes dull. "What's that?"

"The state FBI."

"There's only one FBI."

"The State Law Enforcement Division. It has jurisdiction over the state of South Carolina."

"This here's a national park."

I struggled with the rope that held my hands behind my back. I supposed the boats were around here somewhere, but I couldn't see them with all this bamboo. It was enough to make you think the bamboo had been cultivated, the way it formed the u-shape. Trees grew low and Spanish moss filtered sunlight that broke through. Behind me was the only opening to the water.

"You're obstructing justice." I inclined my head toward the man whose head lolled to one side. "John Ross Wasson is wanted by the authorities."

The girl canted her head to the other side, and still her eyes appeared glazed over. Uh-huh. A dopehead who'd enjoyed her vice. I couldn't see her arms because of her dirty long-sleeved shirt, but her nostrils appeared to be normal. The dope had done its damage long ago, and it was entirely possible John Ross had dried her out by not allowing her to return to civilization.

"Why'd you come if you didn't bring no candy?"

"Candy?"

"John Ross said if I were to sit real still and wait, you'd give me some candy. But I didn't find nothing but a bottle of cherries."

I noticed my small bottle lay on the ground beside her, empty. "I don't know what you think nor do I care. John Ross killed his sister when he blew up that OB/GYN and you're aiding and abetting a felon."

"Killed his sister?" The head straightened up on her neck. "Why would he do something like that?"

"Laura Wasson was having an abortion."

"Laurie goes to school in Georgetown."

I squinted and tried to focus. Sometimes there was more than one of this girl. "No. Laurie Wasson was killed a few days before Christmas." Inclining my aching head in the direction of the man strapped to the pine, I pleaded with her. "You've got to let me go. I can't be here when John Ross wakes up." Well, I couldn't be here with my hands tied behind my back and held in place by this skinny tree.

"But you didn't bring no candy."

What the hell was she talking about? I shook my head to clear it and tears ran down my cheeks. The side of my face felt twice its ordinary size. I had to think. I had to make sense of what was going on. When I could, I tried another tack. "Are you sure you didn't find the candy? It was there when I left the store."

She leaned forward and gripped the rifle in her dirty hands. "What store?"

I tried to remember the name of the general store where I'd met the two swamp rats. The name wouldn't come, but I remembered the stuffed red wolf, and that's what I told the girl about.

She squealed with so much excitement, I thought she might fire off a shot the way she carelessly held the rifle. "John Ross said he was going to buy that red wolf for me. He forgot the last time he went to town."

I wasn't interested in discussing the merits of taxidermy or John Ross's largesse. "What was I supposed to bring you? Peppermint?"

"Lemon drops. I love lemon drops."

"That's it. Lemon drops. Two bags for you."

"They're gone now. I looked."

My lower lip trembled. "Would you . . . would you untie me so I can look?" I glanced at the man slumped next to me. The one who didn't hesitate to strike without warning. *Please untie me before this monster regains consciousness.*

"Not until John Ross and I talk. I have to make this right."

I swallowed and had a tough time doing it. Little of this was making sense. Thankfully, John Ross appeared to be unconscious so I might have a chance with this slow-witted girl. "What's your name?"

"Cindy. Cindy Quillen."

"Where you from, Cindy?"

She glanced at the ground. "All over."

I forced my head to turn this way and that, taking in the canopy, our encampment, and the black water with its occasional cypress trunks and black stumps. Tears ran down my cheeks from moving my head, but there was no time for that.

"Where are we?" Better question: Where was my Swiss army knife? It was supposed to be in my pocket. As I shifted around and tried to reach my pocket, I asked, "How far are we from the highway?"

"The highway where John Ross found me?"

Okay, Cindy, let's go in that direction. "Yes. Where's that highway?"

"I'm not sure. We don't go there much." The young woman held out her arms, showing off her dirty blouse. "John Ross got this for me last time we went out there."

"I thought John Ross kidnapped you."

"That's what I thought at first, but he takes care of me so I don't have to turn tricks."

I had found the knife. It was in my right-hand jeans pocket, and when I moved around, I could feel the soreness under the bulletproof vest. I rose up off my bottom to slip a hand into the pocket of my jeans. This time they were relaxed fit.

"Cindy, why did John Ross shoot me?"

"I don't rightly know. I guess because you were going to make me go home to Daddy."

I found the top of the knife. Now, if my fingers weren't too numb.

"I don't want to go home, and John Ross said you were one of them government people."

"Then why was I bringing the candy?"

Her face broke into a dirty grin. "Why to trick me into coming back with you. But you didn't bring no candy." Now she was puzzled. "How's the trick supposed to work if you didn't bring no candy."

"Sorry," I said with cheerfulness brought on either from getting two fingers around the army knife or sheer hysteria. "He shot the wrong girl."

"He did?"

"Like I said: I work for SLED and I'm here to take John Ross back for killing the two women in the clinic." The knife slipped from my fingers and fell into the sand. What did I expect? They were numb from the rope, which appeared synthetic. Nylon rope. My rope.

The girl stood up, taking the rifle with her.

I froze.

"John Ross didn't kill nobody." She glanced at the unconscious man, lolling against the tree. "He told me how he done it so none of the firemen would get hurt like they got hurt in New York City." She smiled. "He set the whole garage on fire so they couldn't go in there."

I had to break through before Wasson came around. "Cindy, are you wanted by the law anywhere?"

She stared at the ground. "Maybe."

"Tell me about it," I said, flexing my fingers and returning them to agility.

"They caught me turning tricks."

"Where was that?"

"In Georgia." The rifle was shifted to one hand, then to the other as she scuffed her bare foot. Sand sprayed as her foot kicked it like a six-year-old's.

I scrunched down and my fingers closed on the knife again. "John Ross said he'd make sure the people in Georgia never found you?"

She stopped kicking the sand. "My own daddy called me a whore. What was I to do? I didn't want to turn tricks, but I had to when he kicked me out of the house."

"Not anymore you don't." I held the knife in one hand and tried to open the blade with the nail of a finger on the other.

"John Ross said they'd never find me."

"But I found you. Why couldn't others?"

"No, no, we knew you were coming. We found *you.*"

"Cindy, you found me because I went everywhere telling every Wasson I could find that I was coming in here. Someone has to pay for destroying that clinic."

"Them in that clinic were bad to me."

"Them? Who?" I stopped. Something chilled me down deep inside. "The clinic in Myrtle Beach? What did they do?"

"The clinic in Georgia." She stared at the ground. "I can't have no babies. Daddy fixed me."

I didn't want to hear what came next; still, I couldn't resist asking, "Fixed . . . you?"

"Like a stray dog. John Ross said that didn't matter. If we wanted a baby, we could go into town and get one."

"Just go into town and get . . . whatever you wanted?"

"And never have to turn tricks. My daddy was wrong to fix me 'cause I got no reason to be bad."

We were going to have to work this escape angle at a more elementary level. "Cindy, do you ever miss going to the movies?"

She nodded.

"They have candy at the movies. When was the last time you went to the movie and had candy?"

"When they said you were coming after John Ross."

Wasson groaned and tried to sit up.

I glanced at him, trembled, and the knife fell behind me once again. "Cindy, I want you to listen very carefully. You never have to hide again in this forest, you never have to go to jail, and you never have to go home to Georgia. All you have to do is untie my hands and let me go."

"I don't know if I can do that." She was scuffing her foot again.

"Cindy, you have to turn me loose, or the next time the police come, they'll put you away where there's no candy."

"No candy?" Again she stopped scuffing.

I watched the monster roll into a sitting position as my fingers desperately fumbled around for the knife. When I found it, I fitted a nail into the blade again and wrenched the knife open. The violent motion caused the knife to fall into the sand. Or I was trembling too much.

Wasson found his hands tied behind his back and himself to the pine. With the biceps on this guy, that pine didn't stand a chance. He saw me, then Cindy. She was staring at the ground.

"What's going on here?" he demanded.

I started rubbing the rope against the bark of the tree, and I put my back into it. Wasson jerked on his hands tied behind the pine and looked around.

"What the hell are you doing, Cindy?"

The girl looked like she was about to cry. Join the club. "John Ross, I had to," she said.

"Girl, you turn me loose right now. You got no cause tying me up."

He fought as hard with the ropes as I did. I was putting everything I had in it, rubbing the rope against the pine. A moment later, I remembered the knife.

"John Ross, I turn you loose, you'll kill this girl."

"You're damn right," he growled, his blue eyes becoming icy pools of hate. "Right after I bust you one for tying me up this way!"

Wasson's beard dampened as he fought his way to his feet. Sweat broke out on his forehead. Mine, too, as my eyes popped out. I gripped the knife and rapidly sawed its blade against the rope.

"But, John Ross," pleaded the girl, "what about the movies? Are we going to the movies and get some candy? You promised."

Wasson was leaning forward, away from the tree, and erect. His muscles strained against not only the pine, but the fabric of his camouflage tee shirt. "I don't know what you damn women think you're doing . . . ."

"I wanted the candy, John Ross, and she says she can get me more. Lemon drops, she says—"

"I'll kick your ass!"

The man towered over me, and all I could do was work the knife frantically. Evidently I had every right to be operating in the panic mode. Cindy leaped to her feet and ran into the water behind me. There was a distant splash, probably the rifle, then the sound of someone sloshing through water.

Wasson strained against the rope, and the pine followed him as he stepped forward. I blinked as the thin tree snapped in half and Wasson's momentum continued him forward, running into the tent and leaving the tree in his wake. The tree caught at the top of the stand of bamboo and hung there. Spanish moss floated down from overhead.

Wasson had regained his balance. He staggered over, leaned down, and got in my face. With a maniacal look in his eyes, he said, "I'll be back."

Good thing my pants were already wet.

He splashed into the water, and it caused me to work the blade against the rope faster and faster. I don't know what the problem was but I sure as hell couldn't count on brute force breaking me loose. Still, no matter how hard I worked the blade, I couldn't slice through the nylon. What was the problem?

Oh, God! I was sawing with the flat side of the blade.

Calm down! Calm down!

Sweat ran down the sides of my face as I talked myself into fitting the sharp edge of the blade against the nylon. Once again, I went to work on the rope and tried not to look at the pine that had been snapped in two. Behind me, I could hear John Ross Wasson sloshing through the water and the girl screaming.

The rope finally separated!

I flung my arms apart, brought them around in front of me, and rubbed my wrists. Then I clawed my way to my feet, felt the side of my head (it ached), and got my bearings, and hurried into the water. If that monster got his hands on that girl . . . .

Several huge oaks dropped this part of the swamp into shadows, but less than thirty feet away, I saw the froth John Ross Wasson had stirred up. The huge man had flung himself, face first, over Cindy, forcing her underwater by the sheer force of his weight. Only his roped hands stuck out of the water.

Where was the rifle?

Somewhere in the water, dumb-ass. Now get that bastard off her!

I slogged in their direction, looking for some sort of weapon. I tried breaking off one of the black stumps, but nothing doing. I didn't have much time or John Ross was going to drown this girl. I sloshed over, got my hand on his shoulder, and tried to pull him off. He rolled over and snapped at me.

I screamed and let go, then stared at the scratches on my hand from his teeth. John Ross regained his footing and threw himself over Cindy again.

Shit! The bastard was out of his mind.

I roared at him to let her go, reached into the water—both of them were underwater again—and found the top of his head and then his ears. He surfaced and snapped at me with his teeth again. Using his ears, I dragged him off the girl.

Bad idea. Once he got his feet under him, he knocked me sprawling. I fought to get away, but he was cat quick and maneuvered himself across my body and held me down. Now I was the one trapped in the shallows and being drowned. While I fought with my hands and kicked with my feet, John Ross lay across me, the muck of the swamp inviting me into my eternal resting place.

Finally, I remembered he had eye sockets, and when I dug my thumbs into them, the son of a bitch rose up and gave me a chance to catch my breath. He leaped at me again, but this time I was ready for him. I pushed myself up and away from him.

When I surfaced, he rammed me with his shoulder. I took the blow on my side and fell back again and not far away. Wasson sloshed over, coming in for the kill. I tried to kick him, but he stepped back and took the blow on his chest. I did a backwards stroke with both arms and pulled away. That didn't really help either. The bulletproof vest and the water were too much, and Wasson could move faster upright than I could crab walk ashore.

He came down on my legs with his knees, and I had to be quick about it before he got his teeth into me. My effort to kick him was hampered by being under water. By the time I was standing upright, Wasson was springing out of the water again, which, of course, wasn't even waist high to him. He crashed into my torso, knocking the wind out of me. His teeth slid off my thigh, while, for my part, I kicked his shin, but with little result.

I was simply doing too much reacting and not enough thinking. I twisted around and struggled toward the rise. There had to be somewhere I could hide. Evidently not. When I reached land, my legs gave way and I stumbled over the tent and went sprawling.

Sanctuary of Evil

That was John Ross again, taking my legs out from under me. He had me pinned down by one foot, me on my knees and clawing the ground for a handhold. Or the Hibachi. Well, if he was going to throw himself on me like he had Cindy, he'd have to free up my foot. When he did, I rolled away.

He landed where I'd just been, trying to hammer me with his knees. Laboring for breath, I got to my feet and brought along the Hibachi. Wasson was up again. When he came at me, I swung the Hibachi and hit him. He took the blow on the shoulder and the metal grill fell apart in my hands. In shock, I watched Wasson go down. To one knee.

Where the hell was Cindy? Heading for Georgia if she was smart.

John Ross and I faced each other across the clearing. Sweat ran down his face; blood from scratches. The elbows had been torn out of my long-sleeved shirt and my clothing dripped water. Our feet were covered with mud and our pants were dotted with sand.

"It's just a matter of time," he said, gasping for air and giving me a little smile. "I can take you with both hands tied behind my back."

"You know, John Ross," I got out, head throbbing and tears running down my cheeks, "I do believe you."

"Then make it easy on yourself. Untie my hands and I'll snap your neck like kindling."

"It's not . . . the snapping that bothers me . . . ." I said, moving away from the wall of bamboo as he continued to circle, "it's what happens before you . . . take the time out of your . . . busy schedule . . . to break my neck."

It was then that I realized that my only hope of escape was finding water deep enough where John Ross couldn't swim. The Cindy option. I stumbled across the clearing, sloshed into the shallows, and tripped over one of those blackened stumps. As I went down, I bumped into Cindy, lying on her back and staring at the canopy.

Behind me, I heard John Ross holler as he rushed off the rise, built up a head of steam, and leaped at me. It was all I could do to push away from the dead girl and fall to one side. Still, when John Ross came down, the force of the blow knocked me to the mushy bottom of the swamp.

But this time was different. For some reason, John Ross didn't follow me, so I was able to twist around and claw across the mucky bottom. When I ran out of air, I stuck my head up, got more, and willed my arms to throw themselves in front of me, legs fluttering. The soggy, bulletproof vest didn't make it any easier.

I'd only gone a few feet when my head bumped into a cypress. I cried out in pain, tears came to my eyes, but by now I'd learned to roll to one side—to elude the flying body that would be right behind me.

There was nothing behind me.

I rose up cautiously, steadied myself by holding onto the surface of the tree, and looked back. All I could see was the body of Cindy hung up on the blackened stump. Something thrashed near her, and I tried to puzzle out what was happening. I'd been wrong. Cindy wasn't dead, just unconscious, and John Ross was making damn sure he finished one of us off.

I sloshed over to where he lay across Cindy and clubbed him across the back with my hands laced together. "Now that's a sucker punch, you bastard!"

Only gurgling from Wasson, and the man wasn't even under water. He tried to fit his legs under him and stand up. Impossible. He was impaled on the pike-like blackened stump. I took him by the hair and held his face out of the water so he could breathe.

I could only raise him several inches. The rest of his torso was so heavy his weight prevented me from pulling him off the pike. The blackened stump had entered his groin and he could not back off or rise up. With me holding his head out of the water, he wasn't going to drown, unless it was from all the blood gushing from his mouth.

He fought with the rope holding his hands behind him. He fought to get his feet under him so he could gain the proper leverage. Then, with a gasp that sprayed both my hands with blood, John Ross Wasson stopped struggling and went limp.

TWENTY-ONE

I raged at the man. I pummeled him over and over. I sure as hell didn't want him to live, but I didn't want him to die like this. Maybe at the hands of the state of South Carolina but not this. What would be learned if this bastard died where no one could see him?

Where no one could see him? I stopped hitting John Ross and sloshed back several steps.

Where no one could see me.

I stepped away from the two bodies as more squiggly lines of blood drifted by. I looked deep into the swamp and remembered how anxious Theresa Hardy had been to hang something on me. With two more bodies, she'd be even more eager, not to mention I'd embarrassed the hell out of her in that interrogation room. Maybe that's what Mickey DeShields had meant when he said I should be careful.

Would the cops buy the idea that John Ross and Cindy had fought to the death? I really didn't know. I really didn't care. I wanted to go home. But I did have one small problem. I didn't know which direction was home.

Where were the damn boats? Cindy had the brainpower of an eight-year-old so it couldn't be all that complicated. I returned to the rise and forced my way through the wall of bamboo. To someone like Cindy, out of sight, out of mind.

I walked to where the shallows gave way to deeper water. Minutes later, I came upon John Ross's runabout and my skiff. I towed them to the rise and tied them off near the bodies. John Ross's boat had a bow line, stern line, and a long rope trailing in its wake. What was up with that?

I went back to the map, and using the compass that had been ripped off my arm during the fight, I reconstructed where I'd been and how far Cindy might've brought both John Ross and me before we regained consciousness. It couldn't be far. That sucker was one heavy SOB.

Oh, hell. I threw down the map. She'd floated us here in the skiff. That's why our clothing was so wet and that rope trailed behind the runabout.

I collected my gear and dumped it into the skiff. By the time I'd brushed the rise clear of any sign of habitation and sunk John Ross's boat, which was a major chore in itself, I was a nervous wreck. With shaking arms, I picked up the pole and got to work. I was going home, wherever that might be.

By morning light I found a highway. I took all my gear ashore, bathed in the creek, and changed into a new set of clothes. Two days later, as the sun was going down, and as I was contemplating the size of the national forest, I saw a black sports car coming in my direction. Chad Rivers out burning his daily tank of gasoline. Next, to Travis Rice's to let him know where to find the skiff, and then to Evelyn Mooney's seafood restaurant. I told both of them that I'd gone into Francis Marion, lost my nerve, and hid out. Neither one believed me.

Harry Poinsett said there was a standing order for me to report in to Theresa Hardy when I returned home. Since Chad had smuggled me into the Plantation under cover of darkness, I told Harry he should pack a bag and go stay at his girlfriend's. For the next week, I didn't turn on a light or leave the condo until the bruises disappeared and I could stop shaking. Chad had a lot to do with ending my serious case of the shakes.

Theresa Hardy wanted to know where I'd been. I repeated my story that I'd gone into Francis Marion and lost my nerve. After all, I was no Susan Chase.

Then where'd I been the last two weeks?

Camping out. I'd been too ashamed to come home. On a map, I pointed out the place along the highway where I'd spent most of my time. The way I figured it, if no one could find John Ross alive, what was the chance they'd find him dead? That reminded me, I needed to do a net search for "Quillens" and hope the family who got the message about their "Cindy" could receive e-mail.

Chad was waiting for me in the SLED office with Mickey DeShields. The office is nothing more than a room that holds two metal desks and chairs. An extra chair sits next to the door and that's the one Chad occupied. Mickey pulled his feet off his desk and Chad smiled as I crossed the bullpen. I was looking forward to getting to know the person behind that smile.

"What's your status?" asked DeShields.

I glanced at Hardy, who had trailed me into the room and stopped to talk to someone. Probably the person to be sent into the forest to find where I'd camped out. Neither one of them looked very happy.

"I think my status with SLED is up in the air."

"Well, don't tell Theresa that I told you, but the city and the county chief filed a protest against the way she handled your interrogation."

"They did?"

"There must've been thirty people in that observation room when she demanded your badge and weapon. For Christ's sake, Susan, your mother was dead."

I remembered the blond woman I'd never see again, unless it would be in my dreams. Then again, if my memory returned, I might lose her all over again.

"Hardy was caught up in the heat of the moment when she interrogated me. I would've—no, make that, Susan Chase would've made the same mistake."

"And that's what you were counting on, right?"

"Mickey, I don't know what you're talking about. As I've said before, I'm no Susan Chase."

"Well, hon," he said, taking me by the shoulders and kissing me on the cheek, "just don't ever forget that you measured sup to her standards."

Chad took my arm and escorted me past Hardy and out of the bullpen. I didn't know if I'd ever see this place again and I wasn't sure I wanted to.

Going out the front door of the law enforcement center, Chad put his arm around me and pulled me close.

"Now what?" he asked.

I looked up at him and smiled. "Hell if I know. Start all over again?"

About the Author

A member of Mystery Writers of America, Sisters In Crime, and the International Association of Crime Writers, Steve Brown is the author of six Susan Chase mysteries, plus *Radio Secrets*, a novel of suspense about a radio psychotherapist with a secret past; *Black Fire*, the story of a modern-day Scarlett and Rhett facing a church-burning in Southern Georgia; and *Woman Against Herself*, a suspense novel in which a single mom takes on a drug kingpin.

Steve lives with his family in South Carolina. E-mail him about Susan Chase at www.susanchase.com

If you would like to read more about Susan Chase, please ask for her books by title and number:

Color Her Dead	ISBN 0-9670273-1-4
Stripped To Kill	ISBN 0-9670273-3-0
Dead Kids Tell No Tales	ISBN 0-9670273-4-9
When Dead Is Not Enough	ISBN 0-9670273-7-3
Hurricane Party	ISBN 0-9712521-5-7
Sanctuary of Evil	ISBN 0-9712521-6-5

LaVergne, TN USA
03 February 2011
215164LV00003B/13/A